## RAVE REVIEWS FOR KAREN LEE AND *MEREDITH'S WISH*!

"Funny, warm and enchanting are just a few of the adjectives that apply to this delightful novel. Don't miss the magical ride."

—*Romantic Times*

"What a cute book! This story made me smile from ear to ear. The laughter plus the fun, fizzy romance all make *Meredith's Wish* a perfect lazy afternoon read."

—Mrs. Giggles from Everything Romantic

"Great comedy, excellent amore, an independent, feisty heroine, and a hunky hero . . . Karen Lee has a knack for creating humorous character dialogue."

—*The Romance Reader*

"Karen Lee has a fresh new voice that inspires dreaming."

—*The Belles and Beaux of Romance*

## A PERFECT MATCH?

A man stood looking out Chloe's office window, tall, dark and totally unexpected. Dressed completely in black, from the toes of his polished black wingtips peeking out from the neatly pressed black slacks, past the black belt, the black turtleneck and the black silk jacket that nicely enhanced the breadth of his shoulders. Chloe caught her breath and hugged the laptop closer.

He looked very familiar.

The purple e-Cupid pager began to vibrate wildly in her hand. She put the laptop and her Palm Pilot on the credenza, and opened the miniature computer. Yep, there he was, the man e-Cupid had designated as her True Love spokesman, smiling out from the screen.

She looked up. Yep, there he was, standing in her office, large as life and at least as tasty. Damn, these e-Cupid people were good. He was even more attractive in person.

Before Mr. True Love had a chance to respond, dissolve or disappear, Chloe decided she'd play along with E. Rose and Milo. If they'd delivered her True Love, she'd just try him on for size.

She walked across her office, put her hands on his shoulders and kissed him.

Other *Love Spell* books by Karen Lee:
**MEREDITH'S WISH**

# CUPID.COM

## Karen Lee

F LEE

LOVE SPELL

NEW YORK CITY

*This one's for Wendy, the best sister anyone could ask for. And for Kate, because she didn't give up on Chloe or me.*

LOVE SPELL®

December 2002

Published by

Dorchester Publishing Co., Inc.
276 Fifth Avenue
New York, NY 10001



ISBN 0-505-52482-1



Printed in the United States of America.

## ACKNOWLEDGMENTS

Thank you to all the people who stuck with me: Judy Fitzwater, Ann Kline, Robyn Amos, Beth Fedorko, Catherine Anderson, Courtney Henke, Lisa Arlt, Barbara Cummings, Vicki Singer, Laurin Wittig, Denise Timpko, Cameron Nyhen and Felicia Ansty. Thanks to Bob Bradshaw for reading the final manuscript and to Elaine English for her insightful comments.

# CUPID.COM

# *Prologue*
# *"All You Need Is Love"*

*Washington, DC, Tuesday*

Cupid dumped his matched leather luggage on the king-sized bed in the honeymoon suite and looked around. His apprentice, the demigod Milo, followed him into the rooms, laden with more luggage.

"Take a lesson," Cupid said. "This is what comes from making bets." He swept his elegant hand in the air, indicating the ornately decorated room. "Pink flowered bedspreads."

"Bets? What bets?" Milo rubbed his hands in anticipation.

"Psyche, my lovely wife, thinks I'm falling down on the job, that my failure numbers are up. You know the drill—rising divorce rate, couples living together without benefit of wedding vows, relationship therapy overload. She blames it on the arrows. Says I need to modernize, employ some of the new electronic communications, like cell phones, pagers, the web." Cupid paced back and forth. "Technology is the problem, I told her, not the solution. Technology keeps people apart." He sighed, and shook his handsome head. "She bet me I couldn't manage *any* kind of technology to make people fall in love." Cupid opened his sleek black leather attaché case and pulled out two folders. "Called me a technophobe. A technophobe!"

"You reminded her, didn't you, that you're the god of love who's made even hard-core skeptics fall for someone?"

"To no avail." Cupid sighed. "But what can I do? I love her." He sighed again and waved the folders in the air. "Psyche's picked two people for us to bring together. Cupid tossed a blue folder to his apprentice. "The man, subject A, is completely hopeless. Hopeless. He's in love with his car."

Milo read the sheets inside. "Handsome, sort of, although he looks like a bad boy in a suit. How'd he break his nose?"

Cupid shook his head. "You don't want to know." He handed the pink folder to Milo. "The female, subject B, is a business woman with a math deficiency."

Milo thumbed through the few pages. "Hmmm. She's definitely a Creative Extrovert with an Advanced Inability to Say No, what with all these inventions and projects." He shook his head, then held up a photograph. "She's cute, but check out the wild red hair. It's like cinnamon and ginger spun with fire."

Milo stacked the pink folder on top of the blue. "Why these two?"

Cupid shook his head. "Star-crossed lovers. These two are meant to be together, but they've managed to miss each other all their lives. Watch." He snapped his fingers and the air in front of Milo got all foggy. A school materialized. Gray lockers lined the hall, and Milo could see a tall, gangly boy listening to a walkman and jamming books into an already overloaded locker. A bunch of computer game disks fell out just as an awkward girl, red hair curling riotously around her head, approached. The boy bent down to pick up the disks and missed seeing the girl by inches.

"Didn't he meet her later that year? They went to the same school, right?" asked Milo.

"He was a senior and she was a freshman. He spent every afternoon at the video arcade with his friends. She discovered Van Halen and wore headphones from dawn to dusk. Portable tape players," Cupid shuddered, "a hideous invention. These two never had a chance and, of course, in a year, he was gone."

Milo looked worried. "Surely, later in their lives . . . ?"

"You'd think so, wouldn't you? Her first job out of college was with the same firm that employed him. The Fates set that up. But *she* opted to take part in a telecommuting trial, so she worked from home, linked by computer, cell phone, and fax machine. Six months later, when the trial was complete, she came back to the main office to get approval to extend her work-at-home job. Of course, that was the day *he* was out, fighting with the computer people because his laptop kept crashing."

Cupid threw up his hands. "Every time these two have a chance to meet, some screwball technological goof-up keeps them apart," he said.

"But they're destined for each other so, now that you're on the job, there shouldn't be any problems getting them together, right?"

"One can only hope." Cupid paused, his eyes downcast. "Psyche attached conditions."

Milo looked at his boss with extreme pity. "She's serious this time, isn't she?"

Cupid shook his handsome head. "She's threatened to stop sleeping with me." He pointed to the folders. "We've got exactly a month to make subject A fall in love with subject B, propose marriage, and live happily ever after."

"How very Brothers Grimm," Milo said, rummaging around in the luggage. He pulled out a sleek bow and several arrows. "Better warm up the Stealth Model, Boss."

"Put that away," Cupid whispered, snatching the weapon from Milo and shoving it back into the bag. "If Psyche gets even a hint that we're employing twelfth-century methods on this one, she'll really never grace me with her heavenly pleasures again!"

Milo cocked his head. "What then? Poison darts? Guided missiles?"

"Nope," Cupid said, pointing to the black laptop next to the attaché case. "The World Wide Web. Psyche specified *new* technology. Technology has kept them apart, and technology will have to bring them together. That's why we're here." The god of love pointed to the computer. "I've invented this new high-tech, high-touch way to get people together. But we've got to hurry. A month is only so long."

# Chapter One
# "Bring Me a Dream"

*Washington, DC, Wednesday*

*Some days you should simply throw the alarm clock in the trash, roll over, and sleep for a week,* thought Chloe Phillips as she rushed across the street, barely beating the light. Fishing her cell phone from her briefcase, she dialed her office number amid the shriek of car horns and the smell of exhaust. She shoved her black beret more solidly on her head. The breeze was colder than usual for the middle of October and it whipped leaves into brown, orange, scarlet, and gold swirls around her feet.

"Gloria?" she said when her assistant answered. "Has the report from the FDA come in yet?" Chloe tucked the phone between her ear and her shoulder and dug around in her purse for her lipstick and mirror. "The board needs an answer on Spuddy Buddy immediately." The board needed a lot more than that, but her instant potato cooker was at the top of their list. Right ahead of loud worries about profit margins and shareholder value.

"You sound like you're in a wind tunnel. What are you doing?" Gloria Vigil shouted.

"Trying to make my ten o'clock appointment and I'm late. The board meeting ran overtime." Chloe paused as a bus careened around the corner.

"Mrs. Fratelli called," Gloria said. "She's got over a hundred RSVPs for the Halloween Charity Costume Ball. According to her, it's going to be a huge success."

"I know it will," Chloe replied. At the Ball, she was trialing Punkin' Pal, an innovative carving kit. Punkin' Pal was just one of a long litany of ideas Chloe had funded since she'd taken the reins at Creative Investments when her father died two years ago. Not one had turned a profit. At least not one that she, the unabashed Queen of the Math Impaired, could find.

"The vet called," Gloria continued. "Edgar Allan is ready to come home."

She'd completely forgotten. Her father could have left her any number of mementos when he died, but he'd chosen to saddle her with his neurotic cat, Edgar Allan. Stupid thing ignored her almost as efficiently as her father had.

"The mailman hasn't come in yet this morning, so I don't have an answer on the FDA," said Gloria.

Crud. "I'm on my cell. Call me as soon as it gets there." The market had been so erratic lately, the board was worried. Chloe'd just spent two hours reviewing her top opportunities with them and each one was delayed. Spuddy Buddy was hung up in red tape at the FDA. Fish-in-a-Dish couldn't seem to satisfy the EPA. And FrogVision 2100 was in endless review at the Defense Department. Each one over budget and not yet on the market.

"What's the plan, Chloe? You've always got one."

"I'm looking hard at a couple of ideas. I only need one huge success, and the board will be happy. If I don't have one guaranteed moneymaker by the end of the year, I may be moving in with you and your parakeets." Which would make Edgar Allan happy. The board had fired another division president last week for nonperformance. The terms of her father's will protected her for a while, but she was running out of time to prove that she could manage the company.

"You'll find a winner," Gloria said. "Don't worry about the board. Oh, and call Miss Holland."

Chloe closed her phone and slipped it back into her briefcase. She didn't need a report on her friend's latest dating disaster. She had impending foul weather of her own to worry about.

The board of directors had gotten downright insistent that she pay more attention to finances. The one part of life she avoided at all costs: numbers. She shuddered. But, it was the board, after all, so she'd relented. They'd hired someone her brother Oz recommended to assist her in straightening out her books. It was sure to be some stiff, weaselly little guy with thick glasses and a thin, whiney voice who'd lock her in a room with a zillion columns of numbers and not let her out until they balanced. Accountants were the least creative people on the planet and she avoided the noncreative like she avoided brussels sprouts.

Her cell phone rang. All right! The FDA had relented. She popped the phone open. "Gloria, tell me good news."

"Have you heard from Barb?" Leann asked. "She's pretty depressed."

Looked like she was getting the bad-date report whether she liked it or not. "Another newspaper ad gone wrong?"

"This one was especially bad. He spent the entire evening talking about his ex-wife."

*"I've* told her. *You've* told her. People who take out ads in the newspaper are, by definition, desperate."

"Maybe," Leann said, "but it's hard for single women to meet quality guys in this town."

Chloe was silent. She could feel a Leann lecture coming. She never could figure out how Leann segued so quickly into the topic of Chloe's lackluster love life.

"You, for example," Leann continued. "You need to concentrate on finding someone to go to the Ball with."

"You should never end sentences with prepositions," Chloe said. "Besides, that's too Cinderella even for me."

Leann laughed. "You work on coming up with a date and never mind the lessons in sentence construction. You're not in college any more, you know. Good men are in short supply and you need to concentrate on bagging one."

Leann made dating sound like the great Moose Hunt of 2002. Right now Chloe needed to concentrate on running the business her father had left her. Once she got her killer idea launched, *then* maybe she'd turn to the question of her sagging social life. Not until. "Say goodbye, Leann."

"Goodbye, Leann," Leann parroted.

Chloe jammed her cell phone in her pocket.

The overwhelming scent of fresh-baked bread reminded her she'd skipped breakfast. Checking her watch, Chloe ran around the corner and dodged a knot of tourists consulting a map. "Amateurs," she said, and headed directly into the coffee shop. She had time for a bagel and latte.

* * *

AJ Lockhart brushed minute dust off the solid maple dashboard of his classic 1958 Corvette Sting Ray and looked up at his friend. "Don't worry, Tommy old son, this assignment with Phillips International will take us from the brink of disaster back to being a viable company." He settled back into the soft leather seat. Two years ago, AJ had started his own consulting firm with his college roommate, Tommy Morales. They'd set up office in an inexpensive strip mall and he'd been supremely happy. Business had boomed until the economy took a nosedive. Then their smaller clients cancelled their contracts and their biggest ones were always late paying for services rendered.

"It better," Tommy said, running his hand through his short, blond hair. "Joanie will be out on maternity leave for at least three months once she has this baby. We've got to find a temp to replace her. Not to mention insurance and rent and two dozen other bills piling up on my desk." He scowled down at AJ, his tall, lanky frame effectively blocking AJ's view of the peeling paint on the entrance to Lockhart Associates World Headquarters—all five hundred square feet of it. "You should have demanded cash from Biedemeier instead of this wreck." He nudged the Corvette's tire with his toe.

"Charlene? A wreck? Please, don't insult a lady." Tommy was a decent lawyer and great business manager, and AJ respected his talents, but the guy knew nothing about cars. "Once I get her fixed up, she'll be worth three times what Biedemeier would have paid us." The only thing of value AJ had gotten from his father was a love of fine automobiles. He'd dreamed about this Corvette for as long as he could remember.

"So," Tommy continued, "when we hit rock bottom, you'll sell the car to keep us afloat?"

Over AJ's dead body. He'd taken the car in lieu of six months salary and had become very fond of macaroni and cheese because of it. "Won't be necessary," he said. "I feel serious business coming our way. Phillips is connected in ways you only dream of. If we do a good job for them, and it's the only kind Lockhart Associates does, we'll have more of their business and a slew of class-A referrals. Stop worrying." He'd take up dog walking before he'd let Tommy and Joanie face unemployment. All he needed was a quick infusion of cash, which would be coming from Phillips, and then he'd simply grow the business. Somehow.

AJ turned the key and the car started immediately, its finely tuned engine humming. "Listen to that purr. Two-hundred-eighty-three cubic inches of pure love."

"While you're lusting after an antique, Lockhart Associates is facing a financial crisis."

"I know," said AJ, his smile fading. "I'll have a retainer check in your hands this afternoon." It was going to be less than he'd anticipated, but they'd have to make do. "The money we'll make from this job will be more than enough to bring us current and fund the company for the next quarter." He gazed up at his best friend. "Have I ever let you down?"

"No."

"I don't intend to start now." He eased Charlene into first gear and pulled away from the curb. "Phillips is going to be so happy with our work he'll keep us on permanently."

"He better," shouted Tommy, his voice barely audible above the throaty roar of the Corvette.

"Your next appointment is here." Gloria stood in the doorway of Chloe's expansive office drumming her bloodred fingernails on her steno pad. "I put them in the big conference room."

Chloe blinked at Gloria. Today, her assistant was wearing a purple silk dress and a red boiled-wool jacket. Of course, a lime green scarf tied the two clashing colors together. "How do you do it?" Chloe asked. "The clothes, I mean?"

"I have impeccable style." Gloria tucked a jet-black curl behind one ear and raised her penciled-on eyebrows. "The conference room? People? With ideas?"

Oh, right.

"I'm on my way." Chloe gathered her pad, her Mont Blanc fountain pen, and the spiral-bound proposal for e-Cupid.

She squared her shoulders inside her dove-gray wool crepe suit jacket and strode toward her conference room, two doors down. Her straight black wool crepe skirt hung at a fashionable but acceptable mid-calf length and her conservative black three-inch heels made no noise in the thick burgundy carpet. She took a deep breath.

"Good morning, gentlemen," she said, swinging into a large room that faced the Potomac River. She rarely noticed the view from her suite of offices, but today the sun was streaming in wide banners through broken white clouds, highlighting the bank of scarlet sugar maples that ran along the river. The fresh coffee steaming in the corporate mugs, gave the room a warm, friendly smell.

She sat down and faced her clients. One of them was a mere boy, his golden hair haloed by the sun from the window. He looked positively godlike, even though he was dressed in baggy white chinos and a loud tie-dyed T-shirt that announced "Can't Buy Me Love." He focused a pair of impossibly blue eyes on her and said, "Hey, sweetknees."

Sweetknees?

"I see you've reviewed our proposal. Cool." He winked at her. "So, chickee. Whadya think?" He leaned back in the chair, propping his hands behind his head.

She blinked at the name on the front of the folder as if she'd never seen it before. "Excuse me? Mr. Rose?"

"That's me, honeytoes. E. Rose. At your service." He grinned insolently. "You're excused."

"What?"

"You said 'excuse me'. You're excused."

"I beg your pardon?"

"Beg all you want, lambkins. I like it when women beg."

She stood abruptly. "After the board meeting, I didn't think this day could get any worse, but you've proved me wrong." She gathered her things. "This meeting is over."

"Don't be insulted, Miss Phillips," the second figure said. "He doesn't mean anything by it. It's just his style." The person sitting next to Mr. E. Rose looked like one of those tacky plaster figures people stuck in their petunias.

"And you would be . . . ?" she paused, waiting for the gnome to speak once more.

"That's Milo," the boy cut in. "Don't mind him. He's in product testing. I brought him along for the demonstration." E. Rose scooted forward and leaned his elbows on the table. "You know, cutie, you're exactly the sort of customer e-Cupid is looking to help."

"Oh, really?"

He nodded sagely. The gnome nodded too.

"Perhaps you'd explain why by telling me about your product, its target market, and its purpose." Finally, the discussion was under her control. She continued, "Then we can move along to your cash flow and break-even point." There. She'd gotten all of the board's favorite terms on the table before she'd agreed to fund this idea. Pity they weren't there to witness her accomplishment.

At least E. Rose had toned it down to "cutie."

"Whatever you want, sugarlips."

"The product," Milo said, clearing his throat, "is designed to address the extremely sad state of affairs in the world."

She frowned. "The sad state of what affairs?"

"Why, affairs of the heart, of course," E. Rose said. "Too much divorce, lovee, too many people living together but not getting married, too much unhappiness, too much singleness. Too much technology in the way." He stood and paced in front of the windows. "The fine art of love is lost, lost I tell you, in this sound-bite world we live in. Chicks and dudes don't take the time any more to get to know each other," he warmed to his topic, "or to sample the simple joys of being together." He spun around to face Chloe. "No, it's rush, rush here; rush, rush there. Cell phones and pagers, personal digital assistants and remote-control love. Never taking time to do anything well, never spending time wisely." He flopped into the chair, his smile returning. "That's why we've come to you, babe."

They had described her life to a tee. "Please, go on."

"E-Cupid is a fully functional, multiprocessing, completely integrated software program to help people meet people," Milo said. "It's a matchmaker on speed." He sat back, a satisfied smile on his face. "Just think of all those lonely men and women out there"—he waved his hand in the general direction of Washington, DC—"starved for companionship, pining away for a meaningful relationship, alone with their techno-toys."

"Right. They're called politicians."

"No, no, no, no. They're single people who need partners. People want love in their lives. True love. It's what makes everything come into focus. What gives this whole stupid world meaning."

Chloe leaned back in her chair and crossed her legs. "I certainly don't have anything against true love." She gave a small grin. "It's like the song says, all the world needs is a little love, right." Then she sighed. Heck, she could use a little love in her own life. She pushed the thought aside and concentrated on the business at hand. She'd done her homework on this project. Singles had a number of matchmaking options open to them. Newspaper ads, dating services, on-line sites for the lovelorn—she'd studied them all. Most of them were gimmicks to sell someone's books, or perfume, or other stuff "guaranteed to boost your love life." In her opinion, none of them worked very well. Oh, she'd admit the occasional couple got married. But it seemed to be more the exception, than the rule.

Her preliminary reading of the e-Cupid proposal, however, had noted much promise. The air fairly crackled around her. Something momentous was about to happen. Her killer idea was inches away. A bigger, better dating service attached to technology would be perfect for the techno-driven twenty- and thirty-somethings too busy to find their own mates.

Of course, it all depended on the product itself. It had to have great graphics and a super user interface. Lots of visual appeal would be key. She rubbed her hands together in anticipation.

E. Rose looked at Milo. "We've come none too soon, my pudgy friend." He pinned Chloe with his blue gaze. "You, dearie, are in sad need of your true love."

She laughed. "Of course I am. But what I really need right now is a killer idea so successful that the board will stop hounding me about numbers. I've got to secure the future of my company before I worry about true love."

"Aren't you lucky we came along? This *is* that idea."

It was sound enough, she conceded, trying not to get too excited about e-Cupid. A software program that found your true love. Her nose twitched. Definitely a killer idea, promoted properly. After all, no sane person believed that a mere software program could actually match you with your true love. But with the kind of marketing plan she could dream up . . . She knew people would be intrigued just to see who they got paired up with. And if it actually offered high-quality screening of users, and personality testing to make sure of compatibility as the proposal claimed, E. Rose and Milo might really be on to something. They could even make the program available on the Internet, maybe a website called Cupid.com. Chloe smiled to herself as she imagined success within her grasp. She definitely wanted to see their creation in action. "How does it work?" she asked.

"Give it a spin," E. Rose said. He nodded to Milo, who opened a slim black laptop she hadn't noticed before. He turned the screen so it faced her and, stretching out one finger in a dramatic arc, turned on the computer. "Voilà!"

Chloe leaned forward, shivering. If e-Cupid was good—please let it be good—it could be the one invention she'd been waiting for. The board would be happy, Oz could quit worrying about her—and her father, wherever his spirit hovered, would finally be proud of her.

Besides, she thought ruefully, it wouldn't hurt to have a little true love in her own life—and if it came via one of her projects, so much the better. She could be her own best testimonial.

E. Rose smiled, cocked an eyebrow, and winked at her. "Sit back and prepare to be blown away, sister."

The computer screen filled with clouds that looked real enough to float right off the computer onto the table. She felt like Jack-up-the-beanstalk, expecting a giant to wander off the screen and *fee-fi-fo-fum* at her. She held her breath. Great graphics. Seriously great graphics.

The scene on the computer had zoomed to a close-up of a Roman-looking villa. She saw movement behind one of the Corinthian columns. A striking youth with gleaming blond hair and blazing white wings walked toward the center of the computer screen. He looked amazingly like E. Rose.

She resisted the urge to reach out and touch the figure on the screen to see if he was as real as he looked.

"Chloe?" The winged boy spoke. "Chloe Phillips?"

She nodded, mesmerized.

"I've come to help you."

"Help me what?" she whispered.

"Find your true love." He held up a silver-framed photograph of a man—an attractive man, with black hair that waved across his forehead, midnight blue eyes that sparkled with mischief and a smile that promised adventure and passion. He looked so real she once again felt the urge to reach out and. . . .

She blinked several times to regain her equilibrium and pull her attention away from the man's image. She hugged herself. Oh boy, this was going to be big. Huge. She calculated the impact e-Cupid would have if the rest of the program was even half as good as this opening. "You should put a warning label on this," she said. "Do not drive or operate heavy machinery while using this software." What a marketing gimmick! Sweet. She could see the board's smiling faces looming. She looked at the picture once more. He was definitely handsome. Even the crooked nose looked great on his face. A perfect spokesman for e-Cupid. Every woman's fantasy.

Including hers.

E. Rose reached into a chino pocket and pulled out a small purple object. "You'll need this." He handed it to her.

Chloe fingered the gadget in her palm and opened it up. It appeared to be a miniature computer with a small screen and a tiny keyboard. "What is this?"

"It's the e-Cupid Rapid Response Unit." E. Rose reached over and turned it on. "It will beep, or vibrate if you'd rather, when your true love is within range. And it doubles as a pager."

Chloe suppressed a chuckle. Add-on sales for pagers. This idea got better and better. "So, how does this work, exactly?" She composed a quick list in her head of the single people she knew who would absolutely love this kind of thing. Her friend Barb Holland was number one.

"Ah, proprietary software," E. Rose said. "I can provide specs after we've come to an agreement that you'll represent e-Cupid."

"I understand your desire to protect your software, but I need details. Screening, for instance. How does the program match people?" She stood and paced in front of the table. "Do you use profiles? Questionnaires?" She frowned at E. Rose and Milo.

E. Rose cleared his throat. "We're very careful to

bring together only people who are destined for one another."

"And this guy?" She pointed to the screen. "How did you determine he'd be the one for me?" Not that she believed for a minute that he was actually her true love.

Milo shrugged. "He just is."

Right. "Security is a big issue these days. I seem to remember your report proposing to make the software available on a website, Cupid.com. I assume the site will be protected?"

E. Rose nodded. "Perhaps we could schedule a follow-up meeting with my technical staff in a day or two. After you've had a chance to play with the program, to really grasp its potential."

"At least tell me if you provide profiles of these people." She waved at the lovely specimen on the screen. "Who is he? Is he employed? His hobbies? His goals? You know, the important information."

"You'll just have to wait and see," E. Rose answered cryptically.

She didn't have that kind of time. "I'm not sure." Chloe frowned. "It has great visual appeal, but I need more information."

"Take the laptop and the pager. Run tests." E. Rose smiled complacently. "You're going to like what it does. I guarantee it."

It wouldn't hurt to let her friends see it. "Okay. We should plan to meet, say a week from today." She flipped open her Palm Pilot and checked. "How's two o'clock next Wednesday?"

Mr. E. Rose and Milo smiled at each other. "You've made the right decision, Sugarlips," said E. Rose, winking.

Chloe ushered her two newest clients out and fairly skipped back to her office. Their idea did have promise. No EPA or FDA or other federal alphabet approval required. Just test it, put together a marketing plan, and watch her problems dissolve. She smiled at Gloria and walked into her office.

A man stood at her window, tall, dark, and totally unexpected. Dressed completely in black, from the tips of his polished black wingtips peeking out from the neatly pressed black slacks, past the black belt, the black turtleneck, and the black silk jacket that showcased the breadth of his shoulders. Chloe caught her breath and hugged the laptop closer.

He looked very familiar.

The purple e-Cupid pager began to vibrate wildly in her hand. She put the laptop and her Palm Pilot on the credenza, and opened the miniature computer. Yep, there he was, the man e-Cupid had designated as her true love, smiling out from the screen.

She looked up. Yep, the very same man now stood in her office, large as life and at least as tasty. Damn, these e-Cupid people were good. He was even better in person.

Before Mr. True Love had a chance to respond, dissolve, or disappear, Chloe decided she'd play along with E. Rose and Milo. If they'd delivered her true love, she'd just try him on for size.

She walked across her office, put her hands on his shoulders and kissed him.

# Chapter Two
# "Stupid Cupid"

AJ had been on a lot of quirky assignments, but he'd never been welcomed like this before.

*Maybe she's simply grateful not to have to worry about all those sticky business issues any more,* he thought as her warm hands caressed his neck and the back of his head.

He shivered.

*She's forgotten her glasses and has me mixed up with her current boyfriend,* he postulated as the tip of her tongue slipped between his lips.

He shuddered.

*She's merely trying to distract me from my mission,* he concluded as she broke the kiss, *and doing a damned effective job of it.* He straightened. It was a test. He'd had to resign his senior position at Lancaster Loudoun Consulting two years earlier because an executive with more ego than brains hadn't done what AJ had recommended. That, and he'd falsely accused AJ of having an affair with his wife. AJ definitely liked women but he never, *never,* violated his rule not to get involved with people who employed him—or with their spouses.

He wasn't going to start now. Not when the key to digging his little company out of the red and into the black lay with completing this job for Phillips International.

The woman's eye lashes fluttered open and she studied his face as though mesmerized. Her eyes, the most wonderfully clear emerald green, were bright with promises.

"Man, E. Rose has absolutely gone over the top trying to sell this idea," she said in a husky voice that sent tingles of awareness shooting through his body. She stepped backwards and nodded her head. "Unbelievable marketing. Really, really effective." She let out a long sigh. "Amazing."

*She* was amazing. The rest of it? He had absolutely no idea what she was referring to. He'd talked with Oswald Phillips, Jr., last week about working with his sister to clear up some financial problems, but he certainly hadn't been prepared for this bundle of sensuality. AJ cleared his throat. "I believe we have an appointment."

"Oh, yes. That we do," she said, her face lighting up with a huge smile. "You are the answer to my prayers, the essence of my success, and the key to my future." She stepped back and grinned at him.

Maybe his reputation had improved. Perhaps she'd talked to some of his satisfied clients—the ones who hadn't paid him yet—and knew his talent for pinpointing and shoring up the trouble areas in a business. She might have heard of his latest success when he'd recommended that a small conglomerate of local restaurants position themselves for takeover rather than fight the increasing competition. He cleared his throat one more time and cocked an eyebrow. "An awfully big burden to put on one guy, don't you think? All those expectations. Might be difficult to live up to."

She moved toward him again, placing her hands on his shoulders and then running them down his arms, a movement that set herds of goose bumps racing to catch up with the heat of her touch. With a strength he didn't expect, she pulled him toward her until they were hip to hip. Gazing into his eyes, she smiled and said, "But you come with the platinum e-Cupid guarantee. And," she went on, "I'm pretty sure you can live up to my expectations. You and I are going to go far together, Mr. True Love."

This had gone too far already. He had priorities and, while he didn't mind an assertive woman, no intelligent man relinquished control that fast. AJ was very intelligent. He'd grown up poor and clawed his way to the top. He relied on his brain. Fairy tales and true love had no place in his starkly realistic world. AJ wrapped his fingers around the woman's upper arms and gently pushed her away from him. "Let's take this one step at a time, shall we?"

"Fine with me." She grinned and ran a manicured finger down his chest.

"Hold it!" She stopped, her lips slightly parted, glistening with moisture. He was an idiot. Lips like those needed to be kissed, demanded it. But there was a job to do. He had a business to save.

The woman frowned. "What? What's wrong? Milo and E. Rose filled you in on their business plan, didn't they? You're supposed to sweep me off my feet, shower me with presents, court me in a way no modern woman has ever been courted, and prove that e-Cupid works so they can get their funding." She reached out to straighten the lapel of his sports coat. "You *are* from e-Cupid, aren't you?"

"Not that I know of," he answered. "Although, if

e-Cupid routinely gives out samples like that kiss, I might be persuaded to join." He smiled invitingly. Maybe one more sample of her delectable mouth wouldn't hurt. Pink cheeks actually looked good with her wild red hair, he realized a second later, curious to see what she'd do next.

"You're not with e-Cupid?" She stepped back and hugged herself protectively, covering up those breasts that had, only moments before, been pressed against his chest. Pursing those very desirable lips that he'd almost tasted for a second time.

"Never heard of them." He dug his business card out of his inner coat pocket and handed it to her. "I'm from Lockhart Associates." He watched as the joy faded from her amazing green eyes, and he felt oddly disappointed, as though he'd let her down. He wanted to sweep her back into his arms and tease her lips back into a smile.

She took another step backward, bumped into the huge glass and brass table, and stopped. "But, but E. Rose had your picture," she stammered. "Right here." She held up a purple gadget that resembled a pager. "Are you sure you're not with e-Cupid?" She read his card. "You're a consultant?"

"AJ Lockhart," he said, offering her his hand to shake.

She ignored it. "Why are you here if you're not the True Love spokesman for e-Cupid? E. Rose didn't say anything about a consultant on this project." She held onto one of the chairs at the table. "I hope you're working for a flat fee, because giving you a percentage of their business is completely out of the question. It's going to be big, Mr. Lockhart. Very big."

"I'm not involved with this Rose person. I work for—"

"Oh, good," she said, obviously relieved. "I really

don't think a consultant would help e-Cupid at all and you'd cost them a lot of money—money they need to invest in their product launch." She straightened, adjusting her skirt with slender fingers. "You must be here to pitch me an idea. Great. I can use all the new inventions I can find." She pulled a chair out from under the table and sat. She fiddled with the stack of coasters, arranging them and restacking them. She brushed invisible specks of dust off the table, off her blouse. "You may begin, although I must tell you I generally require people to submit their business plans ahead of time." She cleared her throat. Twice. She was clearly flustered.

AJ smiled. Who wouldn't be flustered after the kiss they'd just shared? "I expect you do. And, of course you'll want a full-blown financial analysis with that plan, won't you?" He moved to the chair next to hers.

"Absolutely." She nodded. "A business venture is only as good as its projected cash flow."

Oz had told him his sister didn't understand finance, that she practically had hysterics when she had to do anything involving numbers—addition, subtraction, not to mention complex algorithms. "Before I start, could you tell me about your financial analysis methodology? I want to be sure I've prepared my spreadsheets correctly."

She swallowed and gazed at the ceiling. "Umm. Financial analysis methodology . . . would be proprietary, I'm afraid." He watched as tiny beads of sweat formed on her upper lip. Damn. He didn't care about methodology. This woman had made his heart leap without a word. He wanted to kiss her again.

Instead, he leaned back in the chair. If he didn't technically work for her, he certainly worked for her company. "Proprietary. Well, that's unfortunate. It will make my task significantly more difficult."

"Oh, I wouldn't worry about it, Mr. Lockhart. If your idea is sound, I'm sure we can work something out."

"Oz warned me you'd be like this."

"Oz?" she said, her forehead wrinkling.

"You are Oswald Phillips' sister, aren't you?"

Color flooded the woman's face as she stood up, her eyes wide with understanding. "You're the man the board hired, aren't you? The financial consultant."

"That would be me, yes." He smiled and stood. "You are therefore free to share with me your proprietary methodology. I've signed the standard nondisclosure agreement." His smile turned into a full-fledged grin. "I promise I won't share your deep dark secrets with anyone at all."

She narrowed her eyes, glaring at him. "Very funny." She made her way to the huge chair behind the equally huge desk. The combination of mahogany and leather almost overwhelmed her. When she'd settled herself, she leaned forward and put her elbows on the desk. "Please, take a seat."

He reminded himself that this woman controlled a small but significant part of Phillips International, the company whose fat fee would cover his last-month's payroll with enough left over to restore Charlene. He moved to a comfortable chair in front of her imposing desk and squared his shoulders. This was business. He was a businessman. Really. In spite of what his hormones were telling him.

"You mentioned my brother," she began, the color in her cheeks fading.

"He recommended me to your board." He pulled a pamphlet from his brief case. "This will give you an idea of the kinds of support that my firm provides," he said, handing her the glossy tri-fold. "The board was very specific. I'm to review your projects, identify weaknesses in marketing plans, and get your financials under control."

Chloe took the brochure and swallowed, trying hard to ignore the disappointment that settled inside her. For the briefest instant, she'd let herself believe that the man in the software program, the man sitting in front of her, might actually be her true love. She shook off the feeling. E-Cupid was a business venture, nothing more. An exciting, success-written-all-over-it idea to be sure, but business nonetheless.

Oh, God, and she'd kissed him.

Well, it *was* a matchmaking proposal after all. . . . She shivered.

"This e-Cupid is one of your ventures, I take it?" he asked, his eyebrow quirking slightly higher. She nodded. "I rather thought so. What made you think I was connected to this particular project?"

A soft chill settled over her shoulders. "E. Rose showed me your picture." She picked up the purple pager, vibrating still, and flipped it open. There he was, grinning out at her, a bogus true love. "This *is* your picture, isn't it?" She held the tiny screen out to him. If he wasn't part of the e-Cupid marketing team, then why was he in the program?

He took it, brushing her hand with his as he did so. The chill was replaced with a startling streak of red lightning charging up her arm. The same heat she'd felt when she'd kissed him, touched him, pressed against him. God, how could she have been such a complete fool? She jerked her fingers back.

"It certainly looks like me." He handed the pager back to her and she took it, careful not to touch him again. Too much static electricity was bad for her already unruly hair.

"Where did you get this?"

"Milo gave it to me," she said.

"Milo who?"

She chewed on the inside of her cheek, her eyebrows furrowed in concentration. "He didn't say, actually," she admitted. "But his partner's last name is Rose." She knew this wasn't going to bode well for Mr. Lockhart's investigation of her business practices. Any venture capitalist worth her salt-free, flavor-enhancing additive would at least know her client's names. Surely they were listed in the e-Cupid proposal she had. She couldn't remember if she'd seen them or not.

"Uh-huh." Mr. Lockhart didn't sound impressed. "And these people are connected to e-Cupid?"

"Yes. The creators of my latest project." She turned off the pager and stuck it in her top drawer. All that vibrating was more than she could deal with right now. "I'll get you the file if you like," she offered. She could hear the purple gadget still vibrating inside her desk.

"Eventually, I'll need to review all your files," he said. "Why not just tell me about this e-Cupid idea for now."

Chloe watched him watch her, knowing what must be going through his mind. She was impulsive, disorganized, too trusting. Why else would she fail to get—or remember as the case may be—simple information like a client's last name? She took a deep breath. Then, to complicate things, there was that kiss. That heart-stopping, life-affirming kiss. The kind she'd only read about. She closed her eyes and wished she could run the clock back ten minutes.

He was still watching her when she opened her eyes. "E-Cupid's a very promising software program with a web application designed to . . ." What was it E. Rose had said? "Designed to address the extremely sad state of affairs in the world." So she'd kissed him, big deal. E-Cupid was supposed to find true love and what was she supposed to do when her killer idea's spokes-hunk showed up in her office? Discuss French politics? A woman was entitled to jump to conclusions when a man looked like AJ.

"Uh-huh."

"Here, try it for yourself." She snagged the laptop from the credenza and offered it to Lockhart. "Just open it up and follow the pulsing heart."

"Thank you, no." He blinked. Those eyes. The dark blue ones that suggested he might be warmer than his tone said he was. "Did you and Mr. Rose get around to reviewing the revenue projections and cost estimates?"

Chloe narrowed her gaze. That clinched it. He was a business consultant, plain and simple—no true-love frills attached. Any fantasies she'd entertained about him—personal or businesswise were over. It didn't matter how ideal he might be as the centerpiece of her marketing plan for Cupid.com. The man who would represent true love for e-Cupid would never want to talk numbers. Poetry, flowers, music—even exotic gifts—these would be de rigueur. But numbers? Please. And certainly any attraction she'd felt toward him after their kiss was finito. "Fine. I'll get them for you. Say, tomorrow, close of business."

She had her preliminary analysis, of course, but she knew Lockhart wouldn't be satisfied with her gut-reaction numbers. No, he'd want fully developed spreadsheets with footnotes and references. "Definitely tomorrow," she said.

Lockhart sat back and steepled his fingers. "Why wait and spoil all the fun," he asked, with a smile [illegible] didn't quite make it to the edges of his mouth.

[illegible]t tempting, wondrous mouth.

Chloe narrowed her eyes. Something. She was [illegible]mething. She picked up his business card and really read it this time. She remembered an article about Lockhart Associates in some magazine, but, since it'd dealt with finance and other topics requiring numerical acumen, she'd promptly forgotten it. Oh, well. If she could off-load all the reports and math stuff to Lockhart, she could get on with the fun part of the business. The ideas and their people. It was high time she hired a replacement for her last finance manager anyway. Tom Briggs was off perfecting self-sharpening lawn mower blades. Maybe, if Lockhart worked out, she'd keep him on permanently. Anybody this persistent and annoying had to be good for the bottom line.

Chloe turned around and opened the file drawer behind her. As she pulled out a copy of the e-Cupid proposal, her memory came back with a crash like a hundred crystal vases thrown against a brick wall. Lockhart Associates had a huge reputation for closing down struggling businesses.

Not helping.

Not sympathizing.

Shutting down.

She was suddenly very glad he hadn't been the true love E. Rose had promised. She didn't have time for love right now. She definitely didn't need to be distracted by a guy some software program had picked to be her true love. She had a killer idea to launch and a business to save.

And scratch the budding job offer. There was no way—no way—she would hire a man whose primary goal was to snuff the life out of businesses, leaving people's futures to bleed to death as he cut a well-paid swath through their dreams. Well, it wasn't going to happen to her. And it wasn't going to happen to her projects. Her business. She owed the people who trusted her that much.

She owed her father.

Setting her jaw, she handed the file on e-Cupid to Lockhart. "I assume the board checked your references," she said, surprised at the cold sound of her voice.

AJ didn't appear ruffled by the question. "Actually, yes."

The board didn't believe she could succeed, didn't believe she could find that one surefire, really huge idea. AJ Lockhart sat calmly, leafing through the information on e-Cupid. Anger, followed closely by determination, welled up inside Chloe. She would push ahead with e-Cupid; she would prove to her father—and the board, of course—just what kind of a businesswoman she really was.

She had until the end of the year. According to the terms of her father's will, she had to demonstrate that she could turn a profit within twenty-four months, or resign and let the board appoint another manager. Two long years to improve the profit margin. To reduce expenses. To do all those things canny business managers were supposed to do. She shrugged. She had less than three months. Almost.

"I presume you have more complete files somewhere," AJ said.

"For e-Cupid? It's my newest venture and I haven't even decided to fund it yet." A lie. She'd calculated how much she could manage to give Milo and E. Rose about five minutes into their pitch. "I'm still checking out the product parameters, developing ideas for a marketing strategy. That kind of thing."

"Working up revenue projections?"

She smiled brightly. "I believe that's your job now, Mr. Lockhart. Assuming you really *are* here to help." Was that a wrinkle of hesitation on Lockhart's perfect forehead?

Good.

"And the other projects?"

"I reviewed them with the board this morning."

AJ cocked his head. "Do you have a copy of your presentation I could look at?"

"Yes," she said, hesitating. "You should know that their definition of success is somewhat different than mine."

"*My* definition—the one I'll use to judge the viability of Creative Investments—includes careful decisions, complete documentation, and a high probability of profit." AJ shoved back from her desk and stood.

My, but he was tall. Her normally spacious office was somehow smaller with AJ in it. Smaller and definitely warmer, Chloe realized, feeling heat creep up her neck. "You'll be wanting an office, I suppose," she said.

"Thank you. That would be good."

"How long will it take you to find me incompetent?"

He gathered his black cashmere overcoat from the sofa next to Chloe's worktable. "I know you don't believe me," he said softly. "But I'm here to help."

Oh, boy. His voice was warm honey. Quiet, persuasive warm honey. If only he weren't lying through his straight white teeth.

"I'll have Gloria fix up space for you," she said, standing and squaring her shoulders. No honeyed voice would distract her from her mission.

"Great. I'll see you tomorrow then?"

She nodded.

And watched her future walk out the door.

Somehow, that hadn't gone quite the way he'd planned it, AJ thought as he walked to his car. He couldn't stop thinking about Chloe Phillips pressed up against him, how right she'd felt there, how he would like to sample her lips again. Many of his meetings began with scathing accusations, but this had been the first to begin with an incendiary kiss. It had put him off his stride.

It was critical that he maintain that stride, the professionalism upon which he prided himself. His company demanded it. He wouldn't abandon his employees, his friends, the way his father had run out on his family, leaving his mother to work two crummy jobs just to keep food on the table. No. Lyle J. Lockhart might have been his biological father, but AJ would be damned if he'd turn into the lazy, irresponsible, worthless excuse for a human being Lyle had been. AJ took responsibility for his actions. He didn't run away from them.

"Besides, Charlene, how could I expect you to share me with another woman?" He turned the key and Charlene coughed once, twice, then started up. As the familiar thrum of the engine filled his ears, he looked through the proposal on e-Cupid once more. No wonder Chloe had true love on her brain. Was there no corner of a person's life that the Internet wouldn't invade?

He continued to listen to Charlene, loving every subtle sound she made, but his attention was more and more focused on the e-Cupid proposal. He'd concede there was a need for more love in the world, but he doubted a new website was the answer. Worse, as he'd expected, the report didn't include much financial analysis. The most important part about a new project as far as he was concerned. The board was right to be concerned. Phillips International had always been a sound, well-run corporation. He wondered why Chloe hadn't hired a financial manager before.

He backed out of his parking slot and Charlene stalled. "Come on, baby," he said, turning the key once more. The car sputtered, turned over, and purred. "That's my girl." He drove out of the parking lot and dialed Oswald Phillips, Jr., on his cell phone.

"Lockhart. How nice to hear from you so soon. I take it your first meeting went well."

"Well enough. I'll be starting in earnest tomorrow. But Chloe shared one idea with me—some goofy dating service called e-Cupid." He paused. She'd been completely sincere in her belief that E. Rose and Milo had a product that would work. "Her enthusiasm has obviously clouded her business judgement."

"Chloe has more than her fair share of enthusiasm for new ideas, but, without help, I fear none of them will amount to much. I'm glad you're on board, Lockhart."

AJ was glad to be on board, too. And he planned to keep Oswald Phillips happy he'd hired him. He took the corner onto the Beltway with just a little more speed than was necessary. God, he loved this car. "Why isn't there a director of finance working for your sister? Someone who could help out on these reports, do analyses, that sort of thing?"

"She's had several, actually."

"Then why are her books in such a turmoil?"

"Every financial whiz kid she's hired also had some hot invention. She's funded every one of them and let them go to work on their projects. She has a very hard time keeping staff, you see. They keep chasing their dreams."

Uh-huh. "That won't happen with me," AJ assured him. He was already in a race with his dreams.

"You'll do well, Lockhart. Report back to me regularly on your progress with my sister's company, and I'll see to it you that get more business from Phillips International."

Music to his ears.

* * *

This was some joke, Chloe thought. The cosmos must really be lining up against her this time. She'd finally found the one idea that would spell success and it had matched her with the man who was going to put her out of business. There had to an explanation. Perhaps Milo had found Lockhart's picture in some business magazine and figured one professional would be perfect for another professional.

Or maybe Lockhart had done some modeling during his college years to impress what she was confident had been a constant stream of girlfriends. Whatever it had been, she was going to have a serious discussion with e-Cupid's inventors.

She pulled a box of Cracker Jack out of her desk drawer. The sugar-coated treat was her one vice, especially during times of extreme stress. Lately she'd been buying them by the case.

When her phone rang moments later, she answered it without waiting for Gloria to intercede. "Creative Investments, Chloe Phillips speaking."

"Chlo? You never answer your own phone. What's wrong?" Her best friend, Leann, sounded genuinely worried.

"What? Oh, I guess I'm just distracted. I forgot to let Gloria answer." She dug around in the box, looking for peanuts.

"You never forget. Usually, you're too distracted to think of answering the phone. Something's wrong."

"I have just seen my life flashing before my eyes. It was extremely boring." She turned the Cracker Jack box in her hand slowly.

"Tell me about it over dinner, why don't you? A bunch of us girls are getting together at Clyde's around six. Come with us? Please?" Leann begged. "It's been so long since we've seen you."

"I've got a better idea. Come to my place. We'll steam shrimp, cook a little pasta, and try out some new wine." And e-Cupid as well.

"Great. I'll let everyone know."

"Think, Chloe," she told herself after Leann had hung up. If she could show e-Cupid to a couple of test groups, get some positive feedback quickly, she might be able to salvage her business, make the board happy, and get rid of the handsome but annoying AJ Lockhart.

She'd liked him better when he was a mere picture file in a computer program. She shook the prize out of the Cracker Jack box. A tiny silver heart dropped into her hand. She blinked back surprise. Was it a sign that she was really onto something with e-Cupid? She'd know soon enough. She planned to do a little market research tonight, using her friends as guinea pigs.

She walked to the wardrobe in the corner of her office and took out her black cashmere coat. She adjusted her beret, tipping it just enough to give her what she considered a mysterious air. She slipped the laptop into her black Gucci briefcase and picked up her matching Gucci handbag. "Okay, world. Get ready for e-Cupid. Here we come."

Purse looped over her shoulder, briefcase in hand, she strode confidently out of her office. "Gloria, I'm going to dinner."

She caught the elevator to the garage, thinking Gloria would be shocked if she knew that her usually dateless employer had just decided to fund a matchmaking venture.

"That went fairly well, don't you think?" The god of love rubbed his hands together in satisfaction and glanced at his friend.

"Well?" Milo said in disbelief. "They hate each

other! What kind of matchmaking are you peddling here, Cupid? At least with arrows, the people smiled."

"Look, pal, I've just introduced the world's first matchmaker software that actually works."

"That remains to be seen," Milo mumbled.

"So they didn't declare their undying love right off. These days people don't appreciate things unless they have to work for them. Trust me, these two are perfect for each other. And, technology has finally brought them together instead of tearing them apart." Cupid wandered around the hotel suite. "However, just in case I've overestimated this pair, or something in the program isn't quite right, perhaps I should turn up the intensity on e-Cupid." He waved an elegant hand in the air. "There, that should fix things."

"Hey, are you sure you know what you're doing?" Milo looked worried.

"What's to know? A little code here, some ones and zeros there. Don't worry. I'm the god of love. Even computers must obey me." Cupid spun in a circle of golden light.

"Wait! Where are you going?" Milo squeaked.

The spinning stopped. "Hey, this gig is all yours now, pal. I've got a bevy of supermodels to find guys for. Good luck." The god of love disappeared.

"We're in big trouble now," Milo predicted as he slapped the palm of his hand to his forehead in exasperation.

# Chapter Three
# "I Want to Hold Your Hand"

"Matchmaker software? What a great idea." Leann leaned across the table in Chloe's town house so she could see the laptop. "When's it going to be on the web? I've got a list of people who need this, and you're number one." Her brown, shoulder-length hair was pulled back in a pony tail, secured with one of her daughter's orange scrunchies.

Chloe ignored the implication that she had no life. "As soon as the initial product testing and market research is complete and I've analyzed the results. However, since I'm putting up the venture money, I probably won't be participating in the test. But, please give me the names of your friends you think might be interested, and I'll see to it that they're part of the product launch." She didn't want to talk about the fact that Mr. Right, according to e-Cupid, was on assignment to put her out of business. She glanced across the dining room just in time to see Edgar Allan stalk away, her bushy gray tail twitching in indignation. It was almost as though she didn't approve of Chloe having people over. Chloe never could figure out why that cat hated her so much. The animal was just another great legacy her father had left her, she thought morosely, a cat with an attitude. Well, she wasn't about to let the finicky feline or thoughts of her father's last will and testament spoil the evening.

It had been too long since she'd spent time with her friends and it felt good. She took a sip of her merlot. "When are Meri and Barb coming?"

"Soon. Meri had to be sure Jim was home to take care of the twins and Barb is always late." Leann clasped her hands together. "So let me see this guy you mentioned," she prodded, nodding at the laptop.

"You mean *my* true love," Chloe said, trying hard not to roll her eyes at the idiocy of AJ being the guy for her.

"That would be the one, yes." Leann grinned.

Chloe set the demo of e-Cupid in motion once more. She was used to Leann's constant efforts to spread her own wedded bliss to Chloe. It was really encouraging, in terms of market potential though, that even a married woman could get excited over e-Cupid. An intriguing product would inspire good word-of-mouth, which would lead to lots of hits on the website—which would translate to success and the monetary rewards the board demanded. Chloe could hardly wait to try the program out on Barb, the Perpetually Single.

"There. That's him." The hair on the back of her neck prickled and the air got warm. Edgar Allan stretched on the stairs and watched through slitted yellow eyes. Then yawned. She obviously couldn't care less about true love—a game only mere mortals need participate in.

Leann said softly, "God, Chlo. He's perfect for you. Who is he?"

At least his lips had been perfect. "I thought Milo and E. Rose made him up, special for the demo. Then I thought he was a model they'd hired to help promote e-Cupid. But it turns out he works in town." She sat back and considered the photograph once more. A little wine had taken the edge off the surprise of seeing this snake staring out at her. "He's pretty effective, though, isn't he?"

"Can't you just imagine him coming to the ball, dressed as Prince Charming? He'd ride up on his white charger and sweep you off your feet."

"I don't need sweeping, thank you." The only way Chloe wanted to imagine AJ was exiting her life at a full gallop, leaving her business intact. "I need the general population of singles around the world to get swept up in e-Cupid and its website—Cupid.com. Make it the Next Big Thing." Edgar Allan moved from the stairs to the top of the étagère that housed Chloe's collection of porcelain teacups and saucers.

"Get down from there, you wretched animal," Chloe said, glaring at the cat who, catlike, ignored her and started cleaning its face.

Leann looked up at the cat. "Setting aside the question of every other single person on the planet for the moment, I think you need nothing so badly as to be swept off your feet. Adventure is good for the soul, and this one," Leann pointed once more to Chloe's purported true love, "could give you adventure for a lifetime."

"Some other lifetime, Leann." She felt a slight tug of regret at the thought. Being in his arms, kissing him, had felt so very right. So familiar. Like she was safe. And loved. Until she'd found out who he was and what he really wanted. She shook her head. In spite of AJ, she would make e-Cupid work.

Edgar Allan jumped off the étagère and walked into the kitchen. Even the cat had had enough of AJ Lockhart, it seemed.

"God, we don't need this," AJ said, tossing the business magazine on the table. He'd left Chloe and gone straight back to his office, where Tommy met him with a disastrous article about failed consultants, featuring—ta da—AJ Lockhart. He fingered the envelope with the retainer check.

"It isn't good, but it could be worse," Tommy said, opening the tiny refrigerator in the oversized closet that served Lockhart Associates as copy room, storage, and kitchen. "Here," Tommy said, handing AJ a beer. "You need to relax." He paused, cocking his head "We could head to Georgetown, check out the bar scene. I found this great place last week, all the waitresses are gorgeous."

"How can you think about women at a time like this?" AJ picked up the magazine once more. "What could be worse than this? 'Lockhart, once known for his stable and reliable business advice, has stumbled once more, and may not be able to get up.' Can we sue him for libel or something?"

"Not if it's true," Tommy said, taking a sip of his Heineken. "And, unfortunately, it's true. Not your fault, but true. Stop beating yourself up over it, AJ. All you can do is recommend. If the management team doesn't take your advice, or twists it, well, there you are." He stood up. "How did things go at Creative Investments today?"

"Charlene stalled in their parking garage," AJ said. "I don't think she likes these people."

"That car will be the ruin of this company," Tommy predicted.

"Don't mock what you don't understand, Tommy old son. Charlene has heart." AJ set the envelope on the table, keeping it under his hand.

"Yeah, but does she have cash to deposit in our dwindling account?" Tommy asked.

"Excellent question," said Joanie Claiborne, coming into the tiny room with a pile of bills to file. "Little Skeezixs here will need food when he's finally born." Joanie patted her six-month pregnant belly, the growing baby almost overwhelming her slender, petite form. Her sister had obviously been practicing for her cosmetology license again. Joanie's brown hair looked like it had been cut with a lawnmower and was streaked blond and a color that could only be described as cranberry red.

"I take it Eugene hasn't come to his senses and accepted responsibility for fathering that kid?" AJ wanted to punch her ex-boyfriend every time he saw Joanie. Any guy who left his girlfriend high and dry after getting her pregnant deserved a black eye. In Eugene's case maybe a hit to the head would knock some sense into him. Probably not, AJ thought ruefully. He, himself, was very careful to never run the risk of any woman carrying his child.

Which made him think about Chloe Phillips and her amazing welcome-to-my-world kiss. Her turned-up nose and wild riot of cinnamon hair. If ever there was a woman made that he'd be an idiot to get involved with, Chloe was it. Even if he hadn't been working for her. Her wackiness would definitely wreak havoc on the orderly way he liked things. He leaned back and sipped his beer, enjoying the earthy flavor. "Don't you worry about that baby. This new assignment is going to be a veritable gold mine." He pushed the check-laden envelope toward Tommy.

Joanie cocked an eyebrow and sat down next to Tommy.

"When did you two get to be such skeptics?" AJ asked. "It's a no-brainer—do a solid analysis and move on to more challenging projects, which Phillips promised to line up for us." He finished his beer.

"This isn't what they promised," said Tommy, snapping the check with his fingers. "They forgot a zero."

"Or the decimal is in the wrong place," Joanie suggested.

AJ shook his head. "Can we make it stretch until we complete the initial report?"

Tommy looked at Joanie and they both looked at AJ. "If we have to," Joanie said.

"I guess we have to," said Tommy.

"A week. All I need is a week to finish the first report and Phillips will give us another check." Surely they could last a week. "They've got money to burn. To two guys she'd just met, Phillips promised more money than we make in a year—to launch a matchmaking website, when dot coms are falling like flies." He still couldn't believe it. "On top of that, she thought I was her true love." Which, the more times he said it, sounded more and more ridiculous.

Or more and more possible. He couldn't decide which.

"Sorry. Traffic," Barb Holland said when Chloe opened her door. She tossed her trench coat on Chloe's piano bench and leaned down from her almost six-foot height to hug Leann. "What's that?" she asked, pointing to the open laptop on the table. Her straight white-blond hair brushed her shoulders, completing her Norse goddess look.

"It's Chloe's newest project. E-Cupid. Guaranteed to find your true love," Leann said. "And the guy it's picked for her is so yummy I'd be tempted to trade Karl in on him if I didn't love my husband so much."

"Cool. Let me see," Barb scooted around so she could check out the computer screen.

"Let me start it over from the beginning, so you get the full impact," Chloe said. She clicked through the menu and selected "Begin Again." "Here, you navigate while I get you some wine." She handed Barb the mouse.

Barb moved the arrow around until it was poised over the pulsing heart in the middle of the screen. She clicked on the icon and familiar clouds roiled across the screen.

"This is very neat, Chlo." Barb watched, a smile growing on her pretty face as the Roman villa appeared. "Who's that?" she asked when the golden, winged boy walked toward the front of the screen.

"It's Cupid, silly," said Leann, peering over her shoulder. "Just wait until you see what he's got for Chloe."

The youth held up the silver frame with the photograph, but it didn't have Chloe's dream man in it. Instead, a man with sandy hair, glinting blue eyes, and a neat mustache on his upper lip smiled at the trio. Chloe set down the glass of wine she'd just finished pouring and frowned, but Barb gasped.

"Oh, my God. He's beautiful." She exclaimed, then turned to Chloe with longing in her eyes. "Who is he? Do you know him? I just have to meet him. Can you tell me his name?"

"Slow down. Have a few sips of the wine," Chloe said, completely confused. She'd thought it was a demo with only *her* presumed true love programmed into it. She hadn't known there were other photographs in the software. "I think this must be another computer-generated image. Perhaps the program is designed to run through several samples of men." She was certain that was the answer. How could e-Cupid actually *know* what kind of man Barb would be attracted to?

Barb ignored her drink and grabbed her friend's arm in an iron grip. "Chloe Phillips, tell me right now who that man is. You can't tease me this way. You know I've been wandering this town dateless for almost six months." She waved away Chloe and Leann's objections before they could voice them. "Personal ads don't count as dates. He," she pointed to the screen, "is exactly the man I've been looking for. Who is he? Tell me."

Her grip grew stronger. Chloe opened her mouth but didn't have any idea what to say. "I just got this today, Barb. I've only seen the demo with the other man in it. I don't know who this guy is."

With a dramatic flair, Barbara, brought one hand to her heart and the other to her brow. "I'll simply die if I don't meet him."

"I'll see what I can do," Chloe said. "I've got a follow-up meeting with the people who created e-Cupid. I'm sure they can tell me who he is."

"When? I'll be there. Name a time, a place." Desperation had taken over Barb's voice. "Please. I must know." Was that a tear in her friend's eye?

"I don't think that would be such a good idea, Barb. You might overwhelm them. They're just simple businessmen with what is obviously a very good idea." In spite of, or perhaps because of her friend's strong reaction to e-Cupid, Chloe was beginning to feel much better about her newest project. Take that, AJ Lockhart!

"I want to try something," Chloe said, pulling the laptop away from a distraught Barbara. "Let's see if we can coax another image from the software. Leann, you try it." She shoved the computer across the table, between the glasses of wine to where Leann had taken a seat during Barb's minor hysterics over the mustache man. "Select 'Begin Again,' then click on the pulsing heart."

Leann took the mouse and carefully maneuvered the arrow over the pulsing heart. Barb and Chloe moved to stand behind her, each of them leaning over one of her shoulders to get a better view. Together the three of them watched as the Cupid figure moved towards them, an angelic smile on his face.

Three sets of eyes watched impatiently as the boy produced the silver picture frame and slowly turned it until the photograph inside was visible.

The three of them gasped in total surprise, and in unison they announced in awe, "It's Karl."

"I'll be damned," said Chloe. "How did it know? How could it possibly know?" She tried to remember details of her meeting with E. Rose and Milo. They hadn't asked any questions about her or her friends. Of course, it wouldn't be unusual for an enterprising entrepreneur to research her life to make a more effective pitch. But this was amazing. If the actual matchmaking software—the preliminary questionnaire and other tools used to judge peoples' compatibility—were anywhere near as well researched as their marketing demo, e-Cupid would be a huge success.

A silly, warm expression graced Leann's face. "He's so wonderful, my Karl. I do love him, you know. He brought me flowers last week for no reason other than he wanted to. That's true love. After six years of marriage, to bring flowers because it was Tuesday."

Barb had taken the mouse from Leann. "You've got your man, my friend. Let me see mine again." She quickly clicked through the program and her sandy haired beau appeared once more. "Can you print this out?"

"I can try when I get back to the office, or maybe

I can download his image and e-mail it to you." She smiled at her friend. "Would that work?" She realized she had to do something or Barb would be camped at her office door at oh-dark-thirty tomorrow morning.

"Oh, that would be so wonderful. Thanks, Chloe, you're the very best friend." Barbara sighed, long and deep, a dopey, love-struck grin on her face.

Always on the alert for information that would be potentially helpful to her, Chloe shut down the program and observed her friends. Would the warm glow of love fade if the program wasn't running? She certainly hadn't forgotten AJ, although the glow she felt was definitely *not* love. She shivered. "I take it Meri isn't coming?"

"I completely forgot," said Barb. "She called. She and Jim are staying home tonight."

"Three for dinner, then," Chloe said. Barb tossed salad while Leann spooned cocktail sauce into a small dish. The chilled shrimp beckoned.

Chloe, Leann, and Barb brainstormed promotional ideas for e-Cupid while they polished off a little salad, several pounds of shrimp, and two bottles of wine. The mesmerizing effect of the e-Cupid pictures appeared to be able to endure drink and food and conversation.

"Too bad Meri couldn't get away," Leann offered. "I wonder if Jim's picture would appear if she tried e-Cupid."

At this point, Chloe wouldn't have been at all surprised. "I don't know. But somehow the program is able to determine a person's identity, and then retrieve the appropriate image." She shook her head, puzzled still. "I just don't know how it works. I do know it's got to involve incredible programming. Milo and E. Rose must be computer geniuses."

"Well, you said it was supposed to find true love

for whoever logged into it, didn't you?" Leann slid her fork into the piece of mile-high chocolate pie Chloe had picked up at the bakery, and broke off a substantial chunk. "Maybe it actually works."

Frowning, Chloe said, "How could some computer code know who your true love is? It's ridiculous." She didn't bother to tell Leann and Barb that e-Cupid's choice for *her* true love was a snake of indeterminate species who was out to get her. And not in a loving way. "My guess is that there's some sensor integrated into the programming that recognizes who you are and matches you with someone, that's all."

"Then, how do you explain the picture of Karl when I used it? Surely, this program can't spy on people. How does it know who's married to who?"

"Whom," Barb corrected. "If it's a spy program, like something the CIA might use, it would know everything. That you use Colgate toothpaste and you eat Cherry Garcia by the pint when you're watching romantic movies. That kind of stuff." She nodded, solemnly.

"You eat Cherry Garcia a pint at a time?" Leann feigned shock.

"Only when I'm watching old Cary Grant movies," Barb said indignantly. "It's allowed. They're good movies."

Chloe pondered the capabilities of e-Cupid as she waved good-bye to her friends. Okay. She'd concede that true love existed. Leann and Karl were a testament to true love. But it didn't just come popping out of a computer. The only reasonable explanation—and Barb's James Bond spy program theory didn't fall anywhere near that category—was that Milo and E. Rose had done a little research on Chloe and her friends. They had then used that information to create the demo. A demo that seemed able to determine a person's identity. If the program really could recognize a user by touch. . . . She began to catalog the potential for such software. The market in the federal intelligence community alone would be worth millions. Hundreds of millions.

Success like that would impress more people than her board of directors. It might even impress one AJ Lockhart.

# Chapter Four
# "Luck, Be a Lady Tonight"

Chloe raced across the parking garage the next morning. She'd spent the better part of the night thinking about what had happened with e-Cupid. That and chasing Edgar Allan down from various dangerous perches and out of her baby grand piano. The dumb cat had never been that way when her father was alive—she'd been docile, happy to sit in Chloe's father's lap while he read business journals. Ever since she'd come to live with Chloe, however, Edgar Allan had liked high places or dark places.

Chloe'd finally gotten to sleep around three and then she'd slept through her alarm. She was late. Again.

"Good morning," AJ said cheerfully, looking fresh, rested, and annoying when she rushed, breathless, into her office. He was already at work, sitting at her table.

"What does AJ stand for?" she asked, stifling a yawn. "Always Jolly?"

He cocked an eyebrow. "I thought we could review these revenue projections this morning. I've compiled a summary spreadsheet for you." He smiled and handed her a sheet of paper, completely covered by rows of numbers.

E-Cupid may have been able to show Leann her husband. It might be right about Barb's blond hunk, but it was so wrong about AJ. So very wrong. Not only did he enjoy numbers, he was a morning person. She shook her head. No, E. Rose and Milo might be computer geniuses, but they'd really paired her with Mr. Wrong—regardless of how well he kissed.

She took the page, shrugged out of her coat, and tossed it on top of his on her sofa, her black cashmere snuggling down next to his black cashmere. At least their coats were compatible. "This is no way to start a day."

"Really? I would have thought you wanted to solve your finance troubles so you could get back to handing out money by the bucketful."

She narrowed her eyes and glared at him. "How can you criticize when you haven't tried any of my products? Here," she pulled the e-Cupid laptop out of her briefcase. "Why not give this one a quick run-through." She was definitely interested to see what kind of reaction AJ would have if the love software showed him her picture.

"No, thank you," was all he said.

"Chicken."

"You and I need to review the process you use to determine which ideas get funding and which ones are booted out the door."

"All of my projects are carefully chosen."

"All of them?" He picked up a second sheet of paper. "Including Fish-in-a-Dish? Or SatelHat?" He leafed through his own copy of The List. "How about Call-a-Ball or Drink Caddy?"

"You obviously don't attend many cocktail parties or you'd see the immediate benefit of Drink Caddy. It gives you full use of both hands." She sat at the table. "It's a little peculiar looking, but it supports everything from a highball glass to a brandy snifter, suspended from a harness that you wear around your neck, thus allowing you to sip your drink through a handy straw and nibble hors d'oeuvres at the same time," she said, ignoring the look of bemused tolerance on his face. "Have you even looked at the proposals for those products? Most of the inventions are enormously creative with great potential."

"I doubt the PGA would allow remote-controlled golf balls even if it meant not losing them in water hazards." He shook his head. "And this," he picked up the file for Fish-in-a-Dish. "Do you seriously think anyone in suburban America will be anxious to convert their decorative ponds to miniature fish farms just to be able to grill fresh trout?"

"Surveys have shown that over seventy percent of suburban families would welcome ways to improve the nutritional content of their meals. And if they can do it without harming the environment, so much the better."

"Right. I'd hazard a guess that anyone who can afford the luxury of personal water attractions on their property is more concerned with their own image than with ways to save spotted owls. Besides I'm certain there are zoning issues with backyard fish farming."

"We're working on that," she said. If he would just wipe that smug look off his face, she'd be much happier. He could take potshots at any of her projects but he wouldn't be able to squelch her belief in them.

"According to my numbers," he continued, "the

cost to maintain individual family-sized fish farms exceeds the anticipated benefits by at least fifty percent."

It was seriously too early for numbers. "Didn't we assign you an office of your own?"

"It's being painted."

Of course it was. "Explain to me, if you could, how it shows fiscal responsibility to waste money painting an office you're not going to occupy all that long." She waited. He simply continued to smile at her. "How long *are* you planning to stay with CI, *Mr.* Lockhart?" She couldn't decide how she felt about having him around on a more or less permanent basis. On the positive side, it probably meant she'd stay in business, which was a good thing. On the negative side, it meant she'd have to see him every day, which was definitely not guaranteed to leave her singing with joy.

"As long as it takes, *Miss* Phillips." He leaned forward, stretching the fabric of his very proper blue linen shirt across his broad shoulders. "The office you assigned me was unacceptable so I chose another. Right next to yours. It was empty. It was also pink." He sat back, apparently satisfied that pink was explanation enough to hire painters.

"That was *my* office when my father ran the business," she informed him. "*He* liked pink."

"*He* didn't have to look at it every day."

"*He* picked out that color, especially for me." She couldn't tell AJ that she wasn't fond of the color either, that it clashed with her hair, that she'd put up with it because it pleased her father.

AJ shrugged. "Your father was a legendary businessman, Chloe, but he had dismal taste in colors. The pink is gone."

"I suppose you've chosen blue." To match his eyes.

He ignored her. "I can see why your books are in such terrible shape. You can't focus."

"I'm focusing just fine. We're talking about wasting money painting."

"Yes, but we started out talking about unprofitable ideas."

"*You* brought up the subject of painting."

"*You*—no, I'm not getting sucked into another childish exchange with a woman who doesn't know the difference between net profits and gross margin."

She wanted to tell him the only thing gross in her office was him, but she didn't. Not after his remark about being childish. "I am so very sorry to have distracted you from your mission. Please, do go on."

He enthused about cost of goods sold, supply and demand curves. He beamed about basic principles of accounting. Chloe watched his eyes, thought about how strong he'd felt when she'd kissed him yesterday, all those lean muscles hiding under that button-down executive exterior. She wondered if she'd ever get over the impact of that kiss.

"So, you understand why Fish-in-a-Dish will never make money."

"You're looking at it all wrong," she said.

"I'm looking at it exactly right," he said, his voice strained.

She liked how his face went kind of red when he was frustrated. She liked that she could cause such a reaction. "Control, Chloe Ann," her father used to tell her, "business is all about control."

AJ took a deep breath, closed his eyes, and was probably counting to ten. Maybe fifteen. He was the numbers guy, after all. He could count to infinity as far as she was concerned.

"Chloe," he said, his voice calm, his tone measured, "arguing over the merits of your projects is counterproductive. We must address the problems

I've uncovered with your financial reporting."

Okay, fine. She'd talk numbers. But, first, she needed the fortification of caffeine. "You're right, of course. Let's go across the street and get a latte. It'll help me find the focus you're so fond of."

"Coffee. Fine."

On Thursday, Chloe tried repeatedly to contact E. Rose. After a whole day with AJ Lockhart talking numbers, her normally bubbly personality had gone undercover. A good night's sleep and a long workout hadn't helped one bit. She had a headache the size of Nevada and had actually promised to revise the business case for WindowWonder.

It was imperative that she talk with E. Rose. Or Milo. Immediately. Urgently. Now. While e-Cupid was a great idea, it needed work to make it the killer idea she needed to both please the board and get rid of AJ "I-love-numbers" Lockhart. Besides, it still made her shiver that they'd managed to match Leann up with her husband when they didn't know Chloe would try it out on her best married friend. She fished out the contact information Milo'd left and dialed.

No luck. She left them a stern voice mail message. "Call me immediately." No one answered her page, but she left a second, digital SOS. Ditto with the cell phone (another voice mail plea for help), and the fax line (a handwritten note begging them to return her calls). When she finally got through on the toll-free number they'd left, she wound up lost in an endless cycle of "Press 1 for technical help; press 2 for account information, press 3 for customer service. . . ." She pressed none of the offered numbers and simply hung up.

This was not a good sign. If E. Rose and his henchman, Milo, had taken her money and run off, she'd have grounds to head straight to the authorities.

Problem was, she hadn't given them any funding yet. They had simply disappeared. It was almost as though they never existed, except that she had their business plan and their laptop with its amazing software demo. She really needed to find out why AJ's picture was in their program.

"Have you finished with the revenue revisions for WindowWonder?" AJ asked, poking his head into her office.

Think of the devil and he shows up wearing a gray herringbone jacket, gray turtleneck, and black slacks. Not to mention his broad shoulders and soft, wonderful lips.

She tapped her wristwatch. "It's only been two hours. What was your previous job? Whipping galley slaves?"

It was so pleasant looking at him. Why did he have to be focused on ruining her life rather than helping it?

He came all the way into her office. "I'd like to see files on some of your projects, if I could." He handed her a typed list.

She thumbed through it. Not just some. All.

She sat a little straighter in her chair. If not even one of these projects paid off in the next two and a half months, it meant the end of her career as head of Creative Investments. This was it. She either produced at a profit the One Good Idea and kept the company, or turned over the reins of Creative Investments to the board to dispose of as they wished. If only her father's will had given her more time. If only the economy hadn't soured. If only the board hadn't sent her AJ Lockhart.

She clenched her jaw. She *would* keep Creative Investments.

Provided, of course, that her balance sheet balanced and there was more cash flowing *into* her cash flow statement than *out*. Her investments were like children, struggling to grow up and produce a profit and, while she claimed that many of them were doing just that—running around being profitable—only two of them were just barely in the black. The rest had chosen red as the color du jour.

"Fine." She led him out of the office to Gloria's desk.

"Mr. Lockhart needs a key to the file room."

"Very good, Miss Phillips," Gloria said. "It's so nice to have a man around the office for a change."

"Not now, Gloria," Chloe hissed, her jaw beginning to ache from so much clenching.

Gloria raised both her eyebrows and looked from Chloe to AJ. "Right this way, Mr. Lockhart." Chloe watched Gloria lead the Hangman away, wondering what in the world she could do to make AJ realize how wonderful each of her projects was. How, despite the gloomy numbers, each would succeed in time.

Get back to work and make e-Cupid a success, that's what. She closed her office door behind her and sat at her desk. Instead of working on e-Cupid, she sat, thinking, gazing out her window. The large bank of sugar maples was almost all scarlet. With a backdrop of the Washington Monument and the Capitol Building, the trees reminded her of the flames that her business might end in. One more sigh and she flipped open the deceptive laptop.

This time, instead of working through the product demo and coming face to computer-generated face with AJ, Chloe clicked on the pull-down menu and read the product guarantee information.

*E-Cupid is backed by the full authority of the god of love and is absolutely, positively guaranteed to show you your true love. What you do with him or her after that is your own concern.*

"No way," Chloe said, thinking about AJ. She searched for a "help" menu and found one. When she typed "questionnaire" into the search box and hit return, she got a Customer Satisfaction Survey with questions like this: "On a scale of one to ten, with ten being the last eruption of Mt. Vesuvius, how would you rate your true love's first kiss?" Well, that was stupid. If he was her true love, any kiss would be completely off the charts. She looked at the next question. "Would you be interested in e-Cupid's wedding planning kit? (Yes or No)." She frowned. Marriage. That would be the logical conclusion to finding a True Love. She tried to picture AJ coming down the aisle in a tux, toward her. She shuddered. The tux she could see. The man in the suit made her heart pound and her palms sweaty. Not in her lifetime, thanks. The next question advised her to "Click here for e-Cupid's tips on Safe Sex."

"Crud." She pulled her file of research from her desk drawer and thumbed through it. Every website she'd visited had at least asked for minimal preferences in a man. Things like education level, annual income, height. What was wrong with e-Cupid? And how did it work if it never asked the user for information? She tried the product demo once more. After all, it had given her friends different people. Maybe there was more than one true love for her in this laptop.

She wasn't really surprised when AJ's smiling face beamed out at her once more. "Double crud." There had to be some way to make the software cough up a different man. Maybe body temperature controlled which picture you saw. She clutched her mug of coffee, then started the demo again.

AJ.

She had Gloria bring her a glass of ice and cooled her hands to semi-frostbite stage, then set e-Cupid in motion.

AJ again.

"What is it with you?" she demanded, frowning at the computer picture. "Why do I always get you?"

"Your father hired me." Gloria leaned into her office. "If you're not happy with my work. . . ."

"No, Gloria, I wasn't talking about you," Chloe said, slamming the laptop shut. "What did you want?"

"That nice Mr. Higgenbotham is here to see you." Her eyes were bright and her face flushed a pretty pink that clashed with the orange sweater she wore. Definitely smitten. Maybe she should show Gloria the e-Cupid demo and see if Ralph's face popped up. "And Mr. AJ would like to join your meeting, if that's okay with you."

It was Mr. AJ now, was it? She knew it wouldn't matter if it was okay—he'd join anyway. "Send them in, please." She'd get Ralph's opinion of the e-Cupid demo. He was a scientist, used to investigating, grappling with the empirical unknown. She hadn't tried it out on any men yet. It would give her an opportunity to show AJ what a great idea e-Cupid was.

"Chloe, Chloe, Chloe," Ralph Higgenbotham chirped as he scooted into her office, followed closely by AJ. "Thank you so much for this little bit of your precious time." The inventor was a tall, thin man, with thinner brown hair and a nose of Ichabod Crane proportions. He turned an icy stare on AJ. "Who are you?"

Chloe said, "AJ Lockhart has joined our firm *on a temporary basis*. I'm showing him the basics, getting him acquainted with the intricacies of the venture capital playing field."

Ralph leaned closer and whispered, "Is it safe to talk around him?"

About as safe as striking a match in a room filled with gunpowder. "He's cleared, Ralph. If he shares any secrets, I'll track him down and pull out his fingernails with pliers. Personally." She smiled sweetly at AJ, who quirked an eyebrow and circled around Ralph. "Have a seat." She waved Ralph into a chair at her table. AJ sat next to her.

Ralph fiddled with the clasp on his briefcase, his hands shaking. She noticed a few drops of perspiration on his forehead. "What's wrong?"

"Oh, Chloe, it's the manufacturers. They've increased their prices for the flange mounts. I don't know what to do." She glanced at AJ, who was busy taking notes, likely planning to use them against her. She could easily guess his assessment—more cost, less profit.

She patted Ralph's hand. "Let me look at the numbers and then we'll figure out what to do. Okay?" Beside her AJ made a sound that sounded suspiciously like choking before he turned it into a more polite cough. Chloe pinned him with her eyes. "Why don't you tell AJ about your project, Ralph?" Higgenbotham's total belief in his invention was one of the reasons Chloe thought it would be such a success. Unlike AJ Lockhart, she didn't judge a project's worth on numbers alone—a little imagination was needed. If she could just get the hardened consultant to understand that they were dealing with people's dreams, maybe he would lighten up a bit.

Smiling, Ralph reached into his briefcase, took out the prototype model of his brain child, the SatelHat, and put it on. He'd painted the six-inch satellite dish a bright yellow. It was attached to a maroon Washington Redskins baseball hat by a gray flange that held the dish about four inches off the top of the hat.

"This is SatelHat. A miniaturized satellite dish tuned to orbiting geosynchronous satellites used to broadcast major professional sporting events."

AJ, looking somewhat stunned, didn't respond.

"When you combine it with this," Ralph said, pulling a tiny portable television from his briefcase and switching it on, "SatelHat provides any sports enthusiast with full color, play-by-play action while attending football games, soccer matches, or automobile racing events. Pretty much any sporting event." Ralph sat back, giving them a satisfied smile. "It's especially effective for those fans who can't afford front row seats. Try it on, why don't you?"

Ralph took the hat off and offered it to AJ, who took the cap and turned it around once, handling it with all the delicacy one would use for a particularly sensitive bomb, and then gave it right back. Ralph sniffed. He set his invention back on his head and turned his attention to Chloe. "You see? If the flange is any wider, it will not only overlap the edges of the baseball cap, but it becomes much more susceptible to winds of over five miles an hour."

Chloe's heart melted as she watched this awkward man with a satellite dish on his head pleading with his eyes for someone to believe in it as much as he did. How could anyone squash that kind of hope? She glared at AJ. He had a bemused and slightly bewildered expression on his handsome face, a typical reaction to Ralph's invention.

At least he wasn't laughing.

Her inventor continued, "And, since my target market is sports fans who generally would use the SatelHat in the out-of-doors, well, you can imagine." He sat there, this absent-minded professor, narrow shoulders, wisps of thinning hair sticking out from under the Redskins ball cap, looking frightened.

"Okay, no redesign. I understand. Look," she gathered the papers into a tidier pile, "I'll review these reports, but I wouldn't worry. We'll come to some kind of mutually beneficial terms." Actually, this sounded like the perfect project for AJ Lockhart, plotting to close her business. He might as well help Ralph succeed while he was at it.

"Oh, Chloe, thank you so much." Ralph practically jumped into her lap.

"AJ? Could you fit an analysis into your schedule?" she asked, shoving Ralph's notes at him.

He cocked an eyebrow. "Sure. Nothing would make me happier."

Right.

"Ralph, do you have a minute?" she asked.

He nodded. "Anything."

AJ frowned at her, tapping his watch. "I know you've got an appointment, but you're welcome to stay, AJ. We won't be long." She turned her attention back to Ralph. "I'd like you to give me your impressions of a website I'm considering." She went to her desk and got the laptop. "It claims to be able to pair people successfully."

Higgenbotham said, "I'm no expert on love, you understand, but I'd be willing to see what it does."

Good. If e-Cupid would attract even a confirmed nerd, then Chloe could expand her projections for the website's success. She glanced at AJ, who offered her an indulgent smile. Some people had no imagination. "I appreciate your help," she said to Ralph. She opened the laptop. "Just click on the heart and watch." Would he see Gloria, she wondered. The nagging uncertainty of not knowing how the software actually worked was dampening her enthusiasm.

She sat across from Ralph, but she could tell by the way his lips quirked up in delight that he liked the cloud motif. "The realism is astounding," he said. "Cumulonimbus. Very effective." She could tell by the way AJ narrowed his eyes and frowned that he wasn't impressed in the least. Of course, he might have been if he'd been watching the demo instead of thumbing through the file on SatelHat.

As the program unfolded, Chloe watched a variety of emotions shift across Ralph's face. Interest, first, followed by puzzlement, then joy and surprise. Ralph practically radiated a happy glow. "So, what do you think?" she asked. "Will men be attracted to this kind of website?"

Ralph folded his hands in his lap, a broad grin on his face. His cheeks had grown more and more flushed as the program progressed. "Oh, Chloe," he sighed, his satellite hat tipping on his head. "I don't know about other men, but if this program is supposed to show you your true love, then I'm in love." He slid out of the chair directly to his knees, in front of her. "Chloe, my dove, my own, will you have dinner with me tonight so I can sing your praises and tell you of my feelings?"

He gazed at her so earnestly she didn't react at first. Dinner? Praises? Feelings? Confused, she looked from Ralph to AJ's rolling eyes and back to Ralph. What was wrong? "I don't think that would be advisable, Ralph. We are business partners, after all. It wouldn't be seemly."

A few tears dribbled down his flaming cheek. "I quite understand," he sniffed, struggling to his feet, the sunshine yellow satellite dish slipping dangerously to one side. He shoved it back on his head. "Perhaps if I could find funding somewhere else, the barrier to our united joy would be removed. I'll see what I can do," he said, almost cheerfully. "Yes, that would solve all our problems, wouldn't it?" He gathered his briefcase, not bothering to remove his satellite hat, and rushed out of her office, calling after himself. "Never fear, my darling. Love will conquer all."

Wait, what was he saying? He was going to someone else for backing for his idea? He couldn't do that. They had a contract.

"That was masterful. Amazing even," said AJ, chuckling. "Is this how you lure the unwary inventor into your snare?"

"What are you talking about? Ralph is one of my best prospects for success. I didn't lure anyone."

AJ crossed his arms and shook his head. "Making clients fall in love with you is very inventive. It'd be even better if they actually had projects that were worth investing in."

She turned the laptop around. Her own face was smiling out from the silver frame in Cupid's hand. She slumped into her chair and held her head in her hands. "This is not possible," she said. She certainly hadn't signed any kind of release allowing E. Rose to use her picture in their software. And yet there she was. "Ralph can't be my true love and I'm certainly not his." More puzzling was why, after working with her for over a year, Ralph had reacted so strongly to her now? It couldn't possibly be the program, could it?

"Surely you're not abandoning or questioning your latest, award-winning, income-producing project already? Are you?" AJ asked. "No software program, however clever, can make people fall in love. Not now. Not ever."

"Of course you're right," Chloe said. She took a deep breath. But Ralph had certainly acted like he was in love. Stupidly in love, that was true, but entranced nonetheless.

AJ leaned over to take a peek at Chloe's picture, only to have the laptop snapped shut in his face.

"The only good thing about Ralph's reaction is that e-Cupid seems to work for men as well as women," Chloe mumbled, picking up the computer and walking to her desk.

AJ followed her. "Is that the reaction you always get with this program?" he wanted to know.

"I've only showed it to Leann and Barb. And now Ralph. I'm not sure three people is an adequate sample from which to draw any conclusions. Do you?" She smoothed the top of the laptop and looked up at him. "Why do you care? Beginning to believe I *can* pick out winning ideas?" She raised her eyes to his in challenge. "You want to try it?" He shook his head. Whatever.

He wasn't ready to concede just yet. "No." He licked his lips and leaned closer to her. "Just, ah, interested. Higgenbotham appeared to be a levelheaded sort and I found his abject declaration of adoration out of character." He hadn't seen her image. But he knew she'd look just as intriguing on a computer as she did in real life. And just as infuriating. He straightened up and wandered back to the table. "I'll have his flange analysis done by close of business." He picked up his notes and the papers Chloe had given him and hurried out of the office. It had taken all his professional restraint not to laugh the satellite man out of the office. Preposterous.

And then that e-Cupid thing. "Gloria," he whispered. "Have you seen that software Chloe wants to fund?"

"No, Mr. AJ. Is it a good product? Chloe always has such interesting things to work on."

"Stay away from it," he advised. "Stay far away." He turned on his heel and hurried into his office, dismissing the painters. "Come back later," he said, and closed the door firmly after them.

AJ stepped around a tray with paint and a roller brush, tossed the papers onto the desk, and went to the window. Leaning against the frame, he ran his hand up and down the wall in frustration. What did this woman think this was? Junior high? Of all the stupid, baseless, ignorant, crazy ideas he'd read about or seen in the little time he'd spent with Chloe Phillips, e-Cupid made them all look like Nobel Prize winners. Matchmaking software that turned otherwise reasonable minds into putty. Oh, yeah. The world seriously needed this product.

Had there been something like e-Cupid around when his mother met his father? Even when her husband abandoned her, his mom'd still been crazy in love with her irresponsible spouse. Well, AJ wasn't going to fall. Not for a redheaded businesswoman whose kiss invaded his dreams. Not now, not ever. He wasn't going to take the risk that he'd ever let anyone down the way his father had, and the best way to do that was not to get involved in the first place. Love-'em-and-leave-'em AJ, his college friends had called him. Except there had never been any love involved.

Catching his breath, he took his hand off the wall and put it on his chest, just over his heart. There was a throbbing ache of total disbelief inside. If Chloe's business was this screwed up, the board would simply close her down. He looked around the office. Half pink, half the calm cream color he'd chosen, the walls pulsed back at him, in rhythm with his heart.

He wiped his forehead and sank into his chair. "What now?" he asked the prototype Drink Caddy sitting next to his own pair of FrogVision 2100 goggles. In a corner of the office stood WindowWonder, Model 2.2, waiting for him to take it home and wash his windows. What had he gotten himself into?

A way to pay the bills stacking up back at Lockhart Associates, that's what. A way to completely refurbish Charlene in time for the annual Corvette Rally. Charlene. Thinking of her shored up his resolve. He needed to convince the board that Chloe could manage Creative Investments well. He needed for Phillips International to offer him a few more lucrative assignments. He needed advice from someone who had known Chloe longer than he had. He reached for the phone.

A tap sounded at the door and Gloria entered, a glass of ice water in her hand. "You okay, Mr. AJ? You looked flushed. Here," she handed him the water. "Drink this and sit quietly." She smiled. "I'll take your shirt to the cleaner, if you want me to."

Shirt? Cleaner? Was everyone in this office infected with Chloe's overexuberant idiocy? He sipped the water, aware of every drop of its cold moisture inside his mouth, his every sense on high alert. "Sure, whatever." He looked down at the front of his shirt. His new blue linen shirt. There was a large creamy yellow handprint covering his heart, and his tie sported a thumbprint. "Apparently the paint was still wet," he said, feeling more undone with every sip of water. "You'll have to take the tie as well." Maybe it was something in the air in this office—now even he was acting like an absentminded eccentric. How could he have missed the fact that he was covered in sticky, damp paint? He shook his head as though to clear away the madness, and wondered again what he'd gotten himself into. And, more to the point, what was he going to do with one Chloe Phillips?

"I can have them back tomorrow," Gloria offered. "You want me to bring you a cloth to wash your face?"

AJ nodded and dialed Oz Phillips. Surely Chloe's brother would have some advice.

* * *

Chloe hadn't been prepared to be the love interest for her nerdiest of clients. Having AJ around, previously tagged to act the role of true love, was entirely enough. In fact, how did her picture get into the program in the first place? And, if *her* true love was theoretically the dark, lethally handsome man working in the office next door, then how could she be Ralph's true love?

As more and more unanswered questions piled up around e-Cupid, she realized it was just possible that E. Rose was playing a huge trick on her.

"We've got to talk, Chloe." It was AJ, back to scoff at her troubles yet one more time, she was sure.

"Let me guess, you weren't at all impressed by either Ralph's hat or e-Cupid," she said, looking up from the papers strewn across her desk. "What happened to you?"

He was standing in her doorway, tie undone, shirt partly unbuttoned, with paint on his forehead and all over his clothes. One black curl had escaped his neatly coifed hair and hung just above his left eye, demanding that someone run her fingers through it. She closed her eyes and took a deep breath. Damn e-Cupid anyway for putting all these preposterous ideas in her head!

"Oh, the paint. Nothing. It appears it wasn't completely dry." He shrugged and brushed the errant curl off his forehead. "You need to get the e-Cupid people back in here."

"You liked it?" she asked, hardly daring to hope that AJ might have seen potential in her most promising project.

"We need to talk to them," he said, regaining composure before her very eyes. Turning back into the erudite executive. She sighed. She liked the undone man much better, the curl on the forehead, the wild look in his blue, blue eyes. "I've been trying all day to contact them. When I do, I'll set up a meeting."

"As soon as possible," he said, moving into her office and sitting on the sofa. "You may have stumbled onto something with e-Cupid."

He'd come around much too easily. He was up to something.

"Do you have any thoughts on SatelHat, and how to get Ralph back? Since you've decided to take an interest in my business, I thought I'd ask."

"The break-even point on that invention was too long anyway. You're better off without him."

Ah, showing his true colors. "You are a heartless vampire, AJ Lockhart. Ralph believes in his project and I believe in him. And never mind about his reaction to e-Cupid. I don't need break-even points to know when something is good."

"Maybe, but now that he's seen e-Cupid, who knows what he'll do next. Be glad he left."

"Beginning to believe?"

"In e-Cupid? No, it's still a simple software program that any halfway creative high school kid could have written." He paused. "But something made Ralph turn into a bad imitation of Rhett Butler," he mumbled.

"Yes. E-Cupid."

"I'm not prepared to adopt your Pollyanna attitude, Chloe. Software can't make people fall in love."

"I suppose you don't believe in love," she said. "Unless it comes with a complete set of financials."

He stood in front of her desk. "May I?" he asked, pointing to a chair.

"By all means. Please, give me the Lockhart assessment of love." She'd about had it with AJ. He might not wear nerdy glasses, but he was as uncreative as they came.

"Love is a figment of your imagination, a convention cooked up by some medieval poet out to peddle his songs from castle to castle."

"I see. So you don't believe in attraction between men and women?"

"Oh sure, but that can be explained by chemistry." He steepled his fingers and leaned back.

"Chemistry?"

"Pheromones. And a chromosome-programmed need to keep the species going."

Chloe blew a curl off her own forehead. This guy was hopeless. "So you wouldn't use a website like Cupid.com then?"

"Absolutely not. Don't get me wrong, Chloe. I like women and it's fun to be with them, but love is a fantasy. There is no such thing."

She watched him shift in the chair. He ran a hand through his hair and a finger in the neckline of his T-shirt. She smiled. He was nervous. This frank discussion made him uncomfortable.

Good.

"All that aside, AJ, how do you explain the whole music industry? Name me one hit song that doesn't involve love."

He scratched his cheek. "That's business."

"Oh, so people buy CDs to help the economy? I don't think so."

"People write love songs because they know they can make money selling them to a public that will buy anything that promises to make them feel better."

"What about great love poems? What about Shakespeare?"

He hesitated. "That's different."

"Why? Because he's a zillion years old?"

"Because it's different, that's all."

"Well, I believe in love, no matter what you say.

It may not come with a money-back guarantee, and it probably doesn't start with a computer program, but it exists." She nodded. "I've seen it for myself."

"Lucky you."

Was that sadness in his voice? Interesting. "Have you changed your assessment of my competency?"

"I never said you weren't competent," he retorted.

"But you're here to prove that I don't know a balance sheet from a colander, aren't you?" The paint all over his forehead was very distracting. He was trying to be so professional, but he looked more like an errant little boy who'd been up to mischief.

"I'm here to confirm that your business decisions are sound ones. Which is why we need to talk to the e-Cupid people. The board has a significant stake in your success, you know."

Ah, the board. So that's what was driving the sudden change in AJ. Of course, he'd talked to the board. "And a bigger one in my failure."

"How so?"

"If the board finds me incapable of managing CI, they'll force me to give up everything I've worked so hard to accomplish."

"Look, what if I try out some of your less wild ideas, say Spuddy Buddy, and then we'll discuss any troublesome areas I pinpoint, and together we can try to find ways to make some of your less troublesome projects lucrative."

"If you want to. Fine with me. Of course, I don't think you'll find any *troublesome* areas, but knock yourself out." She paused. "I doubt you've ever loved anything as much as I love this company."

He thought about Charlene, sitting at the far end of the parking garage so no one would hurt her. "Don't jump to hasty conclusions," he said. "Are you implying that I'm heartless?"

"No, heart-locked." She smiled sweetly at him and

stood. "Don't you have an analysis for SatelHat to complete?"

He blinked twice.

"And don't forget your hot potato," she said, tossing him the prototype for Spuddy Buddy. "I'll expect a full report tomorrow."

# Chapter Five
# "Somewhere, My Love"

Her "true love" didn't believe in true love. Or love of any kind. Why was she not surprised? Chloe opened her e-mail box, hoping for a reply from E. Rose or Milo to her plea yesterday for help. When she found nothing from her ersatz matchmakers, she opened a message from her brother, Oz.

*Chlo*, it began. *I understand your meeting with the board went OK, and that they've sent you a consultant to provide advice. Good. It's about time they offered. Sorry I wasn't there to support you, but my network company needed my attention. I know you want to do this all on your own, sis, but one of the smartest things I ever did was to ask for help with the companies Dad left to me. Don't worry about Webster. His bark is a lot worse than his bite. I know. As Chairman of the Board, he's challenged me more than once. Hang in there, Chlo. You'll succeed. We still on for our weekly dinner? Love ya, Oz.*

Chloe smiled. She and Oz hadn't been that close

growing up. They had never had much in common. He had always gotten along better with their father, sharing his all-consuming interest in the corporate world. Oz, two years younger, had inherited the bulk of the Phillips companies and had thrown himself into living up to his father's reputation as a shrewd businessman. From all reports, he was succeeding.

Recently, he had put forth a lot more effort to stay in touch with Chloe, something she really appreciated. It had been nice to feel a little closer to her brother. She looked forward to their dinner each week. He was all the family she had, after all.

If you didn't consider Edgar Allan, and she didn't.

Perhaps she should show e-Cupid to Oz, get his take on her latest project. If Oz gave it a thumbs-up, she knew it would succeed. She typed a quick answer to her brother and worked her way through the rest of the messages in her in-box.

There were the standard reports from her various clients. And some not-so-encouraging news from the Pentagon. While they were intrigued with the potential for FrogVision 2100, they were requesting two hundred units, at no charge, to do an extensive field test. FrogVision was one of her cutting-edge technology projects—a set of goggles that allowed the wearer to see one-hundred-eighty degrees without turning his head—just like a frog. Quickly she calculated the cost to produce two hundred FrogVision units in time to satisfy the Defense Department. A lot. But, if they liked it, every soldier, sailor, and marine in the country would be issued one—and that was worth the cost of manufacturing two hundred.

She shot off an affirmative reply and copied it to her FrogVision development team. At least they'd be happy. She spent the next half hour updating her files on FrogVision. No need to irritate the already irritating AJ—Aggravating and Jaded—Lockhart with incomplete files, she thought. She'd decided the best way to handle the man testing WindowWonder next door was to keep him out of her office. If that meant giving him prototypes to play with, so be it.

There was a flurry of e-mails from Barb, demanding that Chloe find the hunk of her dreams e-Cupid had promised to deliver. The messages started out rational and became more and more incoherent. The last one informed Chloe that Barb would come looking for her if she didn't produce one true love. Chloe shook her head. She'd give Barb a call later.

Gloria stuck her head in the doorway and scowled. "Mr. Higgenbotham is here," she said and stood back to let Ralph enter Chloe's office.

"Ralph," Chloe said. "Give me good news on SatelHat."

Ralph leaned against the sofa, a stricken expression on his face. "Chloe, I am whole once more in your presence."

Oh, boy.

He pulled a sheet of pink paper from his pocket and smoothed it against his knee. Balanced on one foot, he reminded Chloe of a crane or a flamingo, except he wasn't nearly as attractive. Dark circles under his eyes and thin hair awry told Chloe that Ralph had spent a restless night. Apparently he hadn't spent it working on SatelHat.

"Ahem," he said, holding the pink page in front of him.

AJ chose that moment to come into her office. An office, Chloe thought ruefully, that in the last few days had begun to feel more and more like Grand Central Station. "Oh, hi, Ralph," he greeted the inventor. "I think I've fixed your flange problem."

Ralph ignored him.

AJ looked from Ralph to Chloe and back again. "Ralph, buddy, I've solved all your problems."

"I have no problems, now that I've found true love," Ralph announced.

"Oh, please." AJ practically groaned.

Ralph sank to one knee in front of Chloe. "My love," he began. "I've penned a poem for you."

"Oh, my God," Chloe said.

"This ought to be good," AJ said.

*"My heart took flight when I saw your face*
*Like a lonely bird who longed to be free*
*I found my love in this very place*
*And knew then what my future would be*
*In the arms of my one, my only, my Chloe."*

"Your rhyme scheme doesn't quite work, does it?" asked AJ.

Still ignoring the other man, Ralph sighed and put one hand over his heart, a broad smile splitting his thin face. He adjusted his glasses and looked at the pink page once more.

"Please, Ralph, no need to continue," said Chloe.

"But, my dove," implored Ralph. "I must sing of my devotion. It's required. All the great poets have done it."

Ralph hardly qualified as a great poet, but she wasn't going to be the one to tell him. Having never been the subject of a love poem before, Chloe was quite at a loss for what to do. She knew she shouldn't encourage Ralph, but his effort was sweet—in a saccharine, slightly worrying kind of way.

"Why don't you leave the poem here so Chloe can contemplate it at her leisure?" suggested AJ and took the pink page from Ralph's hand.

Quicker than she'd thought he could move, Ralph snatched it right back and handed the poem to Chloe. "It isn't appropriate to sully my love song with him in the room." Ralph, indicated AJ, with a nod of his head. "Take this as a token of my passion," he said and grabbed her fingers. He went to his knee once more and kissed her hand. Then, with his glasses fogging up, he rushed out of her office.

"That was unforgettable, if for no other reason than the sheer bizarreness of it," AJ noted, moving farther into the office and slouching on the sofa.

"I thought it was sweet," Chloe responded, setting the poem on her desk.

"You can't be serious. It was sophomoric at best, something guys do in high school."

"You've probably never written a love poem," Chloe said.

"You'd be wrong," AJ said. He'd been in poem-writing lust only once, in high school. It'd also been an assignment for his English class.

"Really? And how did your lady love react when you read her your great work?"

AJ stood up, set the file folder he'd been holding on the table and took three steps toward Chloe. "She loved it," he said, a cocky grin on his face. "Showered me with kisses and suggested we elope immediately." He took both her hands in his. "Did my heart love till now? Forswear it, sight! For I ne'er saw true beauty till this night."

Chills ran up her spine. Shakespeare. *Romeo and Juliet*. Her favorite play.

AJ stopped quoting and looked down at her hands. "Except it's the middle of the afternoon. Which one did your pal Ralph kiss?"

Chloe backed up a step. "The right one," she said.

AJ dropped her right hand and brought her left one to his lips. He kissed it gently, softly. "I'd hate for you to be unbalanced," he said, giving her fingers one small squeeze before letting them go and backing away. "I *have* solved Ralph's flange problem," he said. "You might want to review it before you get swept away by his poetry." He picked up the folder and handed it to her. Then he spun around and marched out of her office.

"You didn't write that," she called after him. But he'd quoted it to her.

Chloe compared Ralph's innocent kiss to the sizzling touch of AJ's lips on her hand. Intense heat flowed into the very center of her being, where it curled and set up housekeeping. She put her hand over her stomach, about an inch below her belly button. She felt his impact there, warm and satisfying. She shivered.

Ralph's kiss hadn't done anything but make the back of her hand wet.

She could see AJ's eyes as clearly as if they were staring into her own right now. Dark, mysterious, and rich with the promise of passion. She shuddered.

What was going on in her world?

The intercom in her phone crackled. "Do you have time for an unscheduled appointment?" Gloria asked.

Maybe the golden boy and his gnome had decided to come back. Good, she had a number of very direct questions to ask them. "Yes. Show them in, please."

"Him. Singular." Gloria added, "With uniform."

Chloe stood up. Into her office walked a police officer, tall and blond with a tidy mustache. He smiled at her and removed his hat, tucking it under his arm.

"Good morning, ma'am. Sorry to bother you, but I have reports of a band of purse snatchers operating in this area, and my lieutenant asked me to talk to all the executive women in the building."

Purse snatchers? Oh, good. Someone to steal her credit cards while AJ stole her business. Was nothing safe? "Certainly, Officer. Would you like some coffee?"

"No, thanks. Just a few quick questions and then I'll let you get back to work." He gestured to a chair at her table. "May I?"

"Oh, sure. Please, sit down." She joined him, bringing along a pad of paper and a pen. "Now, how can I help you?"

He pulled a picture from his uniform pocket. "This person has been identified as the ringleader. Have you ever seen him before?"

She glanced at the picture then shook her head. "No."

"Have you been approached outside your building?"

"No, sorry." At that moment, AJ returned. Could the man not concentrate on any given task for longer than five minutes? "Perhaps my colleague has seen your suspect."

The officer frowned. "So far the perpetrator has only shown interest in women. Women with briefcases," he clarified.

AJ stood next to the officer's chair and examined the picture. "Pretty scruffy looking. What'd he do?"

"He's organized a band of youngsters to snatch purses and briefcases. Does he look familiar?"

"I'm not sure," AJ said. "Is his name Fagan?" The officer and Chloe frowned in unison. "Okay, it was a stretch, but it worked for Dickens."

Chloe picked up her pen and began doodling on her pad. The squiggles quickly turned into loopy hearts. What if she tried e-Cupid on a complete stranger?

"How do I contact you, if I see this person?" she asked. The officer gave her his card. "Officer Andrew McKinnett," she read.

He nodded. "Just call the precinct and ask for me. Any help you can offer would be appreciated." He stood to leave.

"Wait." She liked Officer McKinnett. He'd make a great guinea pig. Better than Ralph. He was a complete innocent who appeared fairly normal, and she really did want to test out e-Cupid on more men. "Perhaps you'd be willing to help me?" she began.

"To protect and serve," McKinnett said. "Right here on the badge. What can I do?"

Before she could speak, Barb Holland, face glowing with excitement, burst into her office.

"Chloe, have you got any more information on the man from e-Cupid yet?" she demanded, pushing past AJ. "I haven't slept for days, thinking about him." Then Barb turned and saw the man in uniform and shouted, "Oh, Chloe! You scamp. You knew who he was all along!" She rushed across the office and stopped just short of embracing the policeman. "I'm Barbara Holland and you," she sighed, "are my true love."

For his part, Officer McKinnett handled the declaration fairly well, Chloe thought. His face lit up like a kid getting a pony for Christmas. He put his interview pad and pencil on the table, stood and took Barb's hands in his.

"Don't tell me," AJ said. "Another of your e-Cupid experiments?"

"Yes," Chloe said. "Aren't they cute?"

"No."

Seconds ticked into minutes as the couple stared into each other's eyes, trying to memorize the shape of eyebrows and noses. Either that, or they were counting pores and freckles. Enough was too much. Chloe coughed.

Nothing. This was why Chloe had such strong feelings about mixing love with business. The pheromones made you stupid. So did Shakespeare.

She coughed louder. "Excuse me, Officer. Did you have more questions you wanted to ask me?" There was only so much sweet she could take in one dose, and Barb and her policeman were rapidly reaching Chloe's limit.

"Huh? Oh, no. I think I'm done with you." He let go of one of Barb's hands and, keeping tight hold of the other, led her to the table and pulled out a chair. She sat and he sat. As close to each other as they could manage and still maintain an impression of professionalism.

"Thank you," Barb whispered to Chloe. "He's everything the program promised."

Now, how could she know that? She'd been in this man's presence less than three minutes. Talk about love at first sight. The wheels inside Chloe's head began spinning. Instant romance and all because of *her* killer e-Cupid software. Life was good. Very good. "Officer McKinnett?"

"Right," he said, but he didn't take his eyes off her friend. "Miss Holland," he sighed deeply.

"Barbara, call me Barbara."

"Ahem, Barbara." He said her name with such longing that Chloe thought she might break out in cheers. She picked up her pad of paper and scribbled quick notes to herself. Pictures on the Mall, an ad campaign on radio and TV, perhaps an interview on the various news programs. This was going to be big. Bigger than big.

She stopped short. If e-Cupid was so wonderful, why hadn't AJ reacted to her this way? She'd seen him, and he'd seen her, after all. She chewed the inside of her cheek and worried. Maybe there was something wrong with her. She brushed the thought aside. Barb was the type to fall in love based on a picture she saw on a computer screen. She had always been far more impetuous and daring than Chloe when it came to matters of the heart.

"What's your first name?" Barbara asked, her smile overwhelming her face.

"Andrew."

Barb sighed. "I love that name." She glanced at Chloe's stern face. "This is so weird, because I saw your picture in Chloe's new software. And I knew, just knew, that I needed to find you. And here you are."

From somewhere deep inside Andrew McKennett, a remnant of professional duty bubbled to the top and overcame the blush of the first meeting. "A software program?" He turned to Chloe. "May I see this, please?"

Now they might get somewhere. Chloe retrieved the laptop from her desk. "It's a new product I'm evaluating. E-Cupid. Guaranteed to match people with their true loves." And apparently it was working, because Barb and Andrew looked deliriously happy. *Yeah,* a voice in her head told her. *Just wait until she finds dirty socks in the middle of the kitchen and HoHo wrappers in her lingerie drawer.*

"Are you sure you want to risk this? Remember Ralph." AJ whispered.

"It'll be fine. They're obviously made for each other," she said. "Don't be such a skeptic." She handed the computer to the policeman.

"How does this work?" McKinnett opened the laptop. Barb reached over his arm and turned the program on.

"Just click on the heart and you'll find me," said Barb.

AJ cleared his throat. "Officer, I'd be careful with that if I were you."

McKinnett glanced at AJ and then at Barb. "Don't worry, sir," he said. "I've had computer training." With that, he went back to e-Cupid.

Chloe smiled sweetly at AJ with a "See, I told you"

kind of look. She was certain McKinnett would find Barb, since the pair were so obviously meant for each other. That bit with Ralph and his satellite hat had to have been a programming glitch. A simple anomaly.

Andrew McKinnett went through the steps to initiate e-Cupid, watching with interest as the program unfolded. When he was about to get to the part where Cupid presented him with the framed picture of Barb, Chloe walked behind the couple. She wanted to witness for herself the magic of e-Cupid.

The silver frame appeared and there, where Barb's smiling face should have been, was Chloe's!

Officer Andrew McKinnett looked up from the computer screen with a dumb, love-struck grin on his face and spun around. "Chloe, how could I ever have been interested in this person," he hooked his thumb at Barb, "when perfection was sitting across from me. Are you doing anything for dinner?"

Chloe barely managed to sit down before she fell over.

Half an hour later, Chloe had convinced McKinnett that he absolutely must get back to protecting the fine citizens of Arlington, Virginia. Then, under the scornful eye of AJ Lockhart, she turned to the task of calming down her friend.

In the "if looks could kill" department, Barb had been murdering Chloe for the past thirty minutes.

"How could you! You knew, *you knew,* he was mine, or why would your stupid program have allowed me to see his picture? Can you tell me that?" Barb paced around Chloe's office, refusing to sit, refusing to slow down enough for Chloe to try to explain. "You've already got *him,*" she shouted, pointing at AJ who stood, somewhat stunned, in front of Chloe's window. "You are some friend. I wish I'd never heard of e-Cupid!"

"See," AJ whispered. "This is what happens when you take on projects without a thorough analysis."

Chloe glared at him. "Yesterday you were willing to concede that I'd found some excellent ideas. What happened?"

AJ nodded at Barb, making her sixty-third pass across Chloe's carpet. "She happened. And the policeman. And let's not forget Satellite boy."

"Okay, I'll admit I may have a slight problem with e-Cupid but—"

"Slight?" AJ began.

Barb pushed between them and flung herself on the sofa. "I hope you don't have the same designs on Karl. Leann *would* kill you." Tears ran down Barb's cheeks, obliterating her generally expert makeup.

Chloe grabbed the box of tissues from her credenza and sat next to her friend. "You're welcome to leave," she informed AJ.

"And miss your explanation of what just happened? Not on your life," he said, sitting at her desk.

Chloe handed Barb the box of tissues. "I didn't mean to hurt you, Barb. You're my friend. I think there's something wrong with the software in e-Cupid." She tried to console Barb with no success. AJ she'd take care of later.

"Besides," she continued, "who knows exactly what makes a man decide he likes one woman instead of another?" She thought of Ralph and shuddered, then looked at AJ and swallowed.

"Look," Barbara swiveled on the tapestry cushion, "you promised me my true love. That's what the program is designed to do, isn't it? Right. And Andrew's picture came up. Why did you have to put your picture into the program? You've bewitched him. It's some kind of spell." She buried her face in her hands and wept. "Now I'll never know what it's like to be loved."

Chloe looked at the ceiling, hoping for guidance. "Look, Barb. I don't want your officer. He's yours and you're welcome to pursue him. I promise I won't encourage him. I'll sing your praises."

"How can you do this?" Barb shrieked. She jumped up and ran for the door. "I'm going to be miserable for my entire life, and it's your fault, Chloe Phillips. I rue the day I called you friend!" With that, she fled Chloe's office.

Stunned, Chloe sagged against the back of the sofa. There had to be some explanation. Software or no software, people didn't just fall in love like that. Not from seeing a stupid computerized picture. Not professional law enforcement officers who were trained to keep their emotions in check. Barb? Well, she was the resident Drama Queen and everything was a Big Deal with her. But, Officer McKinnett?

She'd heard of love at first sight. But could it possibly be this strong—this confusing?

"Masterfully done," said AJ, rising from the desk chair and coming to sit next to her on the sofa. He applauded softly. "A true triumph."

"Not now," she said, trying to ignore the heat of his closeness.

*She* certainly hadn't gone goofy when she'd finally met *her* e-Cupid-designated true love. In fact, mild dislike was the closest emotion to love she could manage for AJ Lockhart. Total disgust was closer to the truth. In her mind, his initials stood for Absolute Jerk. Sitting smugly next to her, gloating at her latest disaster.

"Are you going to run and tell the board what a mess I've made of this?" she asked.

"No."

Some consolation that was. She leaned her head

back and closed her eyes. If only *one* of her ideas, her pet projects, would work. Just one. It wasn't so much to ask, was it?

"I tried Spuddy Buddy last night," AJ offered.

Chloe opened one eye. "And?"

"I have two of Idaho's finest bakers plastered to the ceiling in my kitchen in little white potato globs." He rested a hand on her arm and heat flooded her body. "I think the power should be adjusted downward."

Instead of pulling away from him, Chloe turned slightly and looked at him, trying to decide if he was being sincere or just warming up to ridicule her one more time. "I forgot to include the control unit when I tossed it to you last night. Sorry," she said. *Two* potatoes? The heat from his touch made its way into the center of her being. Why would he want two potatoes?

"You know, if you could figure out a way to make it portable, Spuddy Buddy might find a market with campers and hikers." He smiled. His hand moved toward her hand.

He was going to kiss her again, she just knew it. She put aside the question of one potato, two potato. "You really think so?" AJ didn't wear a ring, but men frequently didn't these days. Another kiss wouldn't be all that awful.

"Absolutely. The basic idea is sound, but its current incarnation will run up against microwave ovens and those potato-baker things with the nails that go into conventional ovens. I think you'd have better luck in a market segment that isn't as fussy about how their food tastes because they've been hiking all day."

Chloe gave up trying to guess if he was married and if his lips would feel as good on hers a second time, and thought about what he'd said. "I suppose

I could ask Darrell to consider modifications. Yes, I'll call him tomorrow." She frowned and stood up. Had AJ actually *approved* of one of her ideas? The Devil must be wearing ear muffs. "Now, if I could figure out what to do with the e-Cupid casualties. . . ."

"Can't help you there," AJ said. "It's been a long day and I've got windows to wash tonight." He rose from the couch, looming over her. "See you Monday?" He put his hand on her shoulder and squeezed ever so gently.

More heat. "Right," she said. "Windows." Hmmm. "Is your wife going to try WindowWonder or are you giving it a spin?" She walked behind her desk to try to calm her pounding heart.

AJ cocked his head and gave her an enigmatic look that revealed absolutely nothing. "I'm going to try it. I find I do better analyses if I'm the one getting all sudsy."

She could well imagine him all sudsy, and the image shot heat through her body. "Well, then, have fun."

"It's what I live for," he said and walked away.

She hadn't worded that question quite right. She should have asked him if his wife was going to try WindowWonder and let it go at that. Then he would have had to tell her he didn't have a wife. Or, alternately, he did have a wife but. . . . "Phooey," Chloe said throwing herself back into her chair. There was no way any sane woman would fall for AJ Lockhart, she decided. Not after his declaration that attraction was simply a matter of biologically programmed pheromones, and that love had nothing to do with it. She definitely needed to see the questionnaire for e-Cupid. Why had E. Rose and Milo paired them together?

She wasn't remotely interested in AJ, she told herself firmly. Even if his willingness to test some of her products did make him slightly less despicable, and the thought of him cooking and cleaning with said products was endearing. What would she have to do, she wondered, to get AJ to try e-Cupid, broken though it was?

"Wouldn't make any difference," she said to the Boston ivy on the corner of her desk. "He wouldn't believe he was in love even if he did see me. He's too busy plotting how to close down Creative Investments." But he'd liked Spuddy Buddy, so maybe he wasn't the business version of the grim reaper.

Barb, however, could be a stand-in for Death if Chloe didn't figure out how to fix that little screwup. Her friend had obviously believed in e-Cupid and was love-struck. Chloe had to try to help. She stood up and walked to her door. She leaned out and scanned the suite for Gloria, who looked to be gone for the day. Too bad, her assistant often had good advice when Barb was having what Chloe referred to as one of her dramatic episodes.

Fine. She could fix this herself. She marched to her desk, determined to try one more time to contact E. Rose. As she reached for the phone, it rang. She checked her watch. Ralph, right on time. She jerked the receiver off its cradle and said, "Not now, Ralph."

There was a short span of silence, then her brother's voice answered, "Hey, Chloe. I just wanted to talk. Is this not a convenient time for you?"

"No, I mean, yes, it's convenient." It had been a very confusing day. She opened her desk drawer and pulled out a new box of Cracker Jack. "What's up?"

"Just checking in to see how the new numbers guy is working out. He's supposed to be great. MBA from Wharton. Graduated magna cum something or other."

Oz seemed to know a lot about AJ, but he was on the board, so that wasn't unusual. "He's looking at the company's financial statements and trying out some of my product designs, giving me feedback. You know, generally helping out in a supportive kind of way." She tore open the package and poured a small pile of candy popcorn onto her desk. She left out the part about her new consultant quoting Shakespeare and making her break out in a sweat.

"Good. Good."

She could hear him tapping on his desk with his pen. "Do you know if he's married?"

"He was number two on the Most Eligible Bachelors of Northern Virginia list a couple of years ago. Why do you care?"

For reasons she didn't want to examine, that little bit of information made her smile. "No reason," she said. "So, how are things going with your end of the business? I saw in the paper this morning that construction was delayed again on your Waterford property." She popped a piece of Cracker Jack into her mouth. Heavenly. She went looking for peanuts.

"Damned inspectors," Oz said. "I've got this crew on standby and the county can't find my paperwork. Bureaucratic red tape will be the undoing of this country."

Chloe had her own red tape to worry about. "What are you going to do?" She stopped fishing for peanuts.

"Keep the crew, I guess. Pay them for doing nothing and make up the overruns at the other end of the job."

"Kind of like having a new product, oh, say, Keys-in-Tune, not meet revenue projections because the chip manufacturers couldn't deliver on time?"

"Come on, Chlo. Even you have to agree that the world can wait another six months for keys that sing opera when they're lost. My companies can't afford that kind of delay," Oz said.

"Don't forget, they scream when someone other than the owner picks them up," Chloe added. Keys-in-Tune was one of her favorite projects, and it wasn't working the way she'd planned. Each key came with a programmable chip and a tiny speaker. She'd picked a wide range of songs, both popular and classical, that the key's owner could program into the chip. All the person had to do was say "Keys" and the key would sing.

"Which makes it tough to loan your car to someone, or have a neighbor look in on your cat. Speaking of which, how is old Edgar?"

Chloe had gotten to the prize. "She crawled into the piano last night and refused to get out, even when I played Chopin," Chloe said. "She's obnoxious." She propped the phone between her ear and her shoulder and opened the small paper packet.

"Dad loved her."

True. And, how could she expect to manage one of her father's companies if she couldn't even control his cat? "Come to my place this Sunday for dinner," Chloe suggested. "I'll do fried chicken like Grandma used to make."

"Sure, why not," Oz said. "I'll bring a bottle of wine and you can bring me up to date on all your projects. I understand the EPA is holding up Fish-in-a-Dish."

"I'll give you all the gory details on Sunday." Chloe hung up and shook the prize into her hand. It was a miniature book entitled "The Story of Love."

"Nothing beats a crisp autumn day on the links," said Oz Phillips on Saturday morning as he selected a three wood from his golf bag and placed his ball on the tee. "Just breathe in all that fresh air."

AJ stood next to the golf cart in his sweater and windbreaker, shivering. Chloe's brother wore a light jacket and seemed impervious to the sharp wind. "Yeah, fresh air. Gotta love it." The man must have ice water in his veins.

Oz swung his club and his ball took off, rising in a gentle arc down the fairway, then slicing into the rough. "Damn wind," he said, raking his hand through wavy blond hair that would make any Hollywood hunk jealous.

"Tough luck. I think I can find it, though," AJ offered, taking Chloe's remote-control ball finder out of his bag. "Have you tried this?" he asked, showing it to Oz.

"Another one of Chloe's cute, totally unprofitable inventions?" Oz said. "Don't be fooled by her enthusiasm, Lockhart. She doesn't understand the first thing about business." He stepped aside to let AJ line up for his tee shot.

AJ's swing was easy, gentle. His ball flew straight down the fairway, bouncing a couple of times before it stopped, dead center. Probably not the way to play against Oz if he was serious about doing more business with Phillips. He'd gotten the message early in the day that Oz wouldn't be a gracious loser.

"Lucky shot, Lockhart," Oz observed, climbing into the cart. "Let's go." He pulled away so quickly he almost left AJ behind.

Chloe wouldn't have cared if she won or lost a game of golf. To her, it would be an opportunity to try out her ball finder, or a heat-seeking squirrel identifier, or whatever new idea had captured her imagination that week. She would never have been snide about her brother's business or somebody else's golf shot, AJ thought. She would have been a one-woman cheering section and wouldn't have worried about her own game. Oz, on the other hand, needed to work on his self-image.

"How are things going with my sister and all her goofy projects?" Oz asked, swerving around a small tree on the edge of the course. "She's taken on some doozies, hasn't she?"

"She has identified a wide range of interesting ideas, yes." AJ didn't know what Chloe's relationship was with her brother and wasn't about to jeopardize potential future business by making a wrong comment. She hadn't mentioned Oz in the week he'd known her, although Oz's opinion of his sister's company was clear. In the past two hours he'd called his sister "unfocused," "flighty," and "generally a bad manager."

"My father founded this golf club," Oz said, guiding the cart around a sand trap. "He wouldn't be happy with the way it's being managed today, and he wouldn't be happy with Chloe, either."

"Is she really that bad?" AJ didn't belong to a country club. "I mean, I've been there less than a week, and her projects are in some disarray, but nothing that can't be organized with a little attention to detail." If Oz was representative of the type of people who joined country clubs, he wasn't sure he ever wanted to. "There it is," said AJ, pointing to a golf ball nestled in some tall grass.

"Oh, I've no doubt *some* of her projects are sound," Oz answered, picking up the ball and sticking it in his pocket. "Let's just say my hit came fairly close to yours, okay? Since it's a friendly game between friends." He climbed back into the cart. "It's just that I think Dad made a mistake giving her CI to run."

"You think she'd do better with one of your companies, Mr. Phillips?" AJ had agreed to the game with Oz in hopes of learning more about Phillips

International, in hopes of identifying more opportunities for consulting. What he'd discovered was just how good Chloe was at understanding the essence of business when compared with her brother.

"Call me Oz. We've shared a round of golf and a six-pack of beer. You can call me Oz."

"Oz."

"I don't believe a woman like Chloe should be managing any business." Phillips took out a five iron and managed to keep his ball on the fairway.

*There* was an enlightened, twenty-first century attitude. "Really?" AJ followed him with an arrow-straight shot that landed on the green.

"Really. She's a creative thinker, not a manager. She should be allowed to exercise that creativity and not be burdened by all the reports and tedium of running a company," Oz explained as he drove the cart to his ball.

AJ couldn't argue with that, since he'd come to the same conclusion. "So, if CI had someone to organize the business part of things, Chloe would be free to create?" asked AJ. "I could see that being beneficial." He could just see Chloe, shaking her head and telling him he should mind his own business and let her run hers. *I am,* he said to himself, *I am. If agreeing with your brother means more work for Lockhart Associates and pays the bills, how can I not agree?* Aloud, he said, "I suppose it's possible the board could come to the same conclusion after I make my report."

"Might," Oz said and lined up his putter. He tapped the ball and it rolled slowly towards the cup, veered a little left and stopped just at the edge of the hole, where it teetered.

*Please, please let it fall in,* AJ prayed. *Please, pretty please.*

Finally, the law of gravity won out and the ball

plunked into the cup. "There," Oz said. "That's the way to sink a putt."

AJ cheered. "Excellent."

"Yes, it was, wasn't it?" Oz watched as AJ replicated his putt. "You know, Lockhart, I like you and I like your firm's work. That scenario planning you talked about earlier? Are you doing that with Chloe?

"It wasn't in the scope of the board's assignment, I'm afraid."

"Well, let's change the scope, shall we? You do some forward-looking planning with Chloe, identify the top three ideas and how much they'll be worth in five years. I'll square things with the board, make sure they pay you for the additional work. Okay?"

Like he was going to turn down business. "Absolutely, Oz." His new best friend. He didn't even care that the man cheated at golf. AJ added the new fees in his head. Combined with what the board had agreed to, this new project would definitely keep Lockhart Associates humming along.

"You look cold. Why not say we both made par on these last holes and call it a day?" Oz put his putter back in his bag and smiled at AJ.

It was not a warm smile.

# Chapter Six
# "Who Wrote the Book of Love?"

"Why don't you just take the cat?" Chloe asked Oz after their Sunday dinner. Edgar had climbed into Oz's lap and curled up for a long nap.

"Can't, Chlo. You know Audrey is allergic to cats."

"Audrey is allergic to everything except your money," Chloe said. "I don't see why you date her at all."

"Don't be nasty. She has many gifts," Oz said, stroking the purring Edgar.

Right, thought Chloe. A large bustline and a small IQ. But it was his life. She really should show e-Cupid to Oz.

"I played golf with your consultant yesterday," Oz said. "I practically had to screw up every shot just so he could keep up." He chucked Edgar under her chin and the dumb cat almost smiled. "I hope he's better at numbers than he is at sports."

"I doubt he takes any time for leisure activities," she said. "He's been pretty focused on the job."

"Good," Oz said. "Let's keep it that way."

What did that mean? "What does that mean?" Chloe asked.

"Just that with his kind, you have to be careful."

"You're not making any sense, Oz."

"You didn't read his resume?" Oz shook his head. "Of course not. It's just like Webster to send the man, but not the information about him."

"Well?"

"He did graduate from Wharton, but he grew up poor, Chloe. I admire his work ethic, mind you, but while you can take the man out of his neighborhood, it's hard to take the neighborhood out of the man. I mean, just look at that wreck of a car he drives."

Chloe hadn't seen AJ's car and didn't see what that had to do with anything. "He's been nothing but a gentleman, Oz. And a professional. He kissed my hand, for heaven's sake."

"He kissed you?" Oz put Edgar on the floor and stood up. Edgar wasn't amused. "What did I tell you? Watch out for him, Chloe."

She put her hand on Oz's arm. "Nothing's going to happen, Oz. Nothing. AJ's working on the report for the board and helping me with my projects. Nothing more." It probably wasn't a good idea to tell her brother about e-Cupid and Ralph and Andrew, Chloe thought. And definitely not a good idea to tell Oz about AJ's picture. Or that she'd kissed him.

Oz put his arm around her. "I know I worry too much, Chloe, but you're my sister and the only family I've got. I just want you to be happy."

"Thanks, Oz. I am. And as soon as I find my killer idea and convince the board to let me continue running CI, I'll be even happier."

* * *

Monday morning found Chloe at her desk, turning the tiny Cracker Jack book in her hand. It was blank inside, but that wasn't unexpected. Any fool knew there were no rules to love and Chloe was nobody's fool. Was the book another sign, she wondered, that e-Cupid was the Killer Idea she'd been looking for? Or simply the universe's skewed sense of humor? She preferred the first, thank you, and pulled a list of projects from her top desk drawer just as AJ came into her office. Intensely good looking, radiating sex appeal in buckets.

"Ah, I see you're reviewing the same list I am," he said, sitting in the chair across from her desk. "I assume the successful ventures are listed in bold type, while those that haven't done so well aren't."

"Hey," said Chloe, ignoring the purple pager making vibrating noises in her desk drawer. Whatever had caused AJ to make approving sounds about Spuddy Buddy on Friday had apparently not carried through the weekend. He was the same irritating AJ she'd come to know so well. He'd replaced Friday's paint-covered shirt with a burgundy turtle neck. Which she couldn't help but notice was pulled snugly across his excellently formed chest.

*Focus, Chloe Ann, focus.* "It isn't a bad group of companies and products. Task-tender, Goobers Dot Com, and Mystikwire Computer Cables. . . ." She looked up. "Yes?"

"Where would you like me to put these?" Gloria stood in her office doorway holding a huge vase of red roses. There must have been three dozen. Maybe more.

Chloe gave AJ a smart-aleck smile. "Oh, you shouldn't have."

"I didn't," he said, standing. "Why not put them on the table, Gloria? That way Chloe can admire them all day."

Gloria smiled and handed the bouquet to AJ. "No one's ever sent me flowers," she said. "I'm about done with that job you gave me, Mr. AJ."

"Job?" asked Chloe as AJ took the roses, holding them far away from his body as though they might bite. "Who told you to give assignments to my staff?"

He set the roses on the table. They practically engulfed it, and she could smell their fragrance from across the room. "You gave me an office, you gave me access to your files," he said, pulling the card from in between the little gold handcuffs that attached it to the flowers. "I assumed that meant that I could also make use of your people." He handed her the card.

She sniffed and read it. "Oh, dear."

"Trouble?"

She showed him the note.

"Ah, I see your favorite policeman has squandered a week's wages on you. Want me to leave while you call to say thank you?"

"No." Chloe wasn't prepared for the flood of feelings that overcame her. It was kind of nice to have a man sending her a traditional gift of love, even if he wasn't supposed to care about her at all. "I have no intention of getting between Andrew and Barb," Chloe said. She took a deep breath and walked to the door. "Gloria? Could you have the flower shop come pick these up and deliver them to Barb Holland? Thanks." Better to get them out of the way quickly than dwell on the mixture of delight and sadness that filled her.

"What?" AJ feigned shock. "A woman giving back a gift? Unheard of."

Heartless. He was heartless. "Maybe in your circle of friends," she said. "But these flowers aren't mine, really. Barb and Andrew belong together. It's not my fault he's confused. I owe it to my friend to make things right." She shuffled the papers around on her desk. "Where were we?"

"I think I've been insulted."

Good. "Sorry. I'm worried about Barb is all." She cleared her throat. "We were discussing Task-tender, Goobers Dot Com—and Mystikwire Computer Cables, which, as you know, went public this last year and is moving rapidly into the hefty-profit arena." He wanted to be all business, fine. She could be all business.

He raised an eyebrow. "Really? Hefty, huh? That much?"

"Don't be snotty. It doesn't look good on you," she said. "Success will depend on how Wall Street reacts. You've read the files. But I'm banking on things going very well." She glanced at the roses and then back at AJ. There were no occasions at all for which she could conceive of him sending her roses. Why had e-Cupid inspired flowers in a policeman and spreadsheets in AJ? One of life's unanswered and unanswerable questions.

"Ruthie Wheat," she continued, "the CEO of Task-tender, she's a single mother of two and she really needs this company to succeed. Her boys are both under six years old, so running T-squared out of her house is a real help." She wasn't about to tell him that Ruthie's idea took more time to learn than it saved, and in its present form would never make it to the marketplace.

"Tell me there are solid financials behind tending tasks," AJ said, leaning back in his chair.

Chloe chewed on the inside of her cheek. Well, he'd find out sooner or later. Better get it out there. "No, actually, I'm pretty sure Task-tender won't make any profit at all." She sighed. "It was one of the first projects I funded and I've learned a lot since then."

"That's encouraging," AJ said, smiling.

"Ruthie's my friend. She needed help," Chloe began.

"And you were there, checkbook open, to offer it. Really, Chloe, you can't run a charity. Your duty is to create profits."

"I suppose you've had experience as an out-of-work single mom?" she asked.

AJ's face turned red, and he gazed at his shoe tops. Damn, Chloe chastized herself, hadn't Oz said AJ's family didn't have a lot of money when he was growing up? Who was she to preach about the experiences of a poor single mother? She certainly hadn't meant to embarrass him.

"Look," she started again. "It was a bad decision initially. But, check out the numbers." She pulled a file from her desk. "At least it's breaking even now."

AJ took the file but didn't look at it. How different would his life have been if someone like Chloe had been around to encourage his mother in those early, dark years? The wall of distrust around his heart shook just a little. "Let's chalk it up to beginner's jitters and let it go at that," he said.

"Thank you," Chloe said.

"Don't sound so surprised. I'm not as heartless as you think. I understand how tough things are for single parents." He glanced down at his hands, clenched in his lap. "Maybe there's something we could do to make Ruthie's efforts successful." He smiled at the expression of disbelief on Chloe's face. "If we work together on it."

She choked. "Sure. Why not?"

"Now, this Wallace guy of the infamous Goobers Dot Com. Any profit in his future?"

If only he'd decide whether he was going to be a

tough, no-nonsense numbers guy or a sympathetic, supporting kind of guy. Then she could figure out how to deal with him. "You've seen the numb You tell me."

AJ opened his mouth to answer when a uniform flower delivery man poked his head in the office an pointed at the roses. "Excuse me, I understand you want these delivered to a different address?"

Now there was an effective way to break whatever minimal spell she and AJ had begun to weave. "Yes," Chloe told him and wrote Barb's address on a sticky note. "This is where they really belong."

"If you say so," the man said, taking the sticky note and the roses and leaving. "I hope you didn't send these," he said to AJ on the way out.

"Where were we?"

"We were discussing barriers to market entry, and your pal Whitman Wallace," said AJ. "Who, as luck would have it, looks like he's about to run out of money. Oh, but I forgot. He's got Chloe Phillips in his corner. Money won't be a problem."

She glared at him. These were her favorite projects and he was making fun of them. And, by extension, her. What had happened to his support for Spuddy Buddy? His unexpected offer to help Ruthie Wheat? She revised her already revised opinion of AJ—he really *was* out to take her down. The nice words about her automatic potato cooker were simply that. Words. "Fish-in-a-Dish," She continued down the list of promising inventions, pointedly ignoring his uncalled for barb about Wallace. "Fish-in-a-Dish and WindowWonder are on the brink." If Ralph could stop mooning over her long enough, she was certain SatelHat would join the list of really good decisions she'd made in the past two years.

"What, no family history on the chief executive,

chief financial, and chief operating officers of your fish and window projects?"

"Look, Lockhart. Get used to it. I get involved with my investments. I'm very hands-on."

"Ralph obviously wants you to be more hands-on."

She ignored his comment, unsure why Ralph's attention seemed to annoy him so much. He couldn't be jealous, could he? And why did that very possibility send shivers of delight down her spine? She forced her attention back to the matter at hand. "These people come to me because they're not comfortable with the full court press of big business. You know, people like you. I make them feel like family and I love them the same way." She could tell by his blank look that he wouldn't give a damn about Al and Annie Prescott, her resident fish farmers and their soon-to-be child, or that Wanda Wonder, of WindowWonder, had spent the past fifteen years perfecting her idea. He obviously refused to let himself care. "Besides, I promised them that I'd help them succeed. I always keep my promises."

"I'm glad to hear that," AJ said, cocking an eyebrow. The one under the slightly askew hair. "There's nothing wrong with believing in something, as long as you use good judgement." He leaned forward. "Take your latest venture. Do you really think mere software, even dressed up in fancy graphics, will make people fall in love?"

"It certainly has potential. It's a much more appealing approach to matchmaking than those Spam e-mails touting pheromones by the gallon. I've never ordered any, mind you, but I picture plastic jugs filled with sticky blue glop for your fifty-dollar money order (no checks, please)." She considered AJ. "You can't deny the impact e-Cupid has had on at least three people you've witnessed personally," she said. Not that she herself had any clue as to why Ralph and Andrew had reacted the way they had. (Barb she simply chalked up to being free-spirited Barb.) But maybe if she goaded AJ enough he'd come up with a reasonable explanation.

"Sorry to interrupt again, but what shall I do with these?" Gloria asked, pointing to another delivery man carrying an enormous bouquet of flowers and a wrapped package.

Chloe looked at AJ and he looked at her. "The table," they said in unison.

The delivery man handed Chloe the present, bowed and walked out whistling "Some Day My Prince Will Come."

"Let me guess," said AJ. "Ralph?"

Chloe nodded. She undid the purple bow on the box and removed the lid. She took out a thin purple book titled *The Brief History of Love in Flowers.* Under the book was a note that read *A world of flowers to commemorate our budding love.* Chloe coughed. AJ might not think e-Cupid worked, and Chloe didn't know what she believed any more. But something was definitely making Ralph stupid.

"Hey, look at this," said AJ, standing beside the huge bouquet. "Ralph's attached a little tag to each flower with a page reference."

"Great," said Chloe, thumbing through the slim volume. "I'll bet it goes with the book."

"Probably."

"Still skeptical about the power of e-Cupid?" she teased.

"Look, I'll admit Ralph and that policeman appeared to be influenced by your product, but nothing's happened to convince me that some software can make a man act differently than he wants to. Nothing."

"Tell the florist that, AJ." She'd seen some unbelievable things in her day, but having two men as distinctly different as Ralph Higgenbotham and Andrew McKinnett declare their undying love for her in the space of four hours really topped the list.

How could she have not one, but two men, who seriously believed because they saw her picture in a computer program that they were in love with her? Were single people really getting this desperate? As part of the MTV generation were they more susceptible to the power of suggestion via technology? She didn't know if this boded well for the future of e-Cupid and Cupid.com. People were open to finding true love—but there was definitely something eerily scary about Ralph and Andrew's reactions. She laughed to herself at the image of a group of lovestruck single zombies inhabiting the nation's capital after logging on to a website. Tone down the old imagination, Chloe, she told herself. All the stress must be getting to her.

"What is that sound?" AJ asked. "Some of your fish escape from their dishes?"

"No." She opened the desk drawer and removed E. Rose's purple gizmo. "Merely a reminder from the e-Cupid program that you don't think has any potential." She set the pager on the desk, and they watched it vibrate to the edge.

AJ grabbed it as it fell. "You don't believe in it either," he said. He handed the pager to her, obviously uncomfortable being that close to something involving both love and Chloe. "Take the batteries out," he suggested.

"Already did. Doesn't help." She held the purple gadget, wondering what to do with it. It simply made noise in the desk drawer. It wouldn't stay on her desk. AJ didn't want it. She swiveled in her chair and dropped it into the potted philodendron beside her credenza. At least it didn't make noise there. Maybe vibration would stimulate the plant to grow better.

But such speculation would have to wait. She had a balance sheet to balance, and inventor's interests to protect. She looked at her watch. She and AJ had been at it for four hours and they had accomplished exactly zip.

"Do you want to give this one more try, or wait until the parade of flowers stops?" she asked.

"I've asked Gloria to send out for lunch," he said. "We've got a lot of ground to cover, in spite of the flower show." He set several files on her desk. "These projects should never have been funded," he said.

Chloe took the folders, barely glancing at them. "What did you order for lunch?"

"What?"

"Lunch, you know, the meal in the middle of the day. What did you order?"

"I don't know. Gloria took care of it. She showed me a couple of take-out menus and I picked something. You'll love it," he said.

"I better," she said. "Gloria?" No answer. "Not pizza, I hope. Too much fat."

AJ looked at her, his head cocked to one side. "You could cut me some slack, you know. I've got recommendations here that will make the board happy with you instead of contemplating showing you the door."

Chloe settled back in her chair. "Okay, recommend something."

"Those projects," he said, pointing to the two files he'd given her. "Pull the plug on them immediately, before they cost you any more money."

She picked up the folders and looked at them. "I can't do that," she said. Why did his eyes have to be so enticing when he was talking about doing away with her projects?

"The board will insist."

The two he'd singled out were a couple of her favorites. "And what will I tell Armando and Eliza?"

"That you made a mistake. That you've gotten a directive not to waste more cash. I don't care. Just do it."

Chloe sat quietly. "But I promised to help them," she whispered.

"Unpromise." AJ pulled his chair closer to the desk. "Look, I understand about keeping promises, but sometimes in business, promises don't mean the same thing they do in the rest of our lives."

"Oh, really?" Chloe asked. "What about your business? When you take on a job, do you promise to do your best?"

"Sure, but—"

"And, when the going gets a little bumpy, do you simply fold your arms and say, sorry, business is different than real life?"

AJ sat back as if she'd slugged him. She was implying that he'd run out on a client, on his company. He would never turn his back on Tommy and Joanie, they depended on him. And he didn't run away from people who needed him. Unlike his father. He swallowed the lump in his throat and looked at her. "You're right," he said. "We'll just have to figure out a way to make those projects more lucrative." He leaned forward again. "I'd like to review your analyses and plans before you *do* anything, though. Okay?"

"Fair enough."

AJ detected a hint of a triumphant smile around her mouth as he scooted a blue file folder across her desk. "Take a look at this."

She opened the folder and took out a few pages. "More numbers. "What is it with you and the numerical?" She glanced at the pages. "What am I looking at?"

AJ couldn't figure her out. One minute she was bragging about profits and insisting that she keep promises to her clients and the next she wanted nothing to do with one of the most important parts of running a company—the finances. "I told Oz he couldn't be right about your lack of business sense, but it seems I was incorrect."

"Just because I can't read a balance sheet the way some people read books doesn't mean I don't have any sense." She scowled. "Oz can't complain too loudly," she said. "He helped me set up the spreadsheet you're so worried about."

"Really? Well, someone must have fiddled with it because it's not reporting correctly. These figures here," he pointed to one column, "represent your projected expenditures, including investments, for the last three years. These," he pulled out the second sheet and pointed. "These represent the actual numbers. Notice anything strange?"

"The actuals are bigger than the estimated? So what? This happens all the time. It's why they're called estimated numbers and not set-in-concrete numbers. Oz was very firm. I was not to change anything on the spreadsheet."

"Something did change. Don't you see a pattern? Each month, the excess is exactly the same percentage, across the board." He sat back. "Now, either Oz did something stupid when he constructed the spreadsheet or someone is mucking about with your finances."

"Or maybe *you* can't add two and two and arrive at four consistently."

"Fine," he said, standing. "I understand why you love Creative Investments, why you have passion for your work. But, if you can't see what is staring you in the face, then . . ." He shrugged. "I've offered, twice, to help. If you don't want to work together, there is little I can do but make my reports to the board.

"Wait," she said. She didn't need him running off to the board, telling them she wouldn't accept his assistance. Besides, if she really was winning him over to her side of the room, maybe he'd give up on closing her doors. He had said he was there to help, and for the most part all his suggestions today had seemed well intentioned. "Perhaps I was hasty."

"More like Indy 500 record-breaking speedy," he said.

"I thought executives were known for their ability to make quick decisions."

"Quick, but not stupid."

"Sorry." She counted to ten and only made it to four. "I'm juggling a bunch of events that I have no experience with here." She had grown up around businessmen, but she'd never met one quite like AJ. His numerical obsession and just-the-facts-ma'am approach were par for the course, but today he'd also demonstrated he could be sensitive to how his decisions affected other people's lives. Which was not at all typical of the other businessmen she'd been exposed to.

"Now we're making some progress."

"Don't push your luck, Lockhart." She fiddled with her pen, looking once more at the black e-Cupid laptop beside her phone. She shook her head. How could Milo even begin to think that she might be attracted to this irritating person telling her she had no business sense?

"I meant the troubles I'm having with this." She patted the e-Cupid laptop.

"Really?" Damn his eyes. They sparkled with

badly disguised humor, as though he knew he were taunting her and succeeding big. Like she had all her hot buttons labeled "push here."

"For your information, Mr. Cool, E. Rose and Milo declined to accept my funding until I had a chance to try out the product." She didn't bother to tell him that neither E. nor Milo was answering messages, pages, or e-mails. She figured that bit of information would simply complicate things.

"Excellent. And I assume you're sending it back to them now that you've discovered it's broken, right?"

She frowned. "Maybe it's like Spuddy Buddy and simply needs a power adjustment." She swiveled in her chair and stood up. "Besides, I can't abandon Ralph and Andrew and Barb. I'm not going to use it again, if that's what you mean, but I have an obligation to straighten things out." She watched him, daring him to disagree.

When he simply smiled, she decided she was either going to slap that smirk off his handsome face or kiss it off. She hadn't decided which. "Oh, please. Quit. This is serious. Remember that Ralph has stopped work on SatelHat because he thinks he's in love with me."

AJ's reaction surprised him. A stab of what he recognized as pure, unadulterated jealousy lodged in his gut. Right next to undisguised lust. He examined these feelings, pausing for an instant to wonder if any of his other clients could be talked into paying their bills. If he acted on his attraction to Chloe, he'd have to stop working with her. He shook his head. He studied the woman in question, standing behind her desk, the afternoon sun turning her hair into a mass of flame. Sure, she was cute, pretty even. And, sure, she'd occupied his thoughts an inordinate amount of time since she'd kissed him hello. And, sure, he remembered the shock of electricity when their hands touched, the heat from That Kiss. But it didn't mean he should be jealous. He had a job to do and it didn't include romance.

"Uh-huh," he said.

"And Officer McKinnett?"

What if this silly program actually worked? Did that mean she was going off with Ralph? Or Andrew? He pushed the thought away. He couldn't let Chloe's idiotic projects distract him. He had people depending on him too. "But," he continued, "I'm convinced that the only thing that happened was subliminal suggestion." Or mass hallucination. Had to be.

"Have you ever been in love?"

That caught him up short. "I told you, I don't believe in love, not the romantic kind anyway." He gave her a wolfish smile. "But I've been in lust lots of times."

"Right." Her tone dismissed his good-old-boys routine with barely a thought. She continued, "These two are beyond loony and moving directly into total madness. They aren't passing GO and they certainly aren't collecting two hundred dollars."

"And?"

"Men," she muttered. "If we could send one to the moon, why didn't we send them all." She smiled. "If I'm busy fending off the advances of two guys who shouldn't be advancing on me, my business will suffer."

AJ nodded. "I see. Why not simply tell them to go away?"

"I'm sure that has worked for the women in your life, but these guys act like they're on drugs. Simple requests won't work."

Now she was being personal. "Have you tried?"

"No."

Nothing surprising there. Based on everything he knew about her so far, she didn't have it in her to be tough. Soft, beguiling, enchanting? Yes. But not tough. "Well? No time like the present."

"You want me to do this while you're watching?"

"Why not? I'm a guy. I'll give you pointers." Why was he doing this? Encouraging Chloe on any of her flights of fancy would take him further away from his own objective. After all, he wasn't being paid to daydream.

"Like the ones you've given me on my business?"

"Exactly." Was it his fault he'd been sucked into Chloe's fantasy world and couldn't think clearly?

"Fine." She grabbed the phone and dialed. "Ringing once, ringing twice. Contact. Hello? May I talk with Officer McKinnett?" She wound the phone cord around her fingers. For some reason, the movement made AJ imagine what it would be like for her to wind her fingers in his hair. He took a deep breath. And, then another. He fiddled with a paper clip in his lap.

"I see. Could you have him call me when he gets back? Thanks." She hung up. "He's out on a call."

AJ dropped a badly mangled paper clip on her desk with a large amount of relief. That surprised him. Why should he care whether she talked to the good Officer McKinnett? Heck, he'd suggested it.

"Excuse me," said Gloria. "Lunch is here."

"Great," said AJ. Something he could handle. Gloria brought a box of pizza into Chloe's office.

"You ordered pizza," Chloe said.

"And a salad for you," Gloria said to her. "I haven't forgotten what you like just because a handsome man is working here now." She smiled and set the salad in front of Chloe. "Low-fat dressing in the bag." Gloria grinned at AJ and left the office.

"At least Gloria likes me," AJ said.

# Chapter Seven
# "Love Is a Many-Splendored Thing"

Lunch had been an uncomfortable truce between AJ and Chloe, but he managed to polish off an entire sausage and black olive pizza while Chloe picked onions out of her salad. "Tomato sauce is almost as attractive on you as paint," she said sweetly. "Although it doesn't show up nearly as well."

"I'm not usually this sloppy," AJ said.

"If you say so."

"You simply startled me with your comments about after-tax profits and shareholder value, that's all."

Chloe was about to answer with a snappy retort when a commotion outside her office distracted her. "Gloria, what's going on?"

Into her office burst Officer McKinnett followed closely by Ralph Higgenbotham, arguing loudly. "You see," said Ralph. "*My* flowers are here while yours are not."

"Yours are all weighted down with identification tags, like a bunch of lost dogs. They look stupid," McKinnett said.

"They're not any more stupid than three dozen roses with handcuffs attached," Ralph said.

Instead of answering him, McKinnett turned to Chloe and asked, "Where are my roses? The florist assured me they'd be here before *his* botany lesson in a vase."

"I saw her first," said Ralph, clutching a hardback copy of *The Complete Flower Garden* in his left hand. It wasn't a huge volume, nor was Ralph a particularly threatening man, but Chloe didn't want to know what might happen if he decided to use McKinnett's head as a target.

*So, this is what it's like, having men fight over you,* Chloe mused. Not nearly as romantic as the movies and books led you to believe.

And the whole thing was a mistake. A computer flaw. The latest issue of *The Web Is Wide* had blasted headlines from her in-box: "How to Protect Your Software from the Love Virus." Had to be what was wrong with e-Cupid. A virus.

"I don't happen to think that who fell in love with her first has any relevance here. I'm obviously the better qualified to protect her." Officer McKinnett puffed out his chest. "I've already proved that to her."

"Warning her about crimes that haven't happened yet doesn't count. *I've* known Chloe for almost a year."

"Yeah? Why didn't you fall in love with her earlier, then?" Andrew hitched his gun belt up a little higher on his waist, a suggestion even Ralph couldn't refuse to acknowledge.

"Look, you two. It doesn't matter who knew me first, or who saw the program first, or who has the bigger claim," Chloe said, stepping between the two of them. "I'm not interested in either of you. Period."

Two unbelieving faces looked at her. "But, Chloe," Ralph began, "I thought you believed in SatelHat?"

"I do, Ralph. It's a winner for sure."

"Then, how could you not like me?"

"I didn't say I didn't *like* you, just that I wasn't interested in a romantic involvement."

"Which means I'm the one she wants, Four Eyes, so beat it." McKinnett elbowed in front of Ralph, a fairly easy task, given his blond-giant physique.

"Are either of you listening to me at all?"

"Absolutely," said Ralph.

"Hanging on your every word," said Andrew.

"You," Chloe said, turning Ralph around and giving him a gentle shove. "You go work on your flanges." She spun around to face Andrew. "And you, go prevent some crime or something. AJ and I have work to do."

Ralph toddled off, eager to do whatever she suggested except give up this ridiculous software-induced stupidity, while Andrew merely smiled and said, "I see. You want me to protect you. No problem." He grabbed her shoulders and tried to kiss her, but she dodged and the kiss wound up on AJ's arm. Which he had inserted between Andrew and Chloe a second after Andrew had grabbed her.

"Beat it, McKinnett. The lady asked you to go away." AJ took the officer's elbow and guided him to the door. "So go."

"Are you sure, Chloe?" Andrew asked, a plaintive, lost-puppy look on his face.

"Absolutely. Nothing would make me happier," she said. He saluted her and left. She looked at AJ, suddenly glad he'd been there. "Thanks," she said. "Not a bad rescue, even if you don't have a horse and shining armor."

"You're welcome," he said. "They're quite a pair, aren't they?" He started to clean up the remnants of lunch. "What are we going to do about them?"

She cocked an eyebrow and closed her salad container. "We?"

"Sure," said AJ. "You said it yourself. If they're bothering you, you won't be able to concentrate on your business, and I've had experience with executives who don't concentrate on my recommendations. Believe me, it isn't pretty."

Okay. She could understand that. He was a high-powered, expensive consultant who expected to be taken seriously. "Good idea," she said. "I do want to get my money's worth from you."

AJ didn't stay late. He and Chloe had worked through three of her many projects and she had a long, and growing, list of things to do to bring them into line. Every time he looked at her, he saw the Doubtful Duo fighting over her and remembered the shocked look on her face. So he'd left early, pleading a need for some analysis tools back at his office.

He couldn't concentrate on work without picturing Ralph and Chloe, head to head over some book of poetry in the dark corners of a quiet restaurant. Or McKinnett and Chloe at a baseball game, munching on the same bag of peanuts. Neither was a pretty sight. He told himself he was simply overreacting to the absurdity of e-Cupid and that he was going to recommend she not proceed with it under any circumstances. E-Cupid was a clear example that she needed to implement tighter controls when she evaluated ideas. And he planned to offer to create those controls when he made his report, because it was clear setting parameters wasn't Chloe's strong suit.

It was clear she was making him crazy.

Usually, driving Charlene, even through the

traffic-clogged streets of DC, renewed his faith in himself and the world in general. Not today. Today, he worried about Chloe. Then he worried about his own business and Joanie and her unborn child. He worried about Tommy's reaction if AJ didn't complete this assignment satisfactorily and their little firm sank any deeper into debt. He screeched Charlene to a stop in his driveway and got out. "Sorry, gal," he said, patting the gray primer on the driver's door. "We'll make it to the rally. Don't you worry your pretty little camshaft over that. And you'll have a brand new coat of paint." He fished in his pocket for his house keys.

Once the door was open and the alarm system was turned off, AJ headed straight for the kitchen. He took a beer out and popped the top. He'd known Chloe Phillips less than a week and she was all he thought about. Her *company* was all he thought about, he corrected himself. He sat at his table, enjoying the flavor of the dark, hoppy brew and reminding himself of his goals. He was not at CI to fall for the scatterbrained optimist trying to run it. He was there because he was responsible for two other people.

Chloe Phillips was the key. He pushed aside his unfinished can of beer and loped up the stairs, thinking of how he could help her to be the CEO the board wanted. He just had to be sure not to get tangled up with her and her goofy ideas.

An hour later, dripping sweat from an exuberant workout with his punching bag, he definitely needed a shower. A hot shower to relax his body. A body stressed because of a screwy, albeit charming, redhead who thought letting people follow their dreams was a substitute for business management.

On his way to his bedroom, he kicked off his shoes. He peeled off his shorts, then stripped off his boxers as well. The sweat-damp T-shirt went next, along with the socks. He hurried into the bathroom, and turned on his shower. It was large and decadent, with light streaming in through a trio of skylights. From the knotty pine cabinet beside the shower, he pulled out a thick towel in a manly shade of navy blue and a wash cloth to match. The towel he tossed over the warming bar; the wash cloth went with him into the shower.

Water, hot and exhilarating, crashed over his head and chest and steam roiled around him. He sluiced soap over his shoulders, under his arms and along the length of his torso. His over-sized shower had been built to hold at least two, and sported multiple showerheads, but he'd never been tempted to have anyone join him. Showering with someone was too personal.

As he rinsed shampoo from his hair, he remembered Chloe's eyes when she explained her trouble with McKinnett and Higgenbotham, how her green irises had sparked with passion. In a flash, he pictured her standing in front of him, rubbing soap across his chest, rivulets of water running over her breasts and down her legs. The image disappeared as soon as he'd called it up. Ridiculous in the extreme.

"Ridiculous in the extreme," he repeated out loud for good measure. "The plan is to work with her, not get her into bed." He thought about the two men who were tripping all over each other to impress Chloe.

Damn.

AJ turned off the water and reached for the towel. How had he gotten himself into this situation? He absolutely couldn't lose sight of his purpose—a purpose that in no way included falling for a tempting redhead.

He had his future to work on. The only woman he made room for in his life was Charlene.

Back downstairs, wearing clean black jeans and a black T-shirt showing spots of water from his still wet hair, AJ dumped his half-finished beer in the sink. For some reason, after all his thinking about Chloe, beer didn't sound good. Getting up close and personal with her did.

His phone rang.

"Hey, Tommy," he said, reading his friend's name off the caller ID box.

"Hey. How are things going? Does it look like you can spin this assignment into a permanent retainer?"

"Possibly. Today was interesting. Challenging. Definitely not dull." He could have added stimulating, enchanting, and confusing, but he didn't want to get Tommy started.

"Good. I haven't been idle either," his friend said. "The reasons I invented for why we haven't paid the phone bill should be in the *Guinness Book of Records.*"

"Phone bill," AJ said quietly. "How big this month?"

"Not to worry. Ma Bell is happy to wait until next week before they shut off our service. You should congratulate me."

"Congratulations. How much?"

Tommy mentioned a number significantly larger than AJ was prepared to deal with. "Can we make a partial payment?"

"I sent them a check today."

From his own account. Tommy had done this before. "Be sure to leave an IOU in the petty cash."

"Along with the others. Don't worry, AJ, the company can take its time paying me back."

"How's Joanie?" She was the only one he wouldn't let subsidize the company from her meager funds.

"I went with her to Lamaze today. Interesting experience. She actually glowed. I think she's going to be a great mom."

"I swear I'm going to kill Eugene next time I see him," AJ said. "What was his excuse today?"

"I didn't ask. Didn't want to upset Joanie any more than being pregnant and not married has."

"She should be grateful she's *not* married to that bum."

"Hey, not every guy is like your father, you know. Some of us are responsible."

AJ wasn't in the mood to review his father's sins.

"Want to grab some food, shoot a little pool?" Tommy asked.

"Not tonight. I've got to put something besides beer in my frig."

"You feeling all right, AJ? Since when do you go grocery shopping?"

"Tom? I want to run an idea past you." AJ gave Tommy the abbreviated version of the two unwanted suitors and the trouble with e-Cupid. "So, I thought if I helped Chloe make these two guys go away, well, it would make work easier."

"Better be careful, AJ. Remember what happened last time? And that was a frame. If you're chasing the boss lady for real this time, well. . . ."

"I'm not. What makes you think this has anything at all to do with me chasing Chloe?"

"That certain tone in your voice, like a hound on a scent."

"I'm not chasing her."

"Whatever you say, buddy."

"I know what he's up to. He's trying to keep me away from my projects so he can prove to the board that I'm incapable," Chloe complained to Leann. The sky was bright and clear, the breeze perfect. Opting for exercise of the physical type rather than more number crunching, she'd taken Tuesday afternoon off to go in-line skating. Chloe maneuvered a corner on the trail. "It won't work. I have a plan."

"This should be entertaining." Leann skated around her friend and grabbed a tree. "Tell me again why I'm taking my life in my hands by putting wheels on my feet?"

"I figure if I invite AJ to sit in on all the meetings with my projects and their creators, he'll have to come around and begin to care. He'll have to see how important these ideas are to the people who thought them up. And," she stopped next to Leann, "he'll begin to understand how all these products could succeed." She was probably being unfair, lumping AJ in with other heartless businessmen, but she was really pissed at him. He was the embodiment of all that was wrong with American business today. He didn't care about the *people* involved in building a successful company. For her, the people were the most important part.

"Oh, that sounds like fun." Leann did sarcasm so well. "Why not take him skiing in Aspen instead," she suggested. "Get him away so he can't fiddle with your projects."

Chloe took Leann's arm, supporting her as they went back onto the trail. "I thought about that. But he could accuse me of neglecting the company." Not to mention that she was stymied as to how to make the e-Cupid duo of Ralph and Andrew go back to being normal.

Chloe skated to a bench and sat down. "Also, Oz has been awfully chummy lately, calling and asking about AJ and the business," Chloe said. "I don't know what to do, Leann. I'd almost come to terms with the fact that Dad never thought I could hold my own in business, and Oz was tripping down the same path until last week." She sat and looked out over the Potomac. "Now all of the sudden he seems to think maybe I can run CI. It's very weird; he's being incredibly supportive and encouraging. He actually agreed to go over the spreadsheets tonight. At my place."

Leann collapsed beside her. "Whoa," she said. "I have an idea. Why not invite AJ to join you? Then you could see the two of them together and maybe figure out what's going on."

"An interesting idea," Chloe conceded. "You don't think that would be too much like walking into the wolves' den?"

Leann watched sailboats navigate the choppy waters of the Potomac. "You always insist that people stand on their own. If this guy AJ can't be strong, if he's a total bum, you'll drop him like a hot rock. As for Oz, you can run the loafers off him without breaking a sweat."

"Maybe. That was *eons* ago when we were kids. Anyway, AJ and Oz will probably prove easy to handle compared to the two goofy, but very persistent, men swooning over me."

Leann greeted that statement with a wrinkled forehead.

"I haven't told you, have I?" Chloe said. "E-Cupid? The program that showed you Karl and made Barb dewy-eyed?" She leaned closer. "It's broken. Or something." She gave Leann the Cliff Notes version.

"First, we've got to get Barb together with Andrew," said Leann. "I love that name. If Karl and I ever have another baby, I want to name him Andrew."

"I'm sure the good officer will be honored. How do I get him together with Barb?"

"Let me think about that."

"I know I have to do something or Creative Investments will be a footnote in the next annual report for Phillips International, and I will have lost one of my best friends. Ralph needs to focus on developing his SatelHat, and Andrew needs to court Barb." She stood abruptly. "And I need chocolate. Exercise is wonderful, clears the mind and all that, but it's entirely too virtuous to handle this kind of crisis."

"You want chocolate, then let's go get chocolate. We can stop by the Godiva place in Tyson's and then head over to Ethyl M's. And we can finish up with Ben & Jerry's." Leann looked hopeful. "Nothing like chocolate to stimulate the old brain cells." She stood and grabbed Chloe's hand. "Let's go spend some money. We can plot the pairing of Barb and her policeman on the way."

Brightening, Chloe nodded, "Okay. Let's." She rarely indulged in chocolate, but the last few days had been very trying. Software bugs, swooning scientists, a heartless Accounting Jackal—a girl could take only so many disappointments.

If chocolate could clear her muzzy head, maybe she'd be able to understand this squiggly ache she felt every time she remembered kissing AJ. And the empty hollow she felt when she considered that he probably wasn't the person e-Cupid had set him up to be.

"Lead on."

An hour later, the sweet taste of chocolate lingering on her tongue, Chloe and Leann had laid out a basic plan. "Let me make sure I understand what we've decided to do," Leann recapped. "You're going to invite Andrew to meet you for dinner, and I'm going to call Barb and offer a shoulder to cry on."

"Right. They'll conveniently "bump" into each other and sparks will fly, making Andrew realize his mistake," Chloe concluded, hoping she was right. "I thought we were doing ice cream next," Chloe complained as Leann headed into a costume shop at mach nine.

Leann ignored her whining. "I'm sure we'll be able to find the perfect outfit for you in here. Look at this," Leann said, pulling a medieval gown from a rack. She held it up in front of Chloe. "You could go to the Halloween Ball as Rapunzel. Or Cinderella."

"Or not," Chloe said, putting the dress back. "I'm planning on wearing my old standby."

Leann snorted, fisting her hands on her hips. "Not if I have anything to say about it."

"Why not? What's wrong with my chicken costume?"

"It's a *chicken* costume, that's what's wrong."

"I like it."

"You, the woman who only moments ago were in high matchmaking mode, want to wear a chicken costume? *Please.*"

Chloe nodded.

"Well, how many Prince Charmings do you know who would come rushing across a crowded room to dance with a chicken?"

She didn't need a prince. She had a financial wizard, a nutty professor, and a cop. She couldn't deal with a prince. Chloe blew hair off her forehead and followed her friend to the rear of the shop. Once Leann got something into her head, Chloe had learned from long years of experience, it was better just to be quiet and go with the flow. Leann could be very single-minded.

Like Chloe had been since her father had left CI to her. Single-minded. But creative, she reminded herself. Could she help it if she was more right brain than left? Was it her fault that the people who came to her for funding had curious and funky ideas that she just adored? Surely one of them would pay off sometime. And there was the outside chance that AJ would catch her enthusiasm. For her projects, she told herself. Nothing more.

"If I'm going to make an entrance as the Swan Princess, what are you coming as?" Chloe frowned at another Cinderella dress. Too frothy.

"I'm going to borrow your chicken suit and make little ones for the girls. I'll go as a mother hen and her chicks. Karl can come as himself, a rooster."

Chloe narrowed her eyes. "So, this wasn't about getting me a new look so much as you needing my old one? Chicken."

"That's me." Leann shooed her back into the dressing room. "Try these and I'll go get the clerk." Leann shoved an armload of costume pieces at Chloe and grinned.

"Then can we get some ice cream?"

"Tell me about this AJ guy," Leann prompted, around her double scoop of fudgy ice cream. "What's his real name?"

"Who knows?" Chloe responded. "Abbreviated Juvenile? I don't know. He showed up on the software and then he was standing in my office. I don't know how he got into the program, but my brother recommended that the board hire him to help me out."

Leann teased. "Maybe your brother hired him, *thinking* he was going to help, but really the e-Cupid magic *made* him pick AJ." She smiled devilishly. "I mean, there must be a hundred consultants in this town. A thousand."

Why AJ? It was a question Chloe had chewed on since she'd kissed the man hello. "At this point, I'd believe almost anything."

"He likes some of your ideas, doesn't he?"

"He seems tolerant of a couple, but, Leann, the man is so stiff. There's not a creative bone in his lovely body."

"So, you help him create," Leann said. Once she was warmed up on the topic of matchmaking, it was impossible to get her to stop.

"Could we talk about something else? You're almost as irritating as he is."

He *was* irritating, Chloe thought, even when he wasn't in the office. Irritating and hot and dangerous. Not dangerous as in he might make a lunge for her Gucci bag. No. Dangerous as in if he ever decided to be friendly instead of adversarial, she'd be in big trouble. She took a bite of her hot fudge sundae, hoping that cold ice cream would help her body cool down.

She couldn't really put a word to it. She kept comparing her reaction to AJ with Barb's to Andrew. If AJ was her true love, shouldn't she be doing cartwheels around the restaurant? Shouldn't she feel fluttery butterflies?

She'd never been good at cartwheels, even as a child. Besides, the ice cream shop was too crowded for a good gymnastics display. And the butterflies had formed squadrons and were dive-bombing her stomach. Her head felt as if it could voluntarily float away, making any stab at a rational thought all the more difficult.

If this were true love, it was a lot like riding a roller coaster.

She hated roller coasters.

Tomorrow, she'd try again to phone E. Rose and Milo. She needed answers.

She took a spoonful of chocolate and ice cream. AJ, Chloe thought. How appropriate. Her twin inventors, Rose and Milo, had paired her up with initials. Maybe it was her just desserts; maybe she didn't deserve a whole person. Her heart sank at that thought. For just an instant, when she'd first seen AJ, she'd begun to believe that there might actually be someone in the world with her name tattooed on his heart and emblazoned across his mind. She sighed.

Her purse started vibrating and, puzzled, she opened it and reached in. Surprise didn't come close to her reaction when she pulled out the purple pager thingy Milo had given her. She looked at Leann and said, "I left this in the potted plant in my office."

"What is it?"

"Something the e-Cupid people gave me to let me know when my true love was in range."

She stopped pushing chocolate sauce around her dish when the door to the shop opened and in walked AJ and another man. Thinking about him had been one thing. Seeing him set off a whole different set of images in her head. Confused images of her cleaning out her desk, of Oz smirking as she left the building, of AJ holding her, kissing her. She swallowed. That kiss had been better than ice cream.

She nodded to the doorway. "He's here."

Leann looked up and smiled. "He's much better in person." She waved.

"Don't do that!" Chloe said, pulling Leann's hand down.

"Why not? He's your true love, isn't he? Why wouldn't you want him to know you're here?"

"Because," Chloe started, and then smiled up as AJ arrived at her table.

"Somehow I knew you'd be a chocolate sundae kind of gal," he said. "Can we join you?" Instead of waiting for an answer, he pulled out a chair and then snagged one from the next table for his friend. "This is Tommy Morales," he offered.

What could she do? Leaving was too rude. Besides, Leann was grinning up a storm beside her. "Hi," Chloe responded. "This is my friend, Leann. Leann, AJ Lockhart."

"So pleased to finally meet you," Leann said. "Chloe has told me so much about you."

*Don't say anything stupid,* Chloe begged silently, giving Leann one of those looks.

"Really?" AJ cocked his head and blinked innocently at Chloe. "I didn't think you knew that much about me," he said. "What is that infernal rattling?"

"It's Chloe's Love Alert," said Leann, taking the lead in the conversation, now that she'd been properly introduced.

"Love Alert?" Tommy looked perplexed.

Leann leaned closer, and said, "Yes. It tells her when her true love is within kissing range."

Tommy grinned at Chloe. "You been holding out on me, AJ? This is just the kind of woman I could learn to like."

AJ shook his head, looking at Chloe with supreme pity. "Sorry, Chloe. I don't generally bring him out in public. Forgive him?"

For what? For trying to be charming? "Sure," said Chloe. She dropped the pager into the trash behind Leann's chair. That should end the interruptions.

The door to the ice cream shop burst open and Ralph Higgenbotham spilled in. Close behind him, arguing loudly, came Officer Andrew McKinnett.

"She's here and she's mine," insisted Ralph.

"Not if I have anything to say about it, she isn't," Andrew shouted, shoving Ralph aside. Quickly he scanned the room, his gaze lighting at last on the table where Chloe sat with Leann, Tommy, and AJ.

"There, there you are," Officer McKinnett exclaimed. He moved swiftly towards the table, stopping short when he saw AJ sitting next to Chloe. "Oh, right. You work with her." he said.

"I'm trying to," AJ replied. "Why are you here?"

"I'm here to see Chloe," the officer said, fixing his adoring gaze on her.

She shifted uncomfortably. Ralph skidded to a late halt beside McKinnett. "My love, my life," he said, wringing his hands. "Come away from this rabble with me."

Chloe cleared her throat. "No."

"But you must," Ralph insisted.

McKinnett elbowed him aside and went down on one knee. "Tell him it's me you love, Chloe. Me."

"Stop this!" she shouted. "I don't love either of you. And you're interrupting my sundae."

AJ stood, his height dwarfing both Ralph's narrow form and Officer McKinnett's kneeling one in a single motion. "Gentlemen, the lady wants to finish her ice cream and I think we should allow her to do just that." He nodded as McKinnett stood, then he put one hand on Ralph's shoulder and one on McKinnett's. "Let's go find some place else to talk about this, shall we?" He smiled. "You ladies will be safe with Tommy."

"Who do you think you are?" Ralph Higgenbotham demanded, squirming under AJ's strong grip.

"Me? According to Chloe's purple early-alert device, I'm her true love."

# Chapter Eight
# "I Believe in Miracles"

There were many things AJ didn't profess to understand, but his ability to manage tough situations wasn't one of them. Until his reputation had been trashed by a couple of reporters trying to make a name for themselves, he'd been known for his disarming smile and agile brain. Actually, the bad news coverage hadn't dimmed the smile, and his brain worked as well as it ever had.

For the most part.

What he couldn't quite figure out was why his talent had suddenly abandoned him at this particular moment. Why Chloe's ersatz suitors wouldn't listen. Why he couldn't seem to keep his mind off Chloe. What was wrong with the world?

He paced back and forth across the scarred floor of the dark bar to which he'd dragged Ralph Higgenbotham and Andrew McKinnett. They sat, rigid and unsmiling, on opposite sides of a table, and glared at each other.

Fine, if that was the way they wanted this to be, he could play that game.

He stopped pacing and leaned on the table. "Gentlemen, and I use the term loosely, the object of your mutual affection appears to be stubbornly resisting each of you. I propose we call a truce and figure out where your mutual interests may lie."

"What the hell kind of nonsense is this?" McKinnett scowled at AJ. "Who do you think you are, trying to horn in on my action?"

"Your action?" inserted Ralph. "She's *my* woman."

AJ could see a huge fight growing rapidly. "Sit down and shut up, both of you," he said, ignoring the fact that they were both already sitting. He pulled up a chair and turned it around, leaning on its back as he straddled it and sat. An idea formed, full blown, in his mind. One that, if it worked well, would at least keep the silly suitor antics to a minimum and allow Chloe time to focus on her business. "Please, let me buy you a drink." He gestured to the waitress who hurried over. "What can I get you boys?"

McKinnett grumbled, "Coors."

"Fine," said Higgenbotham, "I'll have a wine spritzer, with a slice of lime. Oh, and water." He relaxed slightly.

AJ handed the woman his credit card and said, "Scotch, neat." A serious discussion called for a serious drink. She placed three cocktail napkins on the table and took AJ's American Express Platinum card with a smile.

"Okay, Lockhart, we're here. What's this about you being Chloe's true love?" McKinnett demanded, bunching his fists. "Her program clearly showed her to be *my* true love."

AJ leaned forward, satisfaction spreading warmth

in his chest. He knew he could handle the scientist; it was McKinnett he'd been worried about. "It's not that simple. Both of you want Chloe." He choked a little when he said it, still not comprehending how mere software could turn a man's better judgement to mush. "E-Cupid aside, she professes not to want either of you." Two pairs of eyes followed him, heads nodding. "Admittedly, it's hard to understand, but that's how things are."

The waitress brought the drinks, gave AJ back his card, and said, "Anything else?"

"No, thanks. Start a tab, would you? This may take more than one round." He took a substantial sip of the scotch and turned back to the subject at hand. "Consider the facts. Officer McKinnett, she's known you all of four days. Yes, her program showed you her picture. Still, she scorns your suit. And you," he turned to Ralph. "You're an intelligent, even brilliant, inventor who can make her business or break it. What woman wouldn't appreciate what intelligence can bring to a relationship? Especially one like Chloe?"

Ralph straightened his bow tie and lifted his chin. Ah, the geek wasn't completely impervious to compliments. "True, so true. But why are you interested in helping, Lockhart?"

"Because the software doesn't work. Although I'm not the least interested in Chloe romantically, it appears I'm the guy *she* saw in the software. Go figure."

"No, I'm sure she wouldn't have seen you. Especially when *I* saw *her.*" Andrew took a drink of his beer.

"It's sad how software has taken control of our daily lives, isn't it?" AJ leaned back. "I'm not sure why I'm part of this equation, fellows, but I am, and Chloe did see my picture while you two saw hers.

Okay. Given that situation, you two should be jumping at my suggestion."

McKinnett took a long pull from his beer while Higgenbotham squeezed the lime into his spritzer and stirred it gently with the orange swizzle stick.

"What suggestion?" said Ralph.

AJ picked up his scotch and saluted his worthy competitors. "A contest, gentlemen, of wit." He normally didn't go up against people so ill equipped, but he was desperate. Ralph and Andrew presented a perfect opportunity to showcase his problem solving skills, not to mention creative process development. If he could solve Chloe's suitor headaches, there might be more work for Lockhart Associates. End of discussion.

"I don't understand," Ralph grumbled, his hand tight around the spritzer glass he'd taken fewer than three sips from.

McKinnett sighed and swung his chair around to look Ralph squarely in his weak-chinned face. "It works like this, Science Boy. AJ is proposing that we agree to a contest of sorts—a treasure hunt and the treasure is Chloe's heart. We'll both be competing for her affections." He looked at AJ. "That's what you were suggesting, right?"

"Yep. Each of you is free to court Chloe in any way you think might cause her to choose one of you. If she outright rejects either or both of you, that person agrees to drop out of the competition."

"Wait," Ralph protested. "She already rejected both of us. Just now, at the restaurant."

"I don't count that, Ralph. She hasn't actually *been* courted yet, masses of flowers and poems aside. And it will be each man's skill in wooing that will turn her head." AJ gathered both men with his look. "To continue then. Any man rejected agrees to drop out of the competition. Neither will that rejected candidate harbor ill will to the remaining contender, nor will he assist the remaining suitor. And no one can tell her what you're doing." AJ had begun to list the terms of their agreement on a cocktail napkin. "Agreed?"

Andrew McKinnett nodded. Ralph Higgenbotham pushed his horn-rimmed glasses back up on his nose and frowned. "I suppose this is the only way to make you go away, so, yes, I agree."

"Great," AJ said, shoving the napkin across the table. "Sign here." He offered Ralph the pen. "I'll have copies made and sent to each of you." He watched as Ralph signed the napkin and passed the pen to McKinnett.

"Don't you think we should specify a time frame for the end of this game?" McKinnett asked. "Otherwise, we'll be dodging each other forever."

"Interesting idea, Andrew," AJ said. "How about at the Halloween Ball that Chloe and her friend are involved with? It's on Halloween, appropriately enough. If you're clever in your suits, you should be able to convince Chloe to choose one of you by then, don't you think?" He looked at Ralph. "It's for a great charity, so your tickets will be tax deductible and in any case your evening won't be a total waste. Higgenbotham?"

"Agreed. You'll need to add that to the napkin, to make it binding."

"Done," AJ said, snagging the napkin and adding the time limit to their impromptu competition. "There," he said, showing both men. "I'll sign it as a witness," he scribbled his name below Ralph's, "and Officer, you sign as well." He gave the amended napkin to McKinnett.

The sandy-haired policeman signed the napkin with a flourish and a grin. "May the best man win," he said, giving the document back to AJ. "I'll expect a copy of this no later than tomorrow." He extracted a business card from his shirt pocket and gave it to AJ. "Courier it to me, please."

Ralph offered AJ his card as well. "As soon as possible, Mr. Lockhart. I'd like to get on with this adolescent game so Chloe and I can begin to plan our future together."

In a day filled with strange things, the idiocy of a cocktail-napkin contract didn't phase AJ in the least. In fact, it seemed somehow appropriate to the absurd nature of the whole agreement. "Very well, gentlemen. A Tale of Two Suitors, out to capture the heart of the maiden fair." He raised his empty glass in salute. "Last man standing gets the girl."

"More flowers?" asked Chloe on Wednesday morning.

Gloria grinned broadly. "Aren't they wonderful?"

"If they're from Andrew, you'll just have to send them to Barb again."

"They're not actually for you," Gloria said. "They're for me." She handed Chloe the tiny card from the bouquet of bird-of-paradise. *"Beautiful flowers for a beautiful lady,"* Gloria quoted as Chloe read. "Mr. AJ sent them. Isn't he wonderful?"

"Wonderful," Chloe agreed, thinking how kind it was of AJ to send her assistant flowers. And how unexpected. She handed the note back. Maybe he had a heart after all.

"Let's see," Gloria said, thumbing through a pile of phone message slips. "The chairman of the board called, that policeman called—something about dinner tonight—and Mr. Higgenbotham called." Gloria stopped and turned sad eyes on Chloe. "You're not really dating Ralph, are you?"

"Absolutely not."

Gloria nodded, satisfied. "Your esteemed brother

called as well. Twice," Gloria said. "Something about not being available to review spreadsheets and he was sorry. Oh, and how were things working out with the finance man." She handed several pink message slips to Chloe and squinted at her over purple half glasses.

"Yes?"

"The board wants an update as well."

Uh-oh. Since AJ had come to help, she was further behind on the obligatory reports than she'd planned. "I'll give Oz a call."

"Actually, he's waiting for you in your office," Gloria whispered. "Good luck."

Wonderful. A buggy software program, an inventor *and* a policeman with love on their brains, and her brother to remind her just how not like her father she was. What a great day this was shaping up to be, and it was only nine o'clock!

"Hello, Ozzie," Chloe said, grinning as she walked into her office. Her brother was seated at her desk, scrolling through files of documents on her computer. "Can I help you find something specific?" she asked, setting down her briefcase.

"What? Oh, no. I was just looking for that dratted spreadsheet. Since I can't look at it later, I thought I'd see what was wrong with it right now. But I can't find it."

"I've renamed the file," she said, shooing him away. She slid into the black leather desk chair her brother had abandoned. "But AJ and I think we've found the flaw in it, so you don't have to worry any more."

Oz sat in one of the chairs across from her. "A flaw? Oh dear."

He looked rather pale, Chloe thought. "It's okay. AJ fixed it."

"Excellent. Then you're making progress with the

third-quarter results?" He stood and paced to the other side of the room.

Well, actually, no. She'd been much too busy playing couples counselor to keep her mind on business. "Of course we are. Don't worry, Oz. I think you'll be very pleased with the plan we've come up with." She lowered her voice to a whisper. "I think I've found the one killer idea."

He came to sit on the edge of her desk, his long patrician fingers steepled, his brow furrowed, his steel gray eyes drilling holes in hers. "Really? And what would that be? A variation on FrogVision 2100? Or have you invested in earthquake prediction equipment, or expeditions to the Amazon to find rare depression-curing herbs?"

Where had that tone come from? "FrogVision is coming along very nicely, thank you. Hans Karlsrud just completed a briefing at the Pentagon, so don't be saying it wasn't a sound investment. Just because it hasn't made a penny of profit yet doesn't mean it isn't cutting edge technology with plenty of earning potential." She adjusted her glasses on her nose so she could see her brother's disapproval more completely. "In fact, the Defense Department is definitely interested in our latest refinements."

Oz raised both eyebrows at this bit of news. "I assume Lockhart will cover this development in his report?"

"Yes. There could be a contract in it, a really, *really* big contract." She might use FrogVision to keep track of the men pursuing her.

"I'll call Senator Salton on Defense Appropriations and see what he has to say about that," her brother said.

"Please, don't. I've already set up demonstrations at Fort Myer. If you chat with the senator ahead of time, it might cause the whole deal to go bust."

"Excellent. Well, you know how to find me if you need my help," Oz said, standing abrubtly and giving her a quick peck on the cheek before heading for the door.

"Thanks for stopping by," she said, puzzled by his almost confrontational mood and his sudden hurry to leave. She tried to dismiss the chilly feeling she had by reminding herself that her brother was very busy with his work and probably had an important meeting.

Still, he'd seemed very anxious to find that spreadsheet. And to help on FrogVision. It was half an hour later that she realized she hadn't yet seen AJ this morning, which was odd. She'd known him just long enough to identify the words "precise" and "on time" as his permanent guidelines. Plus, he was never in the office very long before he found some pesky numbers question to discuss with her.

She grimaced at the figures in regimented columns on her computer screen. They had a story to tell and she wasn't any fonder of its plot now than she had been thirty minutes ago.

She got up to stretch her legs and was drawn to Ralph's bouquet. It dripped daisy petals onto the shiny teak surface of the table underneath it. Each of the blossoms in Ralph's collection of flowers contained a small, hand-lettered tag identifying both the common name of the bloom and the correct botanical nomenclature, with the centerpiece being several lovely orchids. *Thanatopsis Orchideae*, or so the label indicated.

It was so very Ralph.

She hadn't heard from her poetic inventor yet this morning and that worried her as well. Unless AJ had managed to talk some sense into both him and Andrew yesterday, she should be hearing from him about now. When the phone didn't ring immediately, she decided she needed a latte.

"Mr. AJ is on line two," Gloria announced before she could leave. It was the absolute last thing she needed.

AJ calling her with some lame excuse as to why he'd been late for work. Or worse, some new, detailed report for the board on how she Wasn't Doing Well. Not that she really considered him an employee, or minded if he was there, but she didn't want to talk to him right now. She'd had a very frightening revelation studying the spreadsheet that AJ had fixed. The numbers were beginning to make sense. She'd just identified the problem with revenue projections on WindowWonder. And she'd managed to open some hidden part of the database, which was full of more numbers.

She snatched up the phone and said, "What?"

"Is that any way to talk to the man who just uncovered your killer idea? Especially when that man is, theoretically at least, your true love?" AJ asked.

"The fact that you rescued me from Andrew and Ralph yesterday afternoon hardly qualifies you as my true love."

"Hey, you're the one who accused me of being your true love based on a computer picture." He laughed good-naturedly. "But listen, as much as I enjoy debating my merits as your true love, I've been working from my own office this morning and I've got good news."

She was just about to answer him when Barb burst into her office. "Barb, I can explain," Chloe started.

"Explanations aren't what I came for," Barb said. "Leann called and I came to find out what you're going to do. Andrew is mine. You know it and your computer program confirms it. Now, tell me. What are your intentions?"

"AJ, I can't talk now." She hung up on him, all her attention focused on her distraught friend. "Oh, Barb, I have no interest in Andrew. You should know that, you're one of my best friends."

Barb sat straighter in the chair at Chloe's table. "I used to think all you really wanted was to succeed in business, but now I'm not so sure."

"God, Barb. Andrew is a lovely man. Handsome, brave, employed. But he's not my type. Not vaguely."

"Then why is he head over heels for you and won't return my phone calls?" Barb started to sob.

Chloe sat next to her friend and put an arm around her. "Don't cry, Barb. I'll do anything. Absolutely anything to get you two back together." Like wring Milo's chubby neck if she ever made contact with him again.

Barb stopped crying and said plaintively. "Oh, Chloe, I've never felt this way about anyone. I think I'm in love with Andrew and if I don't get him back, I don't know what I'll do."

"Fine, then we'll just have to get him back for you, won't we?"

"How will we do that? He's bewitched by that stupid computer thing. I never did trust computers and now I know why I hate them," Barb said.

"Well, the bug in the program that made my picture come up when Andrew was watching instead of yours should be fixed by tomorrow." A lie, but she *was* working on it. Actually, the FrogVision team had agreed to look at it. "We simply get Andrew to look at the program once more and, bingo, your picture comes up and he's wildly, madly, insanely in love with you and can't remember my name." Chloe thought she sounded very convincing, even if she did have a small doubt as to anyone's ability to fix the problem. She did have a weak Plan B, just in case. It involved adhesive tape, Barb's picture, and the screen of the laptop. She was desperate.

Barb sniffed. "Are you sure?"

"Absolutely. Guaranteed. Trust me. When have I ever let you down?"

Barb smiled and headed out the door. "You're a wonderful best friend, Chloe. I don't know why I thought you were interested in Andrew for yourself. How silly. You've never really been interested in being in love."

"You're welcome."

How sad and how true, Chloe thought. Trust your best friends to recognize the patently obvious when you yourself couldn't see it with searchlights. Her focus always had been business, and that wasn't going to change simply because a pretty face popped up when she looked at a stupid computer program.

Focus. Business. She reviewed her brief conversation with AJ. What had he said just ahead of "true love"? Something about finding her killer idea? "Oh, my God," she said, grabbing the phone and dialing. "What have I done now?"

# Chapter Nine
# "The Shape of My Heart"

"I wondered when you'd call back," AJ said when he answered the phone. "I trust you got whatever pressing problems distracted you straightened out?" He leaned back in his creaky secondhand chair.

"For the most part, yes." Chloe's voice sounded strained, choked, and unnaturally tight. "Why aren't you here today?"

"I'm having my town house painted and I had to pick out colors." He'd already paid for the work, or he would have taken the money and put it into his company, his office. The tiny and cramped space, was such a contrast to Chloe's spacious work area. But it was his. "Missing me already?"

"No." He heard her blow the hair off her forehead in frustration. "I, um, I've made some adjustments to revenue projections on WindowWonder. I wanted you to look at them."

"Really? Selling out to the enemy so quickly?" AJ chuckled. He pictured her, twirling the phone cord around her index finger. He swallowed.

"No."

"Sorry. Tomorrow, first thing," AJ said.

"Tomorrow. Okay." She paused. "Um, before, when you called?" Now her voice was quiet, coy.

"Yes."

"You said something that I ignored but shouldn't have."

"Is this an apology?"

"No, I just thought we should talk about it."

"You mean the bit about me being your true love?"

"No, the bit about killer ideas."

He closed his eyes and visualized her getting angry, the color in her cheeks rising and her eyes snapping green sparks. It was so satisfying, getting to her.

"Ah, yes. Killer ideas. There are several possibilities, really. You see, even though most of the stuff you take on is beyond impractical, inside are nuggets that might actually work."

"I knew it! Which ones? It's WindowWonder, isn't it? And Keys-in-Tune. This is so cool."

"Slow down, Mario Andretti. WindowWonder has potential, especially since it has a small but growing base in consumer sales. But I'm more interested in Spuddy Buddy."

"Sweet. I can't wait to call Darrell. He'll be so thrilled."

"You can wait and you will. There's a lot of work to do here. Plans to be made. Research that should have been done before you agreed to fund it."

"Oh."

"Yes, oh. Look, I'm tied up here all afternoon. Why not meet me somewhere this evening and we'll have dinner and go over my preliminary assessment?"

Chloe hesitated before answering. "I don't think that would be a good idea, AJ. Can't we talk about this tomorrow?"

"What happened to your unbridled enthusiasm? Your impulsive, let's-go-for-broke attitude?"

"Maybe I'm learning to slow down and look at things before I jump in. That should make you happy."

"It does, but I'm busy tomorrow morning—"

"You said you'd look at the revenue projections for WindowWonder first thing."

"And tomorrow first thing is going to have to be after lunch. I have a business to run, you know. You aren't my only client." Only a small fib.

"Tomorrow afternoon, then?"

"I'll be there with bells on."

"I'd pay money to see that," she said. " 'Bye."

Tommy leaned against the door to AJ's office. "That was interesting. I assume that was Phillips on the phone and wearing bells has something to do with increasing our income with that company?"

"Not exactly, Tommy old son. But I do have Chloe's interest piqued and I'll have a new contract in hand before the week is out."

"That's very good news," Tommy said, coming into the office and slouching in the chair in front of AJ's desk. "Here's some bad news to balance your good mood." He handed AJ a thick envelope.

AJ pulled the pages out and began to read. "You know, it's about time our luck turned, don't you think?"

"My dad always said if he didn't have bad luck he wouldn't have any luck at all."

"Yeah? So it's your fault? All that paternal bad luck rubbing off on us both." AJ tossed the pages onto the desk and held his head in his hands. "Wintertree was the only one of our clients that promised to send us a check, and now they're declaring bankruptcy."

"True, but we're twenty-third down the list of creditors, so we should get at least ten cents on the dollar when the courts get done."

"Ten cents won't pay the bills." Ten cents was about what his mood was worth. He couldn't wait until tomorrow afternoon to convince Chloe to increase the scope of his work. He needed to do it tonight.

AJ hustled around his town house. He'd selected a camel-colored cashmere sports coat for his first official out-of-the-office meeting with Chloe. He needed to look every bit the successful business consultant he was beginning to doubt he was to make this work. He wasn't a man to go back on his word, and he'd promised Tommy. And Joanie. He checked himself once more in the mirror. Yes, the black turtleneck and black slacks worked well. He smiled, trying to hide the strain visible in his face.

He wouldn't think about what would happen if he didn't succeed with Chloe.

He whistled as he walked down the steps and climbed into Charlene. He put the key in the ignition and turned it.

Nothing.

He tried again.

Again, nothing.

"Not now, Charlene. I've got a very important meeting to get to." He tried the ignition once more and the car sputtered, coughed, and stopped.

"Look, this display of jealousy isn't going to get us anywhere. I'm not replacing you, Charlene, I'm working on securing our future. If the lovely Miss

Phillips is happy with my work and is charmed by me, then it's likely she'll toss more work our way and I can refurbish you properly. Understand?" He patted the dashboard and tried to start the car again.

Charlene turned over immediately, purring like a satisfied cat.

"Thank you, darlin'," AJ said, and backed out of the driveway and into traffic. He flipped on the radio and hummed along with Ricky Martin. He was definitely livin' "la vida loca". He headed toward Chloe's office.

She might have said no on the phone, but AJ wasn't a man to accept that answer when what he wanted to hear was yes. Yes, I want you to work on the business plan for Spuddy Buddy. Yes, we here at Creative Investments would like to put you on permanent retainer. Yes, I'd love to have dinner with you. And yes, please kiss me once more. Besides, he'd heard Barb in the background and knew Chloe'd been distracted. Like she so frequently was when people were involved. One of her flaws, getting personally involved. Business was supposed to be business, not personal.

It was going to be a perfect night.

By tomorrow, Chloe Phillips would be his biggest, most solvent client. He rounded the corner into Rosslyn and pulled to a stop across from Chloe's office. He'd wait here until she came out, then intercept her before she managed to get away. That way, she'd have to come with him. He smiled. Victory was within his grasp.

When he saw Chloe exit the building on the arm of Officer McKinnett, he blinked, gaped, and couldn't digest what his eyes were telling him. She hadn't mentioned going anywhere this evening. Chloe, his Chloe, was going out, *out*, with that policeman! This just wouldn't do. She wasn't supposed to be interested in him.

As Andrew McKinnett ushered Chloe into his Chevy Blazer, AJ peeled away from the curb. He'd just follow them, that's what he'd do. There was no way a blond giant like McKinnett was going to get the upper hand with *his* Chloe. He had a business at stake. Charlene was at stake!

He wove in and out between cars in the traffic, following the white Blazer, wondering just where McKinnett was taking Chloe. He stopped at a red light, watching the Blazer turn a corner just past the intersection. McKinnett was taking her to a Pizza Hut! What kind of goof was this guy? He might be a stellar law enforcement officer, but he didn't know the first thing about women.

On the other hand, he was the one spending time with Chloe while AJ sat in his Corvette, alone.

The car behind AJ honked, shaking him out of his contemplation. He stopped just past the Pizza Hut. This complicated things. He reached for his cell phone and dialed. "Yo, Tom."

"Hey, AJ. Thought you were out executing a strategy to get us enough business for a lifetime."

"Yeah, me too. Seems like our friendly Officer McKinnett is in the way."

"Really?"

"He's going all out, though, taking her to the Pizza Hut. Big spender."

"Well, for all she knows, you're off in a quiet corner, digesting income statements and devising business strategies."

Sometimes he was so blind. Tommy was right. Again. Of course Chloe would find McKinnett less threatening. *He* wasn't working for her brother. "Tommy, you're a genius."

"I knew that. What did I say this time that made

you come around to my point of view?"

"Devising strategies."

"So?"

"Tommy, when have you ever known a woman who didn't like a little challenge? Chloe has only seen me at the office. But she has no idea who I really am." He just needed to make a very quick stop at home for a change of clothes, he thought.

"Man, you're not well. I'm coming over right now." Tommy paused. "Where are you, exactly?"

"On my way to save our little company." AJ didn't wait for Tommy's response. He ended the call humming, a grin—a stupid one, he was sure—on his face.

"Let me understand what you're saying," Officer McKinnett said. "The one thing that would make you deliriously happy would be if I quit paying attention to you and spent time with your friend. What's her name again?"

"Barb. Barb Holland."

"Barb. Right. This would win you for my own?"

Chloe closed her eyes and exhaled in frustration. Men in love were more difficult to reason with than men in business, men in sports, or men in any other condition men got themselves into. Dear Andrew couldn't seem to focus on anything but *her.* Too much gooey stupidity in men was not an attractive trait.

"Yes, Andrew. It is my heart's desire. Barb is my best friend and—"

"You would give up my love for your best friend?"

"Well, yes." Gladly. She'd had a golden retriever once and Andrew was beginning to remind her of Casey—all happy all the time. Slobbery and waggy.

The man in question sat back and put down his slice of everything pizza. His handsome forehead wrinkled in thought. Deep thought. He closed his eyes and licked tomato sauce from the side of his mouth with his tongue.

Now, thought Chloe. Now would be the time for my heart to pound away inside me if I were really in love. She pictured AJ doing the same thing with his tongue. And then imagined what else he might do. She shuddered as a coil of white hot desire began to unfold, just at the thought of the gorgeous business consultant.

If she'd been Barb instead of herself, she'd have been across the table and all over her blond giant—in two seconds flat. She sighed.

"I don't think I can do it, Chloe. After all. It's you I love, not this, what was her name again?"

"Barb. Barb Holland."

"Right. Like the tunnel." He picked up the pitcher of beer and offered to refill Chloe's glass.

She shook her head. No need to encourage someone she had absolutely no intentions of falling for. "Thanks, no more for me." Would she encourage AJ if he showed the slightest interest?

Andrew smiled and filled her glass anyway.

She was about to protest when he grabbed Chloe's hand and began kissing it. He stood, pulling Chloe with him. "Chloe, love, let's get out of here. It's definitely too crowded." He dropped a handful of bills on the table to take care of the pizza, beer, and tip.

Adolescent behavior wasn't all that attractive in adolescents. It definitely didn't wear well on adult men. She dug in her heels. "I'm not going anywhere with you."

Andrew looked at her, uncomprehending, and continued his slow, steady pace towards the door. Other patrons were beginning to notice. Conversation around them stopped and people watched the two with mounting interest.

"No. I'm not leaving with you." She grabbed the

edge of the pizza counter on her way past and held on.

"You go, girl," said a woman at a nearby table. "Don't give in to that man."

Across the room, a trio of men started whistling and making improbable suggestions.

Finally, Andrew stopped. She jerked her hand away. "I really think you're taking this love thing way too far." She signaled one of the employees behind the counter. "Would you be so kind as to call me a cab?"

The young man cocked his head, frowned, and said, "Lady, there's a pay phone by the front door." He went back to his pepperoni masterpiece.

So much for chivalry in the twenty-first century. Dead. Dead as door hinges. Dead as her attempts to dissuade Andrew. As dead as her career, her business, her future would be if she didn't get this Cupid thing fixed. She had to get Andrew and Ralph to leave her alone so she could focus on CI.

Forget the cab, she'd walk. She narrowed her gaze and poked a finger in Andrew's solid chest. "Leave me alone. Barb Holland is the one you want. Not me."

They were obviously the best entertainment this pizza crowd had seen in months. One woman shouted, "Way to go." Another, "You tell him, sister."

Andrew smiled. She shook her head and stomped out the door. There was no communicating with the love-struck.

"Hey, pal," one burly man shouted. "I'll help."

In the parking lot Chloe adjusted her coat. A chill wind had started and she wished mightily that she'd worn her hat and gloves. Walking into the wind to her office building would be a cold affair. But there was nothing to be done about it. Maybe in a couple of blocks she'd be able to flag down a cab. She started walking.

And stopped. There was AJ, leaning against an old Corvette, splotched with gray patches of primer, clearly in mid-repair bodywork-wise. He was smiling. And chewing on a toothpick as though he didn't have a worry in the world. He was dressed in jeans, tight jeans, she realized as her breath quickened. And a black turtleneck T-shirt. And a black leather jacket, worn around the edges and at the elbows. And a black cowboy hat.

That brought her up short. Who wore cowboy hats in Washington, DC? Obviously, AJ did. His black hair curled over the collar of the jacket and one strand shaped a defiant comma across his forehead. He looked for all the world like a juvenile delinquent waiting for a Hell's Angel to come riding up on a Harley and offer him a cigarette.

He grinned at her and let her take her time looking at him. Then, he actually touched the brim of the hat in a classic western greeting and said, "I thought you might need some help." He opened the passenger side of the Corvette. "Miss?"

At that moment, Andrew stepped out of the Pizza Hut. He scanned the parking lot, then saw her and called her name. Without a second thought, she hopped into AJ's car.

He cocked an eyebrow, closed the door, and climbed in the driver's side. "Guess I was right on time," he said, and tried to start the car, which coughed but didn't start. "Not now, Charlene," AJ said through clenched teeth. "The cops are after us."

As though the car heard him, it coughed twice and started. "Thanks, babe," AJ said and peeled out of the parking lot.

"Interesting," said Chloe, hanging onto the seat with a white-knuckle grip as the Corvette careened around corners. Where were the police when you needed them? Oh, right. Back at the pizza joint. She swiveled in her seat and glared at AJ. "What are you trying to do, break the land speed record?"

"Hey, I'm a guy built for speed and endurance," AJ said, a wicked grin on his handsome face. He did slow down to mach five, though.

"Are you the same AJ Lockhart hired by the board to close me down?" she asked, then gasped. "Of course. "You're finished, aren't you. You've found enough information to give them the reasons they need to take over the business."

AJ slowed and turned into an alley, then stopped. "Look, Chloe. I'm not at your office to close you down. I'm there to help." He reached into the back seat and pulled a file folder out of his briefcase. "Here," he said. "This is the preliminary marketing plan for Spuddy Buddy. It's what I mentioned on the phone, just before you hung up on me."

His eyes were flint, cold and dark, with just the hint of spark at the edges. She swallowed and sat back in her seat. "Okay, you aren't trying to drive me out of business." She took the folder.

"If you like the ideas, my firm would be delighted to complete the job for you. It's got real potential."

"I'll think about it," she said, hugging the folder to her chest. "You seem awfully anxious to do more work for me, AJ. What's in it for you?"

"The Phillips name is worth a lot to a small company like mine. If we do good work, I anticipate that other companies will want to hire us."

"Oh. What were you doing in the Pizza Hut parking lot?"

He shrugged. "I recognized McKinnett's Blazer. I figured it was just a matter of time before you abandoned him. You're not a pizza fan, if I remember correctly." He pulled forward through the alley and

onto the street. "Just thought you might need some assistance."

"Thank you." She watched the buildings go past as AJ drove at a much saner pace. Scarlet and brown leaves, spotlighted by headlights, swirled in front of the car, whipped by the wind and the motion of vehicles, of people going home to their warm houses. She shivered.

"You want to go back to the office, or shall I take you somewhere else?" AJ asked.

Heaven knew she didn't want to go far with this man who seemed to know where she would be before she did. "Back to my office, please." She could review his work there. "You really think Spuddy Buddy is a good invention?"

"Absolutely. Most of your ideas are sound, at the core. It's just implementation that causes you problems. That and the fact that you never seem to modify any of them after you agree to fund them. Part of your responsibility is to make suggestions, fine-tune new products, help them grow."

"Now you sound like I do when I've found something exciting and new." AJ seemed exciting and new—even more thrilling than usual.

He shrugged. "Maybe I have."

Oh. What did that mean? Had he found a new client or was he genuinely interested in CI? Or maybe he had a new girlfriend? Not that it would matter to her, Chloe tried to tell herself.

Silence hunkered, thick and prickly, between them. "I can't quite see why you'd be interested in something like e-Cupid," he said, finally.

"Don't start."

"I wasn't criticizing, just wondering why someone who has so much to offer a guy would need a program like e-Cupid." He stopped in front of her building.

"Who? Me? I wasn't planning on using it at all, actually. It's just that the research I've done tells me there aren't a lot of good ways for singles to meet, and e-Cupid looked like it had potential. That's all." She looked at him.

He raised his eyebrows. "Really?"

"That whole thing with Ralph and Andrew. It wasn't supposed to happen."

"I was there, remember?" he said.

She felt her face redden. "Oh yeah, sorry about that. I didn't forget. I'm just distracted. I have to get Andrew back together with Barb, and nothing seems to be working."

"Not a problem," he grinned at her. "Consultants are generally dull, but I do like my clients to at least remember when I'm in the room."

If he only knew how aware of him she was, Chloe thought. He would do zero to one hundred in no time flat and never look back.

# Chapter Ten
# "If I Loved You"

AJ watched Chloe, wondering if he should tell her about the contest. Not yet. "Here you go. Delivery to your doorstep." The wavery timbre of her voice when she'd said "I have to get him back together with Barb" sent shivers up and down the length of him, chilling and heating his very soul. And irritating him to no end. He recognized and applauded her loyalty to her friends. It was a quality he demanded of himself, but in business, you had to keep a level of professionalism or things simply got out of hand.

"Thanks again for the ride," Chloe said. "I really appreciate it."

"If you get this e-Cupid love bug fixed, do you really think McKinnett and Ralph will go away?"

She rubbed her ear, thinking. Perhaps this wasn't entirely a bad idea, going out with AJ. Maybe what Ralph and Andrew needed was to see her with someone else. Someone like AJ. On a date, holding hands.

If he'd go along with the crazy plan forming in her brain, the two of them could declare their love for each other, pretend love of course, and the courting duo would be out of luck.

She sighed. "I certainly hope so. I've got so much to do at work, I don't have time for one boyfriend, much less two. I'm sure you understand." She gathered her handbag and opened the door. "Thanks again for the rescue." She patted the worn leather seat, repaired with gray duct tape. "It's not quite a white horse, but it'll do."

"Charlene? She's great, isn't she?" He stroked the steering wheel. "I remember watching stock car races on TV with my dad as a kid and telling him I'd own one of these some day. He laughed at me, but I'm almost through restoring her," he said. He cocked his head and said, "Since you're so busy and we really do need to get things organized for the board, why don't we discuss the plans for Spuddy Buddy over dinner. My guess is you didn't eat pizza with the love police."

"That's for sure," she said, a warm possibility opening inside her. She should be working on a strategy to get Barb and Andrew together and Ralph back tinkering with satellite dishes on hats, but Spuddy Buddy was a good project and if AJ had finally come around to her way of thinking—well, why not talk over food? Besides, there was her plan. . . .

"Sure. That would be nice." She started to get out of the car. "I've got a few files in my office that might be useful. I'll go get them."

AJ turned off the engine, came around to give her a hand, and shut her door after her. "I'll come with you. A new pad of paper is required for a new project," he said.

"Okay."

"Lead on, MacDuff," he said. "Shakespeare," he added.

"Wasn't MacDuff a man?" Chloe asked. He'd shifted to *Macbeth*. Not as romantic as Romeo, but she didn't want romance from him. Really.

"Sure, but his wife certainly wasn't."

"Yeah, but she died." Chloe pushed on the revolving door and entered the lobby of her building. Her brother's building, to be precise. It shone with black and green marble and brass so bright you could use it as a mirror for touching up your makeup. Which she did on occasion, when she was running late.

She pushed the button for the elevator. AJ stood beside her, looking dark and dangerous. The shadow of a beard and slight sheen of sweat on his face made him somehow that much more appealing. A tightness in her stomach matched the small buzzing in her head, which was prompted by her very vivid and out-of-control imagination.

"Stop it," she told herself, trying to be quiet about this personal admonition.

"Excuse me? Did you say something?" AJ asked.

"No. Just reminding myself that I have priorities."

"Don't we all," he replied.

The elevator came and they rode up to the twentieth floor. She used her pass key to enter the high-security area and led AJ into her office.

"Have a seat," she said, directing him to the table and its four chairs. He smiled, cocked an eyebrow, and plopped down on her sofa. Men. Not one that she knew took direction well. Or at all.

"I read the preliminary report on FrogVision 2100," AJ said. "I'm not sure it'll make it through another review in its present form. You really need to be tougher on your people."

"I thought you were through being a business vigilante for the night?" she asked sweetly. "Never mind. That was entirely uncalled for on my part." She took off her coat and tossed it across the back of the chair AJ was supposed to be sitting in.

She cleared her throat. AJ leaned back, putting his arm across the cushions on the sofa. Ohmygod. His black T-shirt stretched across his chest and the resulting bas-relief muscles took her breath away. This was *not* fair.

He grinned at her.

"Here's the deal, AJ." She tried to concentrate on his face instead of his body. He'd stretched his long legs out and crossed them at his ankles. Ankles that were covered in scuffed cowboy boots. He took off his black hat and set it on the sofa cushion beside him. Then he ran a hand through his hair.

She thought she was going to faint.

Well, her reaction wasn't quite that far gone, but he was so yummy looking that it took a great deal of self-control not to leap over her desk and maul him.

What had gotten into her? Just because he'd acknowledged her ability to identify good ideas wasn't a reason to lose control, was it? Absolutely not. She scratched her ear.

*Get a grip,* she told herself. *He's the product of bad software, multiplied by being on contract to your board. A joke E. Rose is playing on you. He isn't really your true love.*

"You mentioned a deal," he reminded her.

Her face flamed and she knew she looked idiotic, staring at him. She cleared her throat once more, trying unsuccessfully to dislodge the large lump that had taken up residence there. "Look, this whole e-Cupid thing is seriously draining my ability to handle business. I could use some help getting back on track. And, since you keep insisting that you're here to help. . . ."

"Go on," he said.

"Barb Holland is one of my very best friends. She's in love with Andrew McKinnett, and I've promised I'll do everything I can to get him to quit showering his affections on me and turn his attention to Barb. Which is where it should be, according to e-Cupid."

AJ didn't answer, just stared at her.

"Right. I want to redirect his interest, thus letting me focus on work." She sat back in her desk chair, swiveling back and forth, through a ninety-degree arc. "I thought if he had some serious competition for my affection, he might get the hint. Direct communication doesn't seem to work."

"But you've got Ralph Higgenbotham panting after you."

"I said serious competition. Ralph is a misdirected inventor who is about as in love with me as he is with peanut butter." That sounded stupid. "What I meant to say is Ralph probably has a soul mate somewhere out there, but she isn't me. I'm not her. Whatever. You get the picture."

"You don't consider Ralph serious?"

"Not as a contender for my heart." This conversation was getting out of hand. "Look, anatomy lessons aside, I propose that you agree to act as a serious suitor and I'll pretend to respond to you, thereby giving neither Ralph nor Andrew any encouragement. Ralph will go away and invent something I can market, and Andrew will focus on Barb. And then you can help me shore up the weak spots in the company, develop a more focused rollout plan for Spuddy Buddy."

AJ rubbed his chin. "Let me get this straight," he said. "You want me to *pretend* to court you so two guys who are, for all intents and purposes, crazy in love with you will go away?" Ohboy, ohboy. She'd offered him the keys to the toy box and it was full of new and wonderful things. If he was able to help her surely he'd be well positioned for a whole lot of repeat business. Which meant repeat checks for a lot of repeat money. Tommy could get back to managing and Joanie wouldn't have to worry about little Skeezix. And, as a bonus, he'd get to spend nonwork time with Chloe.

She nodded.

"That hardly seems fair. I mean, they *did* see you in e-Cupid. Plus the fact that I'm sort of working for you." He wondered if taking Chloe up on her offer was technically cheating with regards to Ralph and Andrew and the contest. On the other hand, if he helped, she would likely succeed with CI, and he knew that was the one thing she wanted above practically everything else.

She scowled. "I don't *need* suitors. I don't have *time* for suitors." She blew out a frustrated breath. "I've got a business to save, and I can't do it *and* fight off misguided swains."

"But you'd take time to help your friend?"

"She'd do the same for me."

"See," he said, shifting from potential lover to business consultant, "this is why you're having cash flow problems with your business. Everything is personal with you. Why not just let Barb worry about Barb?" Why wasn't he jumping all over this chance?

She drummed her fingers on her desk with extreme frustration. "Let's leave the broader business discussion for the daytime, shall we? I told you. Barb's in love with Andrew—or thinks she is—and she's my friend." Besides, while Andrew was a lovely man, all tall and blond, he wasn't Chloe's idea of the perfect match.

AJ came so much closer to her dream guy.

"I'll do it."

"Pardon?" She hadn't heard him clearly, busy thinking about Andrew.

"I said I'd do it. But only until Halloween. After that, I've got other commitments."

She snorted, "Right, I remember. You're spending the huge bonus the board will give you on a trip to Tahiti."

"Tahiti sounds good." His honey voice slid across her shoulders like a caress. "Do you think you can accomplish what you want in two weeks?"

She checked the calendar on her desk. Two weeks. In which she needed to prove to the board that she had been a success with this little part of her father's vast business empire. And in which she needed to ditch two would-be suitors, get Andrew to focus on Barb, and convince Ralph to make the modifications needed to his SatelHat idea so it would actually be marketable. Two short weeks.

No problem.

She walked forward until she stood in front of AJ. She stuck out her hand. "Deal."

He stood up, somehow much taller and more dangerous than she'd remembered. He grasped her hand in a firm grip. "Deal. When do we start?"

That was somehow easier than she'd expected. "And you'll still help on Spuddy Buddy?"

"Absolutely." He picked up a pad of paper. "I'm all ready to go, armed with clean pages aching for new ideas." He smiled.

Okay, so this might work after all. "Good. Dinner is an option I can definitely deal with." She shoved files on Spuddy Buddy into her briefcase and then added the ones for Keys-in-Tune and Fish-in-a-Dish, just in case. She'd have to be careful, but he *had* offered to help.

"Okay, then," he said. "Give me five minutes to

warm up Charlene and then come down. We'll do burgers or something."

After AJ left, Chloe sat very quietly in her chair. There had to be some catch to this. Too many things were going her way all of a sudden.

On the other hand, with AJ's agreement to pretend to court her, she did have the chance, albeit a slim one, to make Ralph give up on this ridiculous behavior and get back to inventing. Assuming that he was bright enough to understand that a woman had only one true love, one soul mate, and Chloe wasn't his. His brain, not his heart. That's what she'd funded, after all.

She jumped when her phone rang. It was late, after nine. Who would be calling her at this hour? She grabbed the receiver and answered, "Creative Investments, Chloe Phillips speaking."

"Oh, Chloe, I'm so glad I found you," Andrew McKinnett said, relief obvious in the tone of his voice. "I was very worried when you ran out. Now that I know you're okay, I'll call off the police."

"Police! Good grief, why police? I'm fine." She heard sirens outside her office. "Please tell me you haven't done anything stupid, Officer McKinnett," she said.

"Please, call me Andrew. Now that we're a couple, you don't need to stand on formality."

"We're not a couple," she said, practically shouting. "I've got a boyfriend."

"Very well," he said, ignoring her. "You may not think we're a couple yet, but after I'm through, you won't see other men."

Maybe this fake affair with AJ wouldn't work after all. Simply saying the words certainly didn't have any effect. "Andrew, those sirens haven't gone away. What's going on?"

"I'm not at liberty to discuss an ongoing investigation."

"Andrew!"

"I thought he'd kidnapped you. What choice did I have? I love you."

"Who kidnapped me? I haven't been kidnapped." She stopped, cold realization dropping into her heart. "Oh, no, Andrew. Tell me you didn't do what I think you did."

"I didn't have a choice. I *am* an officer of the law."

He'd arrested AJ.

She gritted her teeth. "*I* got into his car. Voluntarily." The silence on the other end of the line confirmed her fears. "I want all charges dropped, understand?"

"Are you sure?"

"Absolutely."

"Okay, if that's what you want, I'll get the paperwork done tomorrow."

"Now, Andrew. Tonight."

"I don't know. He looks dangerous."

"He's a consultant working for my company, for heaven's sake. He's not a criminal."

"Fine. I'll take care of it. But I'm also checking on his record, just to be sure. You never know with these people, what they're up to. And, of course, with me around, you won't have to worry about being hassled any more. I'll protect you."

How very noble. "Thank you, Andrew."

She'd never been inside a police station, much less a jail, but she'd seen documentaries on television. She shuddered. "I'm on my way right now, and he better be in good shape when I get there."

"Now that we have that out of the way, when can I see you again?" asked Andrew.

An excellent opening to set her Reunite Barb and Andrew Plan in motion. "Today is Wednesday. Why not meet me at Capitol Grill in Tyson's Corner tomorrow. I'll have a surprise for you." Actually, two surprises. One named AJ and one named Barb.

"Do I have to wait that long?" he said, slightly whiny.

"Tomorrow, Andrew. Thursday. Be happy with that. I'm a very busy woman and I have a couple of extremely important meetings between now and then. If everything works out right, you'll be glad you waited."

"Whatever makes you happy, my angel, my adored one. Tomorrow it is, then." Andrew McKinnett made very unprofessional kissing sounds into his phone and hung up.

Chloe shuddered. Was that really what men in love did? She didn't want to be within twenty feet of that, thank you. She preferred her men, if she had any, to be strong, not mushy.

She disconnected Andrew's call and dialed Barb on her cell phone as she headed out to rescue AJ. Barb enthusiastically agreed to meet on Thursday.

"Thanks, Chlo. You're the best."

Yes, she was, she told herself, as she hung up the phone. The best friend. And, after she straightened all this personal mess out, the best person to run her own venture capital business.

She hefted her briefcase. Too much time had already been wasted on this suitor thing. She'd rescue AJ, sift through his ideas over a quiet meal, and have a draft plan for Spuddy Buddy ready for board review by tomorrow morning so Gloria could edit it.

She straightened her shoulders. "This time, you'll succeed, Chloe Phillips. This time for sure." She put her coat and gloves on and left the office.

But first she had to get her true love out of jail.

* * *

AJ walked the length of his cell for the umpteenth time since the good Officer McKinnett had locked him in. It was exactly nine of his size eleven boot-lengths from the right wall to the left. And twelve boot-lengths from the wall with the door to the wall that should have had a window in it, but had a malodorous toilet instead.

He'd once secretly harbored a rather childish but romantic vision of a young idealist wrongly imprisoned for his brilliant but radical thoughts. It was a picture he'd carried around with him after his father ran out. Dads didn't just leave for any but the most serious of reasons. He'd concocted a story about his father being a spy who'd been captured by the enemy. He'd been locked up somewhere and that was why he couldn't come home.

That particular fantasy had lasted about a year, until the divorce was final and his mother explained that Dad wouldn't be coming home at all. And why. AJ'd been ten. The last words his father had spoken to him ran something like "you worthless, stupid kid, you'll never amount to anything."

He leaned against the bars in the door and looked up and down the length of cells. It looked as if he was stuck here for the night. He supposed his attitude with the police who met him coming out of Chloe's building hadn't helped him. He'd accused them of a number of improprieties, maligned their heritages and suggested that they attempt a variety of improbable physical acts.

He touched his cheek tenderly. They hadn't been amused and had not been especially gentle when they tossed him into the cell. His fingers were coated with black fingerprinting ink.

But it was all worth it. Chloe wanted him to help her get rid of Andrew and Ralph. While this wasn't exactly a victory, it was an interesting development.

And, since he'd been arrested for allegedly kidnapping her, once this got all straightened out, she'd owe him. Big.

He'd just started the list of things Chloe could do for him, to him, and with him when the good Officer McKinnett came sauntering around the corner, swinging a ring of keys. Keys that would open up the door of this miserable place.

"Hey, McKinnett," he greeted his jailer. "Don't you think this is going too far?"

McKinnett didn't look like he was having any fun this evening. His face was solemn and drawn, as though he'd received bad news recently. AJ hoped so. "Don't push your luck, Lockhart. One more smart comment and—"

"And what? I get a set of steak knives? You're the one who arrested me for something I didn't do. I should sue."

"So, I made a mistake. I was concerned for Chloe's safety. You didn't look like you in that hoodlum get-up you were wearing." Andrew unlocked AJ's cell and opened the door.

"Smile when you say that, pardner," AJ said and walked out into the police station.

"AJ!" Chloe said, rushing towards him. "Are you all right? What happened to your face?"

Wasn't this an interesting development? She'd come to his rescue. "I'm okay." He touched his cheek. "I tripped going into the cell. Hit my face on the floor."

Chloe spun around to accuse McKinnett as he came into the room. "Police brutality. Andrew, how could you?"

"Sorry, Chloe. I didn't mean to injure your consultant. I wanted you to be safe."

"I'm safe," she said and brushed AJ's cheek with a kiss. "Don't do it again."

AJ frowned at the officer. "Where'd you take Charlene?"

McKinnett looked puzzled. "You picked up another woman?"

"My car. Charlene is my Corvette and you better not have hurt her or I really will sue."

The officer thumbed through a file with AJ's name on it. "I had it towed to the impound lot on Franklin. You can pick it up tomorrow."

"What's wrong with right now?"

"Procedure." It was all McKinnett would say.

"If there's a scratch on her, you'll pay," AJ said, putting a protective arm around Chloe. He shot Andrew the meanest look he could manage with an injured cheek. "Let's go, Chloe. No need to waste any more taxpayers' money."

"Forget dinner. I'm taking you home," she said. "Where do you live?" Together they walked into the cold October night to Chloe's car.

AJ got into the passenger seat of Chloe's BMW while she slid behind the wheel. "I've got a town house in McLean," he said, "but it's being painted and won't be ready until tomorrow. Tommy's out of town tonight, so he said I could use his place. But I was supposed to call him a few hours ago if I needed the keys. I guess I'm kind of at loose ends."

"I forgot about the paint," she said. "This was all my fault. You can stay at my place tonight."

"Nice digs," said AJ, tossing his leather jacket onto the antique coat tree across from the large grandfather clock in the entry of Chloe's town house. "Very nice place." He leaned down and scratched the head of a large tabby cat busy stropping against his legs. "Who is this?"

"That would be Edgar Allan, the most obnoxious, hateful cat on the planet."

AJ picked up Edgar Allan, who closed green eyes and purred loudly. "Seems pretty friendly to me."

"One of life's unexplained peculiarities," Chloe said. She picked up his coat and hung it in the closet.

He looked around. It wasn't quite what he'd been expecting for the only daughter of a very wealthy man. It was very nice, elegant, and tastefully decorated. But he'd expected more. "I appreciate this, Chloe."

She walked down the hallway and into the kitchen. "You're probably wondering if it's the servant's night off?"

He followed her, admiring the deep reds and blues of the carpet as he walked. "The thought had crossed my mind. Your family . . ." He stopped. He wasn't envious, not really. He merely had certain opinions about the wealthy, and Chloe had surprised him by not fitting his picture of the rich and how they live.

Chloe bustled around her kitchen, moving this and that. Emptying the dishwasher. "Sorry to disappoint, but I don't have a trust fund or any source of independent income. It was one of the conditions I agreed to when I took over CI. I have to live on the salary the board approved, nothing more."

An interesting concept. Living within one's means. AJ promised himself he'd try it as soon as he had means.

Edgar Allan jumped down and headed to a plastic dish on the floor, looking suggestively up at AJ. "Can't help you out, pal. Gotta talk to the boss lady for food."

"She eats more than most children," Chloe said, reaching into the drawer for a spoon. She went to the pantry and brought back a can of cat food. Edgar Allan sat patiently next to the dish, confident in her role as the head of the household.

"She?"

"My father thought she was a 'he' when he got her and named her Edgar Allan before he found out her true gender. I think it confused the poor creature."

"Why don't you change her name?" he suggested. "Maybe Eloise or, in the spirit of Poe, call her Annabel Lee."

Edgar Allan turned her head and looked askance at AJ. She clearly didn't approve.

"Edgar Allan is just fine," Chloe said. She scooped food into the bowl in front of the waiting cat, who didn't eat until Chloe had stepped away. "She hates me."

"She's a feline. They're supposed to be aloof," AJ said. "I wouldn't worry about it." He watched Chloe rinse the can and toss it in the recycle bag. "It's a wonderful place you've got," AJ said again, watching her fiddle with a canister filled with cooking utensils. She seemed awfully nervous, trying not to look at him.

She took wine glasses out of the dishwasher and slid them in their appropriate slots above the wine rack. "I like it."

He looked around the kitchen, absorbing the details that were Chloe Phillips. Soft yellow walls, white cabinets with glass fronts. Inside, colorful dishes added accents to the yellow and white. The wine rack was filled with red wines. "How about a glass of wine?" he suggested. "To calm the nerves. Help me sleep. Stimulate brainstorming on Spuddy Buddy?"

She hesitated, stacking clean bowls and putting them away. "Pick out something," she said, finally.

He walked across the shining oak floor and selected a solid zinfandel. He took two glasses and set them on the glass-topped table in the kitchen eating area. "Join me," he said. "Then we'll figure out how to make people crave baked potatoes." He grinned and pulled out a chair for her.

She watched him through lowered eyelids and his heart rate sped up. Dreamy bedroom eyes, that's what she had. "Sure, why not," she said, taking a corkscrew out of a drawer and tossing it to him. "Here." Her nonchalant tone did little to disguise her nervousness.

He opened the bottle and poured. He handed her a glass, his fingers grazing hers when she took it. She wandered away from the table to lean against the counter. "I really want to apologize, AJ. You were helping me, at my request, and you wound up in jail. Sorry," she said, saluting him with the wine. "It merely underscores the absolute need to point Andrew's attention towards Barb."

"Hey, these things happen," he said, watching her. The careful way she moved, the motion of her finger on the rim of the wine glass. "Look at it this way, now I've got something on which to base my definitive treatise on prison life."

She laughed, and the tension in his shoulders eased. "Was it really that awful? I mean, you weren't there that long."

"Long enough to know I won't be eating boiled cabbage any time soon. Long enough to know I don't want to go back. Ever." He sniffed the sleeve of his shirt, hoping the lingering odors of the jail hadn't clung to the fabric.

She frowned. "Certainly they don't serve cabbage at the Arlington jail."

"No, but I read it in a book somewhere. Or saw it in a movie."

For a moment they drank in silence. "You know, this really calls for something to eat. Got any junk food?" His glass was almost empty, and he remembered the tuna sandwich he'd had for lunch an eon ago. Besides, food and wine should make conversation less adversarial, more collaborative. Okay, he wanted an excuse to talk, not about her work, but about Chloe's personal life. He wanted to know more about her. Seeing her house intrigued him, whetted his appetite for all things Chloe. Besides which, he liked it when she let down her guard, laughed and joked with him. He gestured with the bottle, offering. She nodded and let him refill her glass.

"No, sorry. I try not to stock junk in my larder. I get too much of it during the day at work, but I could whip up a sandwich or something. We were going to have dinner, after all."

"Now that sounds like a plan." He smiled and appreciated her return smile. "Let me help."

Together they assembled sandwich parts—sliced cheese, cold roast beef, a variety of mustards, a little lettuce and tomato for color. Half an hour later, they were laughing over AJ's suggestions on packaging for Spuddy Buddy and had worked their way through the first bottle of wine and started in on number two.

"You want something to nibble on for dessert?" Chloe asked. "Let me see if I can find anything that might suit." She poked around in her pantry. "Oh, how about this?" She came back to the table with a box of Cracker Jack.

"Sure, fine wine, gourmet sandwiches, candy popcorn. Works." He opened the box and offered her some. She settled into a chair next to him.

"Thanks," she said, taking a handful. "I really appreciate your helping me get back on track, businesswise. I guess I shouldn't have jumped to the conclusion that you'd been hired to close CI."

"I've always found conclusion-jumping to be dangerous," he said. "I generally get stuck halfway over the conclusion and look like a fool."

She laughed. "You should really try to show that sense of humor more during the day. It would make you more approachable, easier to deal with."

"Oh, now I'm difficult?" he said, returning her smile. "I thought I was simply being efficient."

She stopped smiling. "You are efficient. And thorough, and very by-the-book. But you're also creative or you wouldn't have thought to suggest for Spuddy Buddy a packaging that looked as if it were covered in dirt. That's awfully right-brain for such a down-to-business kind of guy." She reached across the pile of papers and notes, past the Cracker Jack box, and touched his hand. "You need to relax more. Have some fun."

The sensation of her fingers on his was comforting, warm, sensual, and it scared him. Relaxing only got him into trouble, he reminded himself. He looked into Chloe's eyes. Green, like the cat's. Smiling, open, welcoming.

She patted his hand and then picked up the Cracker Jack box and shook it so the peanuts came to the top. "I think my favorite part of Cracker Jack is the peanuts. How about you?" Her tongue came out to lick some of the candy crumbs from her finger tip.

He made a small, strangled noise and reached for the box. "I like the prize," he said, his voice shaky enough that he noticed it. "I used to collect them when I was small. I think my mom still has them in a shoe box somewhere. Probably in her basement." Maybe if he focused on the candy, his heart would calm down.

Chloe pulled the prize out. It was a yellow whistle ring. "Have you got one of these?"

"Probably. I can't remember."

"Why don't you keep it," she said. "I've put you through way too much trouble tonight. Call it your yellow badge of honor."

He turned the plastic ring in his fingers. She was offering him a badge of honor when his thoughts were distinctly dishonorable. "Okay. Any other thoughts on Spuddy Buddy, or shall we call it a night?" he said, sliding his gaze along her collarbone and then to her lips. *You're going to get yourself in big trouble here, cowboy,* he told himself. *Remember the pile of bills Tommy needs to pay and the baby Joanie will need to support.*

Chloe cocked her head and looked at him. "It's late, isn't it? And you've got lots of reports to do for the board, don't you?" She stood up and started to clear the dishes.

"Let me help," he said standing next to her. Close enough to inhale her fragrance.

"Nothing to it," she said, bumping him when she reached for his plate. "I'll take care of these in the morning."

"My mother would have a fit if I didn't help. She trained me well." If he didn't kiss her soon, he'd burst.

"Do you see your family often?" Chloe finished clearing the table and AJ recorked the wine.

"Often enough," he said, not wanting to talk about that part of his life right now and spoil the mood. He ran hot water in the sink. "Soap?"

"Right here," she said, opening the door under the sink. He bent down and grabbed the bottle. As he stood, he brushed against her and chills rippled through his body.

"You wash and I'll dry," he offered and picked up a dish towel.

She grinned at him. "Your mom did a great job with you."

"I'll tell her next time I see her."

"I really wish I had more family," she sighed, handing AJ a wine glass. "I mean Oz is a wonderful brother and all, but . . ." She hesitated.

"But holidays are better when there are kids all over the place, playing with Legos." He smiled at her. "My mom bought me a new Lego set every Christmas whether she could afford it or not."

"I love Legos," Chloe said. "In fact, I think I've got some stashed away. Oz used to make the most outrageous stuff from them." She handed him another glass. "Brothers and sisters?"

"Just me," he said, wiping it dry and slipping it into the rack.

"And your father?"

"No longer around." A ripple of apprehension shot through his body at the mere mention of his father. "And not missed at all."

Chloe cocked an eyebrow. "As bad as all that?"

"Worse," AJ said. He leaned down and scooped up Edgar Allan. "If the cat hates you, why do you keep her?"

"She's the only thing my father left me in his will besides the company." She shrugged. "I guess I keep her to remind me that my father was capable of caring for some other living thing besides himself."

"That's pretty harsh, Chloe," AJ said and set the animal back on the floor. He moved closer to her. He could feel the ache her father left her. It matched his own.

"Dad was a wonderful businessman, but he didn't have much time for his children, and after Mom died . . ." She shrugged. "He got more and more distant."

"Who raised you?" he asked, just touching her shoulder with his fingertips.

She didn't draw away, just shivered. "My grandmother stayed with us for a while, but she remarried and moved back to France." She looked up at AJ. "I'm sorry. I didn't mean to bore you with sordid tales of my family troubles."

He lifted a strand of hair away from her cheek and tucked it behind her ear. "I don't mind at all."

"AJ?" she asked.

"Yes?" he answered, trailing his finger along the line of her jaw and stopping at her chin.

"What does AJ stand for?"

"Nothing interesting," he whispered in her ear.

She shivered. "Really, what?"

"Absolute Genius," he said and kissed her neck. Maybe it was the realization that she'd grown up with an absent father that drew him close. Maybe it was her completely trusting nature.

Maybe it was chemistry.

He turned her so she faced him and kissed her cheek.

"Genius starts with a G," she said, her voice sounding all strange and tight.

"I flunked spelling," he said and kissed her lips. Lightly at first and then more firmly when she didn't resist. When her arms came up around his shoulders, he broke the kiss momentarily and said, "I've wanted to do that since the first time I saw you and you kissed me."

"That was a mistake, you know," she said softly, stepping closer to him and lifting her face. She kissed him quietly, carefully. "And so is this. Probably." She stepped back, the mood broken.

"I'm sorry, I didn't mean to—"

"No, I liked it," she said, blushing and clearly undone.

"No, I shouldn't have taken advantage. It's just you looked so appealing and . . ." He stumbled to a halt.

"No apology needed," she said. She straightened. "Come upstairs and I'll show you the guest room and get you some towels."

He reached for her hand and kissed it. "Sure," he said. "Lead on."

She lowered her gaze, clearly embarrassed. "Don't forget this," she said, handing him the whistle ring. Her fingers grazed his hand when he took it, and the electricity that shot up his arm made him want to kiss her again and see what might happen.

"How could I forget my badge of honor?" he said. He'd certainly not forget her touch, it was going to keep him up all night. He needed the tiny yellow whistle to remind him that he actually was honorable.

He followed her up a curved staircase. "Here's the guest room," she said, more composed now. "Sorry for all the books." She waved to the bookcases lining the wall and overflowing onto the bedside table. "I like to read."

"Yeah, me too." The volumes on the shelves and stacked in tidy piles ranged across a variety of subjects. She liked mysteries, and romance, he could see. But there was a fair representation of management books, old reliable how-tos, and biographies. You could tell a lot about a person from what they read.

"The sheets are clean and here are some towels. The bathroom is through that door."

"Toothbrush?"

"Ah, yes. In the drawer under the sink."

He sat on the bed and bounced a little. "Nice. Firm." He smiled at her. "Want to join me?" His tone was light. The last thing he wanted to do was frighten her.

"You're kidding, right?"

He grinned. "Yeah. I'm kidding." Himself, maybe.

She walked to him and put her hands on his shoulders. Her touch felt like coming into contact with an electric fence, only pleasurable. "Thank you." She kissed his forehead, then slid her hands down his arms. "I really appreciate everything you're doing for me, what with the report to the board and Spuddy Buddy and especially with e-Cupid." She stepped back and headed for the door.

"That goofy software. Got to love it," he said, standing. "Tomorrow we'll figure out what we're going to do about all your boyfriends."

One corner of Chloe's mouth lifted in a self-deprecating grin. "Yeah, all my boyfriends." She pivoted and headed down the hall. "Sleep tight," she called. "Don't let the bedbugs bite."

To the sound of Chloe's bedroom door closing, AJ took a deep breath. His mother used to tell him the same thing when he was a kid, before his dad deserted them. After that, she was less happy and more tired. But working two jobs would do that to you. "Sleep tight. No problem there." He was having one of those embarrassing male moments where his anatomy wanted him to follow Chloe and his brain was shouting "Don't open that door!" He closed his eyes. He'd listen to his brain.

This time.

He found the toothbrush without Chloe's help even though he was tempted to ask for it. When he'd finished in the bathroom, and hung his clothes in the closet, he went to the bookcase closest to the bed to pick out some nighttime reading.

He looked up at a small movement in the doorway. It was Edgar Allan. "Ah, looking for a sleeping partner, are we?" he said and scooped the cat into his arms. "Maybe we should read 'The Pit and the Pendulum,'" he said. "That should keep our minds off her." He took a volume of Poe short stories off the shelf, but when he opened it, it was "The Telltale Heart" he turned to.

Chloe went through her nightly routine. She brushed her teeth, cleansed and moisturized her face, flossed, combed her hair, and rubbed cream into that dry spot on her ankle. She abandoned the T-shirt that she normally slept in and dug around in her drawers, looking for the flannel nightgown.

"Found it," she said and pulled the ugly thing out. It was red-checked, had long sleeves, a high collar, and brushed the tops of her feet. Exactly what she needed right now.

Fifteen steps down the hallway was a man who'd done more to stir up all her little pink pheromones than anyone else, and she needed the protection, however symbolic, of stern flannel. She tried to blame the hot feelings on too much wine, but she couldn't lie to herself.

*You need to dump this ridiculous night wear and trot your behind back down the hall and do what comes naturally,* she thought.

"I need to go to sleep," she said to the clock radio beside her bed.

*Been there, done that. You need to be reminded that you're a woman, thank you very much.*

"He *works* for me," she whispered, not worried at all that she was having a conversation with her clock. "I shouldn't be interested in someone who works for me." Regardless of how his kisses made her feel.

*Chicken.*

Okay, it was Leann's voice inside her head. She wasn't losing her mind. There was no way she was going to encourage AJ Lockhart to do any more than help her succeed.

But succeed at what? What did she *really* want out of life? Did she really want to run a business, or was there more waiting for her in life? She thought about Leann, her husband, and their two small girls. Leann was happy, which was why she kept insisting that Chloe find someone special. So she could be happy, too.

"But I am happy," she insisted to the ceiling fan over her bed. "Really, if the board wouldn't get all bent out of shape over numbers, I'd be very, very happy."

And very alone.

# Chapter Eleven
# "Love, Love Me Do"

The next day, AJ tried his best to forget how wonderful Chloe had felt in his arms and to concentrate on the business at hand. Talking her brother into additional business. "You know, Oz, your sister is a very talented woman," AJ said, warming his hands around the generous mug of coffee Phillips had insisted he drink. They were sitting in the restaurant in the Willard Hotel. The impromptu meeting had gone reasonably well, thus far. If he could impress Oz, he knew there'd be more work for his struggling little firm.

"Her actions are foolish, AJ. I'll concede she's very creative, but creativity alone doesn't make a successful executive."

"Don't you want to see your sister succeed?" He couldn't understand Phillips' attitude. Chloe spoke so highly of her brother, but he certainly didn't sound like he had her best interests at heart. Sure, she'd made some bad decisions, but they'd always managed to turn out right in the end. Call it luck, call it creativity, call it serendipity. Whatever it was, it worked for her. "Take this SatelHat idea, for example. I'll be the first to admit I thought it was the dumbest thing I'd heard of, but since I've worked on it, I think it's one of the most promising inventions she's funded. And, it's a sight better than her first decision, that Task-tender thing. She admitted she supported that idea because she felt sorry for the woman. But she's improved markedly since then with her screening. Give her a little credit."

Oz sat quietly, his breathing slow and measured. "Any other projects strike your fancy?"

"SatelHat's the best, of course, after Spuddy Buddy. None of the rest has near the same potential, and the latest idea she's considering appears to have a bug."

"Really? Bugs?"

"It's a software program," AJ said. "A website, really." He gave Oz an overview of e-Cupid and the troubles his sister was grappling with, including unreachable inventors and two men swooning at her feet.

"Interesting." The other man sat quietly for a moment. "I want my sister to be happy," Oz said. "Do you seriously believe running a company will make her happy?"

AJ cocked an eyebrow. "It's what she wants. All she needs is a solid strategic plan and a steady accountant who doesn't want to invent something, and she'll be fine. There's nothing basically wrong with the business. My firm is well positioned to write the plan."

Oz sipped his coffee and ignored AJ's assessment of the situation. "Chloe has always needed to care for something or someone. When she was small, she adopted every living creature that came within breathing distance of our house. There was a constant stream of toads, lizards, injured birds, kittens, puppies—you name it, she took care of it. I believe her adoption of these projects, as she calls them, stems from a lack of other places to focus her desire to nurture."

Where was he going with this, AJ wondered. Was he suggesting that Chloe adopt a dog?

"She is a great woman, warm, loving. She needs children, AJ, children and a man to give them to her. These two men who have taken an interest in her? Is either of them a possible match?"

Now it was AJ's turn to be quiet. What was that pang that raced through his heart at Oz's suggestion that either Ralph or McKinnett might be the one for Chloe? Jealousy? He pushed away the thought. "I doubt it. Software can't make people fall for each other. Frankly, I think the whole e-Cupid thing is a crackpot dream of a couple of guys who thought they could get some cash from your sister."

"So you agree she doesn't know how to run a business?"

That wasn't what he meant. "No. She'll reject e-Cupid after she's completed her analysis."

"Perhaps I should simply call a special board meeting and tell them what you've reported."

"It's a little early for that, Oz. But I do know that, if you don't stand in her way, Chloe will make a lot of money with her goofy ideas and silly-sounding projects. Underneath all that seemingly unorganized thinking is someone who believes in the innate goodness of each person she deals with, in the right of every individual to have a shot at their dreams."

"Good work, Lockhart," said Oz. "I think you should stay on the job until this e-Cupid thing is straightened out. Then we'll go to the board. I'm sure they'll follow whatever course you recommend."

"Whatever you say, Oz. You're the boss." AJ stood and shook Oz's hand. With chilling clarity he knew he was the one person who could give Chloe her dream or crush her heart.

Chloe dropped AJ off at the impound lot so he could rescue Charlene, and then she headed downtown to one of those dreadful industry functions she had to attend. The Venture Capitalist luncheon would be a nice change from wrestling with over-zealous, unwanted suitors, however, and would afford her some time to think about what to do with AJ. Other than the obvious, which was to trip him and beat him to the ground.

She patted her briefcase. Inside were AJ's preliminary ideas on how to make Spuddy Buddy succeed. His thinking was nothing short of brilliant. His insights into marketing were clear and simple, and if she took his advice, she'd have the killer project the board was after. Maybe there was something to an organized, disciplined, businesslike approach to ideas. Maybe he wasn't as cold and uncreative as she'd first thought.

His kisses certainly weren't cold.

She thought about AJ digging around in the Cracker Jack box, looking for peanuts. About how silly, and at ease, he looked trying out that ridiculous yellow whistle ring. The warmth of his hand under hers. His smoldering looks.

His gentle, insistent lips. Oh, my, she was going to have to be careful.

Thursday afternoon came, and the meeting concluded, finally. Chloe couldn't have told a soul what topics had been discussed or what she'd contributed. Her pad of paper was covered with notes and doodles about Spuddy Buddy and AJ. In a soft, happy daze, she walked out of the meeting room into the lobby of the Willard and ran straight into her brother. "Oz, what are you doing here?" she said. Her brother never attended industry functions.

"I had a couple of meetings," he said, leaning close to kiss her cheek. "What's this I hear about you funding some kind of buggy software?"

Chloe was shocked at the harsh tone of Oz's voice. He'd been so supportive recently. Something must have happened. "Oz, can I buy you a cup of coffee?" she offered. "We can sit quietly and discuss your concerns."

"I don't have time right now. I'm meeting Michael Flaherty in," he consulted his Rolex, "fifteen minutes."

"Then sit here in the lobby with me while you wait. Michael is likely to be late anyway. Traffic," she said. Flaherty was Oz's financial adviser, and not one of Chloe's favorite people. One of his frequent topics of conversation with her seemed to be how to dispose of CI.

"Michael is never late," her brother stated. But, he did sit in one of the hotel-lobby chairs, folding his pigskin gloves in his lap and removing his dark glasses.

"This new investment is fresh, very marketable. It has success written all over it." Briefly, she reviewed the applications for e-Cupid. "Who told you it had bugs?"

Oz shifted in the chair. "Isn't it normal for new software to have some problems? Look at Microsoft. Look at Netscape."

Her concern eased. Of course, all new software had difficulty in the early stages. Eagerly she leaned forward. "E-Cupid and its web tie-in, Cupid.com, have the potential to be enormous."

"And you've tested the program yourself?"

Warning bells went off in her head, loud, clanging warning bells, accompanied by sirens. "I've checked it out, yes." Where was he going with this?

"And you're convinced the inventors can rectify the problem?"

She wasn't about to admit she hadn't talked with E. Rose and Milo since the day they first met. "Let me assure you that a software fix will be found. This is a can't-miss opportunity, Oz."

Her brother snorted. "Like Spuddy Buddy?" He held his hands up, warding off her protest. "I know about the governmental red tape on that one. I know it's not your fault. But I'm concerned about you and this e-Cupid, especially if you try it out yourself and hook up with someone entirely unsuitable."

"I'm not hooking up with anyone. I simply let a couple of friends try it."

Oz shifted on his chair. "And how did it go?"

"Well, Barb seems to have found someone she's compatible with." Now, if only Chloe could convince him that someone *he* was compatible with Barb.

"I hope you have better luck with e-Cupid, because it appears that you've failed miserably with this one. This letter accidentally got routed to my office." He handed her an envelope.

Chloe took it, unable to understand why Oz's friendly and supportive attitude had disappeared. "Ah, here's Michael." Oz stood up, dismissing her. "We'll chat later, Chloe." He shook hands with his tall, middle-aged advisor. "Michael, right on time, as usual," he said, looking sideways at Chloe as if to say "told you so."

"Hi, Mikey," Chloe said, enjoying the wince of pain on the older man's face. "How's life treating you?" She clutched the envelope tightly, thinking perhaps she could squeeze out all the bad news before she opened it.

"I'm good. How's the whistling key project coming?"

Was there anyone who didn't know her business? "I've got it covered."

"I know people who can help if you need them to." With a quick nod of his balding head, he and her brother walked toward the bar, obviously having more important things to discuss than Chloe and her life.

It was ever thus, she concluded.

She simply had to make Spuddy Buddy meet the potential she knew it had. The potential AJ had helped to identify. Then Oz would have to sit up and take notice.

She opened the envelope and extracted the two slim sheets of paper. It was a notice from the EPA. Her environmental impact study for Fish-in-a-Dish was deficient in a number of areas, and they were going to block introduction of the personal fish farm her friends had worked so hard on until the problems were satisfactorily dealt with. She put the notice back in the crumpled envelope, wondering how she was going to break the news to Al and Annie, and how CI was going to recover from this serious setback. Even AJ had finally seen some potential in Fish-in-a-Dish.

A loud commotion outside the hotel brought Chloe back to reality again.

"What *is* that racket?" the bellman asked, moving to the main door to the Willard.

"I have no idea," Chloe said. "It sounds like a band."

Swarms of people crowded the doors and windows at the front of the hotel lobby. Chloe joined them, thinking this was one of those periodic protests or instant celebrations that were part of life in the nation's capital.

She pushed through a knot of Japanese tourists, all busy taking out their cameras, and leaned around them to see where the sound came from. It was, indeed, a band. A large, noisy band, complete with a flag corps, twirlers, and a huge banner.

A huge banner which read "Chloe, Be Mine."

The flags were red with white hearts on them. Inside the hearts were the initials CP and RH. "Ralph," she said, closing her eyes and wishing for the zillionth time that she'd never heard of e-Cupid. Grateful that her brother and Michael were knee-deep in brandy and cigars and not there to witness her latest screwup. How in the world was Ralph affording all this? The last thing she needed was to feel guilty for bankrupting the guy.

"It's a little early for Valentine's Day. Shall I tell them to leave?" AJ asked, appearing at her elbow. "Or tell them to play something more romantic than Sousa?"

What in the world? "Why are you here?" Chloe asked, the heat infusing her face coming from the mother of all blushes. "Aren't you supposed to be working?"

AJ kissed her forehead, a friendly gesture rather than a sexual one, but it made her whole body respond anyway. "How do you know I'm not?"

So, he'd been talking with her brother. No wonder Oz knew about the software problems with e-Cupid. She guessed she couldn't fault AJ for doing his job. Although why hadn't Oz told her he'd met with AJ. She just couldn't figure her brother out these days. She gazed into AJ's eyes, looking at her all blue and filled with humor. How did he manage that, she wondered. Looking innocent and sexy as hell at the same time.

"I didn't think ol' Ralph was this creative. I mean, flowers you'd expect. Dinner is pretty standard. But a whole band?"

The band in question had stopped Sousa-ing in the street in front of the Willard and had shifted into a jazzy version of *Bolero*. "Wouldn't you know it," she said. "Another man who thinks just because Bo Derek jogged across a beach in slow motion to it that *Bolero* is good seduction music."

"What would you consider good seduction music?" AJ asked softly in her ear, sending shivers up and down her spine.

"I don't know. ZZ Top? 'Nsync? I'm not much into romantic music."

"I can fix that," he said, as the band left *Bolero* and shifted to a waltz. He took her briefcase and handed it to the bellman. "Watch this for me, will you?"

"What are you doing?" Chloe began.

"Helping you understand romantic music," AJ said and took her hand in his and put his arm around her. "Like this." He danced her off the steps and onto the sidewalk.

"You're crazy."

"Quite possibly," he said, waltzing around the huge pots of late-season pansies, all blue and yellow in the afternoon sun. The crowd parted to give them more room. Being in AJ's arms, with the music swirling around them, pressed close to him, was almost more than she could bear. She could almost feel his heart pounding in rhythm with the song, and his warmth surrounded her. Longing coursed through her and she wished she could dance on and on in his arms. But the band stopped and the crowd cheered.

Chloe wanted to reach up and kiss him, but instead she leaned into his chest and laughed. "Certifiable."

"Stick with me, kid, and you'll get used to it. I'll introduce you to my CD collection so we can increase your appreciation of the romantic possibilities in music." AJ kissed her forehead, her chin, and then her lips.

She pushed him away. "AJ," she whispered, "everyone's watching us."

"Good," he said and kissed her again.

"Stop. Oz is sipping brandy not fifty feet away and he'd have a coronary if he knew what a commotion we'd caused." She broke his embrace and hurried back up the steps to retrieve her briefcase. She held it in front of her like a shield.

What would Oz think, she wondered, if he knew e-Cupid had matched her with AJ? Remembering his warning over last Sunday's dinner, she didn't guess he'd be too happy. But she couldn't tell if he was just being an overprotective big brother or if he knew something about AJ that he hadn't revealed to her. It would have to be something that made him doubt the consultant would be a good match for his sister.

Chloe shook her head. She'd spent way too much time today trying to figure out what was going on in Oz's mind. She couldn't help but smile as she imagined how her uptight brother would react to Ralph's latest foray into the world of courting.

She looked up at AJ, glad he was there to see Ralph's excesses—glad he had helped her to enjoy Ralph's embarrassing display.

He'd only offered music, AJ thought, and a quick, impulsive dance. He watched her eyes gleam, and wondered why his thoughts, as well as his body, kept turning to romancing Chloe for real. The more time he spent around Chloe, the less sensible he wanted to be. "Don't worry about your brother," he said. "We can simply tell him we're doing research on e-Cupid." He grinned. "Speaking of business, I've already talked with a couple of friends about changing the product design for Spuddy Buddy. So we need to spend some more time fleshing out its marketing plan. We could start tonight, if you want, after we take care of Andrew and Barb." He gave her shoulders a little squeeze. "You could check out my CD collection and pick some tunes guaranteed to enhance your creativity."

"Sure, that would be fine," she said, wondering about her ability to have more than a business relationship with the man standing beside her. More than the fake boyfriend ploy he'd agreed to. Would this ruse to get rid of her unwanted suitors land her a real suitor? Suddenly, she realized how badly she wished that would happen.

"Great," AJ said, quietly. He held her hand, sending fire shooting up her arm, across the tops of her shoulders, and into the pit of her stomach.

They stood together for a minute or two, listening to Ralph's serenade wind down. After the last strains of the theme from *Star Wars* ended and the snare drum had quieted, AJ released Chloe and walked out onto the sidewalk. "Great job, kids," he shouted. "Now, get lost. You're holding up traffic." One thing the District definitely didn't need any more of was traffic.

The drum major saluted with his baton and walked up the sidewalk to where AJ stood, pulling his coat around him to ward off the chill. "I guess this is for you," he said, handing AJ a large envelope. "Hope you liked the music." With that, he pivoted on his heel and marched back to his band, which launched into a brass version of Broadway hits.

AJ handed the envelope to Chloe. "A message from Ralph, is my guess," he said.

"Thanks," Chloe said. "What do you want to bet

it's a compilation of love songs that the band could have played, along with a history of each and its role in someone else's love life."

"Almost assuredly. Ralph is nothing if not predictable, once you get past his grand excesses."

Chloe opened the envelope and read the letter from Higgenbotham.

*My dearest Chloe,* it began. *I have long cherished music as a fond expression of a lover's feelings and present to you my heartfelt emotions along with the fine musicians who are playing my choices of love songs to you right now. You will see that each selection has a key position in the history of the art of courting, as well as a special meaning for the two of us. Please accept this homage to my love for you. With great affection, Ralphie.*

"Ralphie?" AJ said, reading over Chloe's shoulder. "If this wasn't so funny, it'd be sad."

"It is sad," Chloe said. "He's really a very nice, very smart man. I don't understand why he continues to pursue me. I've told him straight out that he's off track."

AJ said quietly, "Maybe you should tell him once more. I'd do it in writing."

"You're probably right. I'll call him and arrange to meet somewhere. Maybe if I hand-deliver him a letter that gently turns him away, he'll finally get the message." Then she could get Andrew together with Barb.

"He's pretty far gone and may not react well to the whole 'go away' scenario. Want me to come with you?"

Chloe shook her head. "No, I don't think that's necessary. After all, I've been working with Ralph for the better part of a year and I know how to deal with him. It's Andrew where I'll really need help."

"Great. Here's a phone," AJ said, handing her his

cellular. AJ sounded upset, although Chloe couldn't figure out why. After all, she was pretending to be with him, not rushing after Ralph. Men were difficult to understand in the best of times and impossible the rest of the time.

She dialed Ralph and arranged to meet him for coffee.

"You sure about this?" AJ asked.

"You said yourself that Ralph's invention is one of the most promising things CI is working on, right? Then, to succeed I need Ralph focused on satellites, not brass bands. I'll be fine," Chloe said, smiling. "I managed before I met you, didn't I?"

"Yes, but not as well as you're managing now," AJ said, whispering in her ear and setting a wave of take-me-now thoughts flooding her brain. "When do you see our boy Ralph?"

"Four-thirty," she said, her voice husky.

"Great. We've got a whole two hours to fill until then. Got any ideas?" AJ smiled and trailed a fingertip along her cheek.

"We could always go back to work."

"Or we could practice pretending to be in love."

"Ralph, it's not that I'm not flattered by your attentions, but be logical about this. A computer program can't control your emotions. You're not really in love with me." Chloe had tried through three cups of caffeine with cream to explain the situation to her normally calm, intelligent inventor. Today he wasn't engaging that part of his brain. He'd short-circuited straight to illogical.

"Andrew McKinnett put you up to this, didn't he?" Ralph asked, a pleading, stupid smile pasted on his face, his eyes eager, hopeful.

What could Andrew possibly have to do with Ralph? "What will you do when you meet the woman you're *supposed* to be in love with? What then? You should know I don't believe in polygamy and I refuse to make some other woman the 'other woman.' Understand?" Now he had *her* talking in riddles.

"There could never be anyone but you, my heart, my dove, my chickadee."

She liked birds as well as the next person, and chickadees were cute, but being compared to one didn't do anything at all for her confidence in Ralph. It hadn't worked for W. C. Fields, either. "Can we talk about SatelHat?" she asked, hoping to move the conversation back into the realm of reality. "What's happened with the flange problem?"

Ralph straightened, some of the new love gleam in his eyes trading places with his passion for his ideas. "I reviewed your consultant's ideas and I think he may have solved that particular dilemma."

"Good, good. Then you'll make the deadline to deliver plans to the manufacturer."

"I've actually put those on hold, temporarily, you understand, until we make *our* plans."

"*Our* plans are about the manufacture of SatelHat, Ralph. I've made promises, started marketing campaigns. Don't let your misguided feelings for me get in the way of what you've been working toward for two years. Don't." Please, don't. She needed his project. Really needed it.

Ralph sat silently, holding his coffee. Conflicting emotions flitted across his narrow face. His eyes alternately glowed with the eagerness she'd identified with SatelHat, and became dewy with his alleged love for her. "Perhaps we could do both, my dove."

Again with the birds. "That would be very nice, Ralph. Could we focus on SatelHat first, please?"

"I'll need to ponder this, my little wren. If you would permit me? I'll go back to my laboratory and evaluate a dual track development, one my fondest dream to see SatelHat become a reality and one to make you the center of my universe."

"That would be good, Ralph. Go. Evaluate. Let me know." Finally, a man who could deal with this insanity in a rational way. It had been a very good thing not to include AJ in this mix, she realized. Ralph was so fragile that AJ's presence would probably have had disastrous results. Bands in the street were one thing. Fistfights were quite another.

AJ was greeted by a tearful Joanie and a determined looking Tommy when he stopped by his office with the good news that Creative Investments was excited about having them work on a rollout plan for Spuddy Buddy.

"What now?" he asked, putting a protective arm around Joanie. "Is it Eugene? Has he been causing trouble? I've got new friends on the police force who will take care of him."

"It's not that," Joanie sobbed. "Read this." She handed him a notice from the real estate management company who owned their strip mall office.

AJ scanned the letter quickly. He already knew what it would say. They were being evicted for nonpayment of rent. He looked at Tommy. "What happened to the check I gave you from Phillips?"

"The bank put a two-week hold on it," Tommy said sourly.

Shit. And he'd just talked with Oz. Why hadn't Oz warned him. "What for? Phillips International has gobs of money, truckloads. I'm calling the bank," he said, reaching for the phone.

Joanie's hand stopped him. "Read this first," she said, handing him another envelope.

"Oh, this is just swell," AJ said throwing himself into his desk chair. "They've cut off our phone service. Guess your creative reasons didn't work after all," he said to Tommy. He tossed the notice onto the desk and pulled out his cell phone. That, at least, was still working, since he paid for it from his own account. He dialed the bank and asked to speak to the vice president. After a brief conversation punctuated by "yeses" and "I sees," AJ hung up.

"And?" Tommy asked.

"He wouldn't be specific, but apparently the account our check was drawn on has been frozen by the authorities in Fairfax County due to "irregularities" on some construction project. He didn't sound happy," AJ said, running his hand through his hair. He'd counted on this Phillips assignment too much, put all his eggs in one omelet—and they were rotten.

"I've got a suggestion," said Tommy. "And keep in mind, it's only a suggestion. We may not have to be this drastic. Who knows? Maybe one of the other companies that owes us money will come through with a payment any second now." He looked pained.

AJ knew what his friend was going to suggest. "You can't go to your father, Tom, and I'm *not* going to ask my mother for help. I've already taken out a second mortgage on the town house. What else is there?"

"I know this guy in Laguna Beach who would pay big bucks for a classic Corvette—"

"Absolutely not," AJ said, shoving back and standing. "I'm not selling Charlene. I took her in lieu of salary, remember?"

"It was just a suggestion," Tommy said. "I'll take another look at our accounts receivable and make some calls."

"You do that," AJ said, grabbing his coat and his keys. "I've got a date with Chloe to get rid of one Andrew McKinnett and to discuss a rollout strategy.

By the time I'm finished, she'll pay me in advance." He stalked out.

Sell Charlene? He'd do almost anything to avoid that.

# Chapter Twelve
# "It's Almost Like Being in Love"

Feeling just like Cinderella chasing her stepsisters around, trying to get them ready for the ball, Chloe tried desperately to tame her hair. As usual, her flame and cinnamon curls refused to cooperate, insisting instead that they be left free to wander where they would. It was exasperating. It was infuriating.

It made her look very young and very vulnerable.

Not the look she wanted for her first "date" with AJ. She was supposed to be a together business woman, not a blithering school girl. Which was how she felt. Out of focus, off center, and very, very excited.

What did she know about him, really?

She knew his business skills—impeccable.

His dealings with her brother—questionable.

He believed in her projects—laudable.

He kissed like no one she'd ever kissed before.

And he was going to help get e-Cupid unsnarled.

She took a deep breath, and then another one. Focus, Chloe, focus. The key to organizing her life was getting Barb and Andrew together. If she could accomplish that, two things would happen. She could spend more time fine-tuning the projects CI was funding, and she'd have one example of e-Cupid actually working.

With the bad news on Fish-in-a-Dish, her list of inventions headed for quick success had dwindled to two: SatelHat and Spuddy Buddy. And Ralph's starry-eyed insistence that he loved her placed SatelHat's future in jeopardy.

One success. That's all she needed. Just one.

Spuddy Buddy would have to be it.

However. If the Andrew and Barb connection worked, perhaps she should reconsider e-Cupid. It was probably wise to have another project waiting in the wings just in case the government red tape on Spuddy Buddy didn't go away fast enough. In which case she needed more than one example of how e-Cupid worked to make any marketing campaign believable. Which brought her back to AJ. He was her e-Cupid match. . . .

His dark good looks and arrogant attitude were compelling in a primal sort of way. AJ in a suit was easy to look at, but AJ in black leather—whew! Chloe knew, intellectually, that the whole bad boy persona was what intrigued her. That it was typical for a woman to fall for the dangerous and mysterious, thinking somehow that she could tame the wild creature inside. She'd confirmed that with her research prior to e-Cupid. Intellectually, she could cope with AJ just fine.

Emotionally, however, she was ill prepared to meet this man anywhere, and especially not where she had to have her wits about her. But to make her business succeed, what was she prepared to do? She straightened. Her primary goal for this evening was to uncouple Andrew from one Chloe and redirect his testosterone toward Barb. Then, and only then, she'd worry about her attraction to AJ.

"Very well," she told herself. "If I focus on the goal, I should be just fine." Of course, she wasn't fooling herself at all. The image that looked back from her mirror told the truth: Chloe wanted this mock date to be more than pretend. She wanted AJ to sweep her off her feet. E-Cupid had promised her true love and had labeled AJ as such. He hadn't come with instructions or warning labels, but at the moment, she didn't care. She wanted him in the worst, and best, way.

An insistent honking from her driveway broke her pleasant thoughts and brought her crashing back to reality. She was a woman with a failing business who had unwanted suitors she had to shed in order to turn the failure into a win.

Chloe stood, gave her uncooperative hair one final and futile pat, and grabbed her Gucci bag. She took a deep breath. Fools rush in, she reminded herself, and concluded there were few things in her life that she'd undertaken more foolish than this frenetic matchmaking venture.

She raced down the stairs to a persistent set of honks from AJ's Corvette. You'd think he'd at least have the courtesy to come to her door rather than summon her like some common drudge. Even the bad boy in her musings would have extended her that small gesture.

She snagged her Eddie Bauer fleece jacket and glanced once more in the hall mirror. Black ankle boots, jeans, pale green sweater, white fleece jacket. About as casual as she could manage. She went out the front door of her town house.

At least he'd gotten out of the car. AJ was leaning against the Corvette, dressed in his signature black. The driver's window was open, giving him easy access to the horn. "You could have come to the door," she said as she walked around the car and stood at the passenger side.

"Yes, I could have, but, after that incident with the police, I don't leave Charlene alone in strange places." AJ opened his door and slid behind the steering wheel. He leaned over and unlocked the passenger door. "Besides, I like to watch you move."

Chloe gave him her best aggravated look, the one that generally left people shrinking, and slid into the bucket seat. She managed to avoid the duct tape repair, which was coming unstuck, and sat back. Apparently bad boys in black were impervious to her looks.

Or perhaps not.

Instead of driving, AJ sat in his black leather bucket seat, his right arm slung across the back of the seat, and stared at her. She didn't have much experience with men, but she'd have to be comatose not to recognize that something was bothering him.

Chloe swiveled in her seat, being careful not to get duct-tape stickiness on her jeans, and cocked her head. "What's wrong?"

He turned the key in the ignition and the car started immediately. "Nothing," he said. Instead of leaving the drive, he continued to study her.

She pinned him with a narrow glare. "You going to drive, or what?" she demanded. She figured she had a fifty-fifty chance that McKinnett would actually come around and see the wisdom in pursing Barb instead of Chloe. But she couldn't accomplish anything if she was late. And, she wasn't quite sure what Barb might do if she arrived first.

*Quit pretending, Chloe,* said a small voice in her

head. *On your worst day, you could handle Andrew and Barb and six people just like them. It's AJ who's got your nerves skating on the edge of a razor blade.*

AJ cleared his throat and shoved the sports car into gear. He pealed out of her driveway without looking in the rearview mirror, an action too foolhardy to contemplate for Chloe. Before she could reprimand him, he glanced in the mirror, jammed the car into first gear, and stepped on the gas. The aging Corvette let out a throaty gasp and leapt forward.

Fast.

Chloe grabbed for the dash and then for her bag as she was thrown back into the seat. She was beginning to recognize that AJ in his car was a different creature from AJ in the office. Something about men and sports cars and speed. Tonight, however, there was an extra worry in AJ's demeanor. She frowned. Had Oz interfered? "Okay, so it's a fast car," she said. "Slow down. We're not that late."

AJ took the corner well over the advised speed limit and screeched to a halt at the stop sign. *"She,"* he said. *"She's* a fast car and she really likes to do that. And here I thought you were the one who liked to try out new and different experiences. Charlene started right up, did you notice that? It means she likes you." The car sputtered, slowed, and then regained its forward momentum.

"I wouldn't call that total acceptance," Chloe said. "Let's just say she's happy to be out on the road and leave it at that." Chloe couldn't believe she was talking to this man about a car as though it were his lover. But, she told herself sternly, getting him to talk about his car might relax him and she'd find out what was really wrong. Chloe attempted to smooth her hair and settled into her seat as AJ maneuvered onto the highway. "Is it—ah, she—easy to drive?"

He kept his eyes on the road, but his hands tightened on the leather-covered steering wheel. "Most of the time."

Strike one. "What color are you going to paint it, her? When you're finished fixing it, her, I mean."

He shot her a sidelong glance. "I'm thinking the original Panama yellow. And I'd go back to the saddle leather seats as well. Black and yellow seem too much like someone's bad high school colors for me." He relaxed his grip on the wheel.

"I know what you mean. My school colors were orange and brown. I refused to wear any clothing in brown and orange for years afterward."

"I bet you looked cute in your cheerleader outfit," he teased.

"Oh, right. Orange sweaters and brown and white striped skirts. Go Ravens."

"Yeah. Ravens." He sat a little straighter. "What high school?"

"Chapman," she said, thinking she'd finally gotten him to loosen up a little. Progress.

He sat very still and the car began to slow. "When?"

She told him.

"I graduated from Chapman the year you started," he said, finally looking at her.

A cold prickly sensation crept up her back, making the hairs stand up on her arms. "Weird."

"Did I know you?"

She shook her head. "No. I'm sure I would have remembered."

"You're probably right," he said, pushing his hair off his forehead. "I certainly would have remembered you," he said quietly.

Her heart caught and bobbled a beat. "Well, isn't that interesting," she said, trying to fill the awkwardness with words. "We'll have to compare notes and see who we knew."

"Yeah, that would be great," AJ said.

Okay, silence wasn't all that bad a thing, she told herself. This time she counted to one hundred and didn't miss a number. "I know you must think this is a little unusual, this request to help." Chloe glanced sideways at AJ. "I do appreciate it."

He glanced at her but remained silent, concentrating on driving.

"I know you've been talking with my brother. Even though he's supportive, he's never been one hundred percent behind my projects."

"How are his companies faring? I'm just wondering, because I enjoy working with you and thought there might be future business with the Phillips group."

That made her sit back. "You're asking me?" she said, laughing. "You came to CI to help me figure out how I was doing, remember?"

"I thought you might put in a good word with Oz," he said.

He was on a first-name basis with her brother. Figured. "I'll talk to him," she said. "But he's been a little weird the last couple of days, and he's never been that interested in my business opinions. Why don't we wait and see how things turn out with the board? Do you think I'll make the deadline? Will the board decide my management is sound or sloppy?"

He shrugged.

He obviously wasn't going to be able to find out more about her brother's finances right now. "Will Andrew and Barb get back together? Will Ralph fix SatelHat? There are so many questions, only two answers. Yes and no." He stopped at a red light and looked at her. "You've got great instincts for ideas.

Better than many of the most successful men I know. You tell me whether the board will get off your back or not. Only you can know for certain."

"You think I'll make it, then?"

He cocked an eyebrow, smiled and said, "Definitely." He could imagine her in a short skirt, tight sweater, jumping and cheering for the football team to put one in the end zone. She was right. He shouldn't rush things, but his company was falling apart before his eyes. He had to do something. "Where are we going again?"

"The Capitol Grill. Andrew is meeting me there."

"Us," AJ corrected, pulling off the access road and onto the Parkway.

Moments later, AJ was ushering her into the restaurant, his hand strong and warm in the small of her back. Warm was an understatement. This, this was a guy you wouldn't mind having around on long cold winter nights. He radiated heat and his heat transferred to her spine, moving like wildfire up and down, spreading all over her body and turning her bones and muscles into glop. Warm, drowsy, formless glop.

Then she saw Andrew and the glop hardened back into human form. He was at the far end of the room, in the corner next to the huge painting of hunters and hounds.

She waved and Andrew stood, a decidedly unfriendly scowl on his long face as she and AJ approached.

"What's going on here, Chloe?" he said. "I thought we were going to have a chance to be alone." He pulled out a chair so she could sit. AJ plopped into the chair next to her while Andrew sat on her other side.

"We need to talk," she began.

"Good idea. You," he said, poking AJ's chest, "can leave now. Thank you so much for delivering her safely."

AJ shrugged and stood. "I'll go sit at the bar. If you need anything, scream." He nodded at Andrew and walked away.

Okay, this wasn't going exactly the way she'd envisioned. Why was it that lately, nothing in the universe was paying any attention to her carefully constructed plans. She sighed. At least AJ hadn't gone far.

She straightened and faced Andrew McKinnett, bachelor number one. "This is all a huge mistake," she said.

"Bringing your pet felon along on our date?" he said. "I'd have to agree."

"No, not AJ. You. You and me. We're not supposed to be a couple, Andrew."

"Man, what kind of voodoo has this guy stuck on you?"

"No magic," she said. "Love bugs."

Andrew leaned back and scratched his head. "You'll have to give me a little more information, Chloe."

At least he was willing to listen. "Promise you won't ask questions until I get done?"

He nodded. "I promise."

She launched into the twisty tale of e-Cupid, E. Rose, and the romance glitch of the century.

Andrew listened patiently, his demeanor that of a tolerant and loving parent to a child with overactive imagination genes on full throttle. Not bored, but not really listening either.

Chloe knew the look well. She'd grown up with it. One of her earliest memories was of her father wearing exactly that same expression while she explained her plan to attach nonskid rubber to the roof so Santa's reindeer wouldn't slip on landing and takeoff. She'd been four, maybe five.

The topics had changed from helping a jolly old elf have a safer holiday to taking oddball ideas and making them marketable products and services. But her father's low opinion of her imagination and her absolute inability to say no to anyone with an interesting idea hadn't changed at all. He'd never encouraged or approved of either personality trait. Until he left her CI in his will. Maybe her father had been interested after all.

She slowed and then stopped her explanation. "So you see, I'm not the one for you."

Andrew scratched his head again, as though that small rubbing action might help solidify all the weird data she'd just given him. "You're telling me that I'm in love with you because of a software bug?"

She relaxed as relief flooded into her pores. He *had* been listening. "Yes. That's precisely what I mean."

Andrew appeared to consider this piece of information for a minute or two. "It doesn't make any difference *how* we fell in love, only that we *are* in love."

Oh dear. "You. You're in love. I'm not." At least not with you, pal. "Do you want another beer?"

Andrew brightened. "Sure. Can I get you anything?"

"Club soda and an Alka-Seltzer." He hadn't heard her. Just as he hadn't heard her every time she'd tried to get him to understand that they weren't meant for one another. She fisted her hands and ground them into her eyes. It must be some sort of cosmic joke. In twenty-nine years she'd had only one real boyfriend, and now she couldn't get rid of unwanted suitors.

She glanced at AJ, who was sipping beer at the

end of the bar. He smiled at her and shook his head.

Just then, Chloe saw Barb around the corner. Her friend looked tense, holding herself straight, glancing around as if unsure of herself. But she was here and that was the first step.

Chloe smiled at Andrew. "Excuse me, please."

He put a hand on hers and said, "Don't stay away too long, honey."

Honey, indeed. She continued to smile, extracted her hand from his paw, and sprinted towards Barb.

"Oh, God, Chloe," her friend said. "Is he here?"

Chloe nodded in the general direction of the table she'd just left. "Right over there. I told him about the computer glitch, how my picture is popping up for everyone, and he seemed to understand, but he's still insisting that he's in love with me." She left out the detail of him calling her "honey," figuring that would simply complicate an already tense situation.

"Do you have the laptop?" Barb asked. "This won't work without the laptop, will it?"

"It's on the table, next to the victim. One more trip through e-Cupid and he'll forget how to say my name."

Barb straightened her shoulders and took Chloe's elbow. "This better work, or else . . ."

"Or else what?"

"Or I'll never speak to you again."

There were days when that wouldn't be such a bad thing, Chloe admitted to herself. Focus. She had to focus. Barb belonged with Andrew. Andrew belonged with Barb. "Let's go. Once more into the breach, dear friend."

"Huh?"

"Sorry. A habit I've picked up from AJ. Shades of Shakespeare."

"You're seeing AJ?" Barb whispered as they got

closer to the table where Andrew sat, tapping his glass of beer, waiting for his true love.

"It's a long story. Concentrate on Andrew and after we've got that straightened out, I'll tell you about AJ." She arrived at the table, Barb in tow. "Andrew, you remember Barbara?"

Andrew glanced at Barb, and then at Chloe. "I'm confused, Chloe. You want me to date both of you?"

Barb took two steps toward Andrew and slapped him. "How dare you suggest that Chloe and I would ever . . . What kind of girl do you think I, we, are? Is."

All of Andrew's attention was suddenly focused on Barb. Although she wouldn't have chosen physical violence, Chloe had to admit that it was effective. With one simple movement, Barb had accomplished what Chloe hadn't been able to with all her reasoning, cajoling, and arguing. Imagine that.

"Barb?" Andrew shook his head as if waking from a dream. "Barb?"

Chloe noticed a glint of light from the hunting picture on the wall. The hunter was grinning broadly and held a bow with arrows that she hadn't noticed before. She was certain he winked at her. She closed her eyes. She definitely needed more sleep.

"Well, you've got the name right, at least," Barb said.

Officer McKinnett rubbed the heels of his hands into his eyes. When he'd finished pushing his eyeballs back into his head, hopefully to improve his ability to see what was right in front of him, he glanced at Chloe and whispered, "What have I been doing?"

"You don't remember?" she asked.

He shook his head and grabbed Barb's hands. He went down on his knees, kissing first one hand and then another. "I'm so sorry, Barb. I've been such a fool."

So that's how it went, Chloe thought, watching the smile on Barb's face light her eyes. This was what true love was all about. Groveling. Begging forgiveness. She looked over at AJ, who grinned and saluted her with his bottle of beer. Right. Like she could ever imagine any man acting the way Andrew was if she were the subject of all that anguish.

Huh. And he hadn't even needed e-Cupid. There went her ironclad, surefire example of e-Cupid's effectiveness. Probably just as well. When the Frog-Vision guys had looked at e-Cupid they couldn't find *any* code at all, so there wasn't anything to fix.

She sneaked a look at the hunter again. Maybe she'd imagined the bow and arrows, because now his one hand was solidly around a horn while the other grasped his horse's reins.

She joined AJ at the bar. At least she'd managed to get Andrew and Barb back together, and that made her feel good. If her attempts to run her business failed, perhaps she had a future as a matchmaker. She leaned on the bar and smiled at AJ. "Chalk one up in the win column."

AJ nodded. "Yep. Shall we leave these two alone? It'd be bad news two times over if Andrew changed his mind once more. I know guys and all it'd take would be one quick glance this way, seeing you with me, and he might blow." He finished his beer, grabbed Chloe's elbow, and steered her out of the bar.

Heat seared up her arm at his touch and she jerked her arm back, alarmed. He'd just been holding an ice-cold beer. How in the world could his touch be hot?

He took her elbow once more.

Puzzled, she looked up at him.

"Don't worry, Chloe. It's merely a friendly gesture."

Yes, but friendly didn't necessarily mean having flames race up your arm. Did it?

# Chapter Thirteen
# "Then Came You"

One down, one to go, AJ thought as he opened the door of the Corvette and helped Chloe in. He'd had a suspicion that Officer McKinnett would succumb as soon as Barb appeared, all dewy fresh and so obviously over the top for him.

He tensed as he climbed into the car and started the engine. Once more, Charlene didn't give him any grief. Which was good since he was going to need all his attention focused on two things over dinner with Chloe. Probing a little more about the check from her brother that was held up at the bank, and how to secure additional work with Phillips International.

Of course, he hadn't planned on Chloe being quite this appealing. Quite this alluring, quite this downright sexy. "Where to now?" he asked.

She stared out the windshield, rubbing her hand. Cripes. She'd felt it too. That blaze of heat between them. It'd been there the first time, of course. He'd expected such a reaction from a pretty woman. But, as they'd gotten to know one another this electric attraction between them had intensified.

"Look, we've got Spuddy Buddy to review and I've got a few other things I'd like to discuss. Let's find some place quiet to work, okay?"

She looked at him, a mixture of confusion and disappointment in her eyes. "Why did that man spend the last week falling all over himself telling me he loved me when all it took was a smack on the side of his head to make him switch back to Barbara?" she asked. "Why?"

"I don't know, but it's exactly what you wanted to happen. Right?" He glanced over at her. "Look, we need to plan our next steps. You know, figure out how to deal with Higgenbotham. I don't think it's going to be as easy with him as it was with Andrew and your friend Barb." He paused. "Unless you've got a starry-eyed babe stashed in a holding tank somewhere who'll steal his heart away and get him to leave you in peace."

Chloe's reaction to his idea was not what he'd expected. He'd expected controlled enthusiasm. Or cheerful acceptance at a minimum. He'd even contemplated her congratulating him with a kiss.

He hadn't been prepared for tears.

He didn't know what to do, so he reached across her and opened the glove box. Extracting a small pack of tissues, he offered her one. When she didn't react, he pulled one out and gently wiped a tear from her cheek. "What's wrong?" he whispered.

Shaking her head as if coming out of a trance, Chloe took the tissue, and dried her eyes. "Nothing. Thank you for the tissue. We should be going." She leaned back and stared out the window once more.

Women. Couldn't live with them. Life wasn't

worth spit without them. He put the car in gear and pulled out of the parking lot.

After ten minutes of silence, Chloe said, "I agree. It would be a good idea to plan what to do with Ralph. Turn right at the next light. There's a Burger Barn about a block away." She swiveled around so she faced him. "But I'm buying my own dinner."

"Whatever you say, Chloe." She'd recovered pretty fast, he thought, given the look of abject anguish that had accompanied the tears. And he didn't think for a minute that the idea of sitting down with him to talk about how to disengage Ralph Higgenbotham, the Satellite King, was what had made her so sad.

He went over in his mind what might have caused her reaction. He didn't think the idea of eating with him would make her so upset. After all, they'd shared a number of meals in the last week with no problem. In fact, he thought they were coming to enjoy each other's company more and more. And it wasn't talking about Ralph, or plotting his eventual downfall. She was the one who had been advocating a plan of action on that front all along. So what was it?

He couldn't fathom why she'd been sad and then bounced back into the good old Chloe he'd come to know and be confused by.

Well, there was no accounting for the moods of a woman.

He parked in front of the door to Burger Barn and they went in.

Halfway through his Godzilla Burger, it struck him. He'd brought tears to her eyes by reminding her that, once they got rid of Ralph, no man would be pursuing her.

He cursed himself for five kinds of idiot. He should have known. He'd seen similar reactions from his mother over his father, and Joanie was always pining away for Eugene and worrying about raising Skeezix by herself. Although Chloe's relationships with Andrew and Ralph were a lot less serious, he could understand how disconcerting it would be to have a man profess his undying devotion and then change his mind with one slap to the head. It would shake anyone's self-confidence. And it would remind her that she didn't have a special someone in her own life. Which couldn't be easy for a woman who believed so strongly in the idea of true love.

He might be forced to rethink his whole handling of the Chloe Phillips situation.

"How's the Veggie Special?" he asked.

"Fine." She had nibbled at the edges of her garden burger but hadn't made any real progress toward consuming it. Of course, he could understand why. He was all in favor of vegetables, but to grind them up and pretend they were red meat struck him as hypocrisy of the highest order. Besides, all those sprout things got stuck in your teeth.

He suspected, though, that his low opinion of her meal had nothing to do with Chloe not eating.

"So, let's talk about your buddy, Ralph. Tell me about him." He picked up the ketchup bottle and whacked it on its side. He dipped his fries in the resulting glob of red.

"Ralph came to me about a year ago with this idea for a personal satellite system. Everyone else had blown him off, told him either that it was too expensive, and therefore there would be no market for it, or that it was impossible, or just plain stupid. I looked over his notes and listened to his pitch. I thought it was a little far-fetched." She sipped her iced tea. "But you should never underestimate the willingness of the buying public to glom onto an oddball idea and make it a huge hit. Think pet rocks."

"So you agreed to fund his project. Has he made much progress?" AJ had absolutely no idea how to go about inventing anything. He knew how to create impeccable financials. He knew how to analyze a business in five minutes flat—but the creative part, the nuts and bolts of an invention, these were like fog in a low wind. Obfuscating everything.

Chloe nodded, taking a bite of her burger. She continued nodding as she chewed and then swallowed. AJ watched her hands. Her fingers were long and slender, her nails manicured. He watched those manicured nails and those fingers stroke the edge of her iced tea glass. His mouth went completely dry. He was thinking about all the delightful things those fingers could do to him when he realized she'd asked him a question.

"Huh?"

"I really love it when a man listens carefully to what you're saying," she said. "I asked what you thought about setting Ralph up with Gloria."

He stroked his chin. "Has she seen e-Cupid?"

"No. But she's been in love with him since the first day they met. She hasn't said anything because she believes it's the man's job to make the first move." She paused and rearranged the tomato and avocado on the veggie burger. "We could do a rerun of tonight, I suppose, although Gloria will never resort to violence. We should pose as a couple, just in case, but if we're lucky, Ralph will have the same reaction that Andrew did and act two of our matchmaking drama will be concluded."

"I'm in." AJ sat back, wiping his mouth with his napkin. His plate was littered with the detritus of a good meal, and his tummy was happily filled with French fries and Godzilla Burger. "If Ralph can't add one and one to get a couple, namely you and me, then he isn't as smart as you think he is."

AJ pushed the last bit of ketchup around with the only remaining fry on his plate. "But you've got other projects. Like I said before, some of them are really quite promising."

"Yes." She tapped the pile of papers they'd been discussing. "You know the e-Cupid bug ate all the computer code, so I can't even fix it." She stared at her barely touched garden burger, suddenly seeing her life as a series of badly orchestrated disasters. "We need to go," she said, careful not to look at AJ. She'd already cried once and she didn't want.to embarass herself again, especially in front of someone she had to work with every day. Someone she needed to impress with her business acumen, someone for whom she felt entirely too many unbusinesslike feelings.

She sniffed and gathered her bag. She took one last sip of iced tea, now watered down so it tasted like really bad water, and said, "Please, take me home."

AJ blinked at her, then stood. "Sure thing," he said. "Don't worry about dinner. It's on me." He extracted a pair of twenties from his wallet, rubbing them together slightly. He slipped them under his coffee cup. "That should cover it." He put his arm around her shoulders so gently that she wouldn't have noticed at all, except for that heat thing.

She'd been standing beside the table wondering just how awful her eyeliner looked, but not having the energy to check in her small makeup mirror. Standing there, chilled at the prospect of Ralph running so far behind that she'd never make a profit on Satelhat. Then AJ touched her, his arm resting across her shoulders. Electric blankets on the highest setting didn't generate this much heat.

She blinked up at him, shivering.

"You're cold," he said, taking off his coat and draping it over her shoulders. The coat smelled of leather and AJ. His heat seeped into her body with surprising speed, considering it was secondhand. "Your chariot awaits," he said, and steered her toward the door.

She walked beside him, struggling with the urge to snuggle closer, to absorb more of his natural warmth. Heck, if she'd known guys were walking furnaces, she'd have optioned one earlier.

Her personal attempt at humor failed. A single tear dribbled down her cheek. This was what she had dreamed of, this closeness, this mingling of body heat. And true to form, *her* knight in shining leather, was working for her.

Instead of riding home relishing the thought that AJ and she might take this meager beginning and build something interesting out of it, Chloe spent the trip reviewing all her failures. And trying to decide if it would be worth the risk to attempt to make AJ into her true love. When the ship is sinking, why not have one last fling before the waters closed over your head forever?

When AJ pulled into her driveway, she couldn't remember getting there, only that she'd promised herself that she would never give up on CI.

"We're here," AJ said, turning off the engine. "Want me to walk you to the door?"

"No, thanks, that won't be necessary." She got out and walked up the steps. A slip of paper was stuck to her front door. She pulled it off.

*We tried to make a delivery,* it said, *but you weren't home. The neighbor let us in. Hope you enjoy it.*

She looked back at AJ and waved, anxious for him to go. "Some sort of package. Thanks for listening. I'll see you tomorrow at the office."

"Sure," AJ said, not moving.

Fine, he wanted to see that she made it inside safely. Why was it that chivalry popped up when you needed it least?

She jammed her key into the lock and turned. The door opened, she stepped inside, and screamed.

In a flash, she backed out, slammed the door closed, and stood on the porch, shaking. AJ was out of his car and up the steps before she'd sorted out what she'd seen inside her town house.

"What is it?" he asked. "What's wrong? Burglars? Did someone break in and steal everything?"

"No," she said. "Nothing that simple." She'd recovered from her initial fright. She opened the front door slowly and peeked inside. The scene hadn't changed, except for the positions of the players.

She shoved the door open farther and stood back so AJ could go in first. "Welcome to my own personal aviary," she said, beginning to giggle.

AJ walked through the door and she followed him. There were crates and cages strewn all over the house. Each had contained an exotic bird of some sort, although few crate residents were still in their places. And none had smiles on their faces. She doubted birds could smile. But they certainly could talk. The place sounded like a cocktail party filled with overly chatty women. The peacocks shrieked their greeting. Lovebirds cooed in a corner. From atop her glass-fronted bookcases, half a dozen finches twittered.

"Good God, there must be twenty cages," AJ said.

And each one had held a pair of birds of some sort. Which meant there were upwards of forty assorted birds loose in her house. Chloe brushed past him and walked farther into the room, closing the door behind her. "Who could possibly have done this?"

She looked at AJ and AJ looked at her. "Ralph Higgenbotham," they said in unison.

Chloe blew a feather from her forehead where it had lighted as its owner flew from the valance over the bay window to the chandelier hanging in the entryway. The feather was yellow, but Chloe had no idea what kind of bird had shed it. She closed her eyes. She didn't care how successful SatelHat was going to be, she was going to kill Ralph.

As soon as she figured out what to do with the birds.

AJ moved forward through the feathery throng, leaving a wake of squawks and flapping wings. He was headed to a yellow paper on her kitchen counter. Cautiously, she followed him.

He handed it to her silently, and went for the phone, next to the refrigerator.

"For delivery to Miss Chloe Phillips: One Pair of Lovebirds," she read. "Well, they got that wrong." She looked closer at the sheet. There was a smudged part just ahead of a list of winged species, which included geese, peacocks, warblers, cockatiels, parrots, turtledoves, finches, finches, and more finches.

She held the page up to the light. It was possible that Ralph had meant to send only a single pair of birds, in this case lovebirds. The obscured bit appeared to read "unless unavailable, in which case choose one pair from the following list."

Well, this was just dandy. Her house was being destroyed by poor communications. And it was definitely being destroyed. By forty-odd birds that had been there at least three hours while she'd been out mending hearts. Forty-odd birds shedding feathers and pooping and, she included as she looked around her kitchen, eating whatever she'd left out. A loaf of bread and a bowl of fruit.

AJ dialed a number and listened. He hung up, saying, "The county wildlife people are out of the office until tomorrow morning. Want me to call the vet?"

"I don't think a vet will be much help. What I'd like to do is call Ralph and have him come over and trap all these birds."

AJ shook his head. "I don't think that's a good idea."

"What do you suggest then?"

He thought a bit. "We could herd them into a room with a door and leave them there until morning. Or we could attempt to corral them into their respective crates. Or we could just go to my place and not worry about it."

Herding the beasts into a room with a door would require moving them to the upstairs level, since everything on the main floor of Chloe's town house was open. Except for the bathroom and the closet, and neither of them was large enough for this flock. Scrap suggestion number one.

"Let's try to at least get the larger birds into their crates. I'm pretty sure the geese won't fly, nor will the swans, the peacocks, or the guinea hens." She hoped. Taking a step into the room, she tried to identify which crates had contained which birds. There should have been tags.

True to his microscopic-detail-oriented brain, Ralph had specified labeling with the bird's common name, its genus, its species, and its history.

Seeing what she was attempting, AJ waded into the squawking sea of feathers and began looking through the crates. "Here's the swan abode," he shouted above the growing din. The birds objected, loudly, to AJ and Chloe's presence.

"Swan," he read. "*Cygnus olor,* normal habitat lakes, parks and coastal bays. Featured prominently in coats of arms during the Middle Ages and associated with beauty and love." He opened the door to the crate. "All we have to do is persuade Mr. and Mrs. Cygnus to come home." He laughed.

"This isn't funny, AJ," Chloe said, barely able to contain her own giggle. She ducked as a finch of indeterminate gender flew past her ear doing about mach five.

"Really? I think it's a genuine hysterical situation. Registers about seven on my own personal can't-believe-this-is-actually-happening scale. It's a five-point scale, by the way," he said, chuckling. "Here's the crate for the geese."

Yes, but one goose was happily ensconced under one of her end tables, behind a stack of smaller bird-cages. The swans, on the other hand, were in one corner of her kitchen, hissing angrily at what appeared to be a banty hen and rooster, the black-and-white-speckled kind. "Can you move the swan crate?"

AJ looked around. "If I set these finch boxes someplace else, yes."

"Okay, pile the finches on top of the piano." It was going to take a Maid Brigade years to get this place clean, and she'd probably have to have every piece of wood stripped and refinished. "Then open the swan box and I'll try to convince them that they'd be happier inside it than roaming my kitchen in search of smaller birds to terrorize."

"Done," AJ said, lifting a stack of smaller containers and placing them on the baby grand piano. He blew feathers off before he set the boxes down. "You play?"

"A little. Mostly when I'm under a lot of stress," Chloe answered. Like now. "You think a little Chopin would make these guys happy?"

"No, but Cole Porter might work. Or Broadway show tunes, perhaps." AJ looked around. "Where is Edgar?"

She'd completely forgotten about the cat. "Probably wedged between the washer and the dryer. It's her favorite hiding place."

She waded through the birds in her kitchen to the corner where the swans were protesting. "Come, now, be nice swans and go back to your cozy, warm box," she said, trying to get around behind the large birds. The swan closest to her followed her movement with its beady black eyes, snorted once, and then darted its head and bit her arm. "Ow! Not fair."

She backed away, scattering chickens and ducks in her path. She reached beside the refrigerator and grabbed the broom. "Take this, you ugly duckling in disguise." She came at the swans with the broom, trying to sweep them toward the waiting AJ. They took shelter under the kitchen table, protesting loudly.

Of course her actions stirred up every other feathered and winged thing within earshot. All forty or so of them. The resulting racket was almost more than she could deal with. "Now what?" she shouted.

AJ slogged between the stacks of bird crates until he stood next to her. "Do you want to keep any of Ralph's love tokens?"

"No."

"Then open the door to the deck and let them all fly away."

That was entirely too simple. Why hadn't she thought of it? "I'm not sure all of these can fly."

"Chloe, they're birds. They fly."

"Will they survive outside? It's awfully cold and I'd bet none of these is wild." She looked around. "The garage. We can herd them in there."

"It's either that, or set up housekeeping for them in here. If they aren't happy with their newfound freedom, they'll stick around to see if they can convince you to let them back in. Let me move your car first," AJ said. She tossed him her keys and he left her to contemplate the bird sanctuary formerly known as her town house.

It was better than being an adjunct to the National Zoo, Winged Division. When AJ returned, she handed him the broom. "You can act as flight control." Then she opened the door to the garage and stood back.

Nothing happened.

"Move away from the door and help me herd them out," AJ said.

She nodded. Careful not to tip over the unsteady piles of boxes strewn around her house, she followed him out of the kitchen, through the dining room, and into the foyer. "Now," he said, "wave your arms and slowly walk back toward the kitchen."

With AJ wielding the broom and Chloe flapping like a bird herself, they managed to direct most of the creatures through the entryway into the dining room. A few independent thinkers took a left turn into the living room, but she could get them later. As they approached the kitchen, she watched with undisguised relief as the pair of mallards waddled into the garage, followed by several smaller birds in flight.

She couldn't wait to hear what her neighbors would have to say.

Taking a hint, the swans followed the ducks. Within twenty minutes, most of the birds were gone. Well, they were in her garage, bonding with her garden tools. As AJ had predicted, the smaller birds were perched in the rafters, while the larger and noisier ones stuck around the door.

At least they weren't marking their territory inside any more. And the din had dwindled to a dull roar that she could close the door on.

She hadn't laughed this much in she couldn't remember how long. It felt wonderful. She felt wonderful, refreshed, and happy for the first time in ages.

The stress that normally occupied space along her neck and shoulders was gone, vanished with the birds. Her house was a wreck, several paintings had been dive-bombed and wore bird poop proof of the deadly accuracy of most avians. In fact, the entire house had been redecorated in feathers and poop. She eyed the overstuffed chairs in her living room, wanting to collapse onto something comfortable, but they had been host to too many birds.

Instead, she headed for a chair in the dining room that had been protected, being under the table. AJ followed her. As she took a step forward, her foot slipped on a collection of feathers and she fell back into his waiting arms.

Instead of laughing at her clumsiness, or helping her immediately to her feet, he held on to her. He gazed at her with a dark, hungry, and dangerous look.

Then he kissed her.

# Chapter Fourteen
# "Why Do Fools Fall in Love?"

He hadn't really intended to kiss her, AJ told himself as he deepened the kiss. But she'd looked so small and fragile, so innocent and tempting, with feathers stuck in her wild strawberry hair and her face lit up with one of the first genuine smiles he'd seen from her.

It didn't matter. She began to kiss him back and he pushed away speculation about whether or not their embrace was a smart thing to do.

If she was kissing him back, then it must be all right with her.

AJ knew that to rush this particular woman would be disastrous beyond any disaster he'd fomented in the first moments of passion. And, he'd fomented his share of amorous disasters. Instead of heeding the hardening of certain insistent parts of his body, he held Chloe firmly but gently and started trailing kisses down her neck until he reached that sensitive curve where neck joined shoulder. He felt her shudder.

Then he felt her hands exploring his chest and his mood, already pretty confident, soared. Until she pushed him away. Pushed awfully hard for someone that delicate. He opened one eye and looked down at her with a question half formed on his lips.

"I'm sorry," she began. "I didn't mean to do that at all." She stepped away from him and turned toward the kitchen counter.

"Apology accepted. Let's see what happens when you do mean it," he suggested.

She spun around, the fire in her eyes matching the wild flames of her hair. "I beg your pardon? I have no intention of getting involved with you at all. Just because I participated in one kiss in the heat of the moment, don't think it's your charming self working some certain magic. It's not."

She was lying. He knew it. No woman kissed that way who didn't enjoy it and who didn't want to. "Hey, I'm not trying to start anything either. I just figured some mutually enjoyable moments wouldn't hurt." He scratched his cheek. "But, if that's what you want. You're the one working out this true-love problem."

"Yes, I am." She smoothed her sweater, just enough to let him know that her body had liked his kiss. A mere matter of mind over excited nipples.

He could handle that. He'd just wait.

"You want to check around, make sure we got all the birds. There might be a few hiding someplace." He gestured toward the stairs. "Up there, for instance."

She followed the sweep of his arm. "Good thinking. You check under the furniture down here and

I'll go up." She smiled sweetly, her eyes knowing slits. "I'll call if I need help."

"Cool with me."

He watched her go up the stairs, appreciating all over again certain aspects of womanly anatomy. Haute couture designers could worship at the feet of the skinny, shapeless model all they wanted. He was definitely in favor of shapely hips, and Chloe's were a fine example of what made him happy he was a man.

She disappeared at the top of the steps and he sighed. "Under the furniture. Like any self-respecting bird would go there." Nonetheless, he dutifully wandered into the dining room and bent over, checking under the table. Nothing there.

Likewise with the chairs. Lots of feathers. Several birdie messages in the form of poop, but no birds.

Standing, he noticed a sheaf of papers on the table. He picked them up. They were descriptions of the birds, in agonizing detail, with stories of how each creature fit into Ralph's warped sense of love. Mr. SatelHat was nothing if not a walking encyclopedia.

Most of the furniture in Chloe's living room was low to the ground. He got on his hands and knees and lifted the skirt on the sofa. Peering into the darkness, he blew away feathers and determined that there were no birds hiding there. He did notice how comfy the couch was, with big, overstuffed cushions. He could picture Chloe lying there, welcoming him into her arms.

A quick survey of the rest of the room revealed no more birds. He was convinced that they'd captured all of the feathery greetings from Higgenbotham. Might as well get some of this cleaned up, he thought, opening the coat closet in search of the vacuum.

He'd just found an electrical outlet when he heard

Chloe's scream. Within two steps he was at the stairs. Two more, well, maybe three, and he was up them and tearing into the room the shrieks came from.

Chloe was backed into a corner, trying to fend off a very irritated goose. "AJ! It won't let me go."

He allowed as to how the goose had a very good idea. *He* hadn't wanted to let her go, either. "Not to worry. Geese can be very nasty when they're upset."

"Not half as nasty as I'll be when I see Ralph Higgenbotham." She tried to melt into the wall, the goose pursuing her with honks and flapping wings. "Ow!" she said as the creature bit her knee. "Do something."

AJ looked around the bedroom. Hanging from one of the four posts on the bed was a pale blue robe. He grabbed it and moved slowly around the end of the bed. Holding the house-coat open, he stepped behind the goose, and with one quick movement dropped it over the bird. "Hold the material closed while I get its legs and wings secured."

Chloe moved rapidly to help and within minutes the goose stopped struggling. It squawked and honked angrily, but it was defeated. AJ picked it up, still inside Chloe's robe. "Now what?"

Chloe collapsed against her bed. "I don't know. I'd like to shove the dumb thing down Ralph's throat."

AJ patted the side of the struggling bundle he held. "It'd make a nice Christmas dinner, that's the truth."

She shook her head. "No, it isn't the goose's fault Ralph has such a warped sense of how to win a woman's heart. Let's take it downstairs and put it in one of the bigger crates." She pushed her hair out of her eyes and led the way down to the kitchen.

She opened the crate and AJ shoved the protesting main course in. He tried to save Chloe's robe, but was unsuccessful. "Guess we'll have to get you another one. Mr. Goose has grown quite attached to this robe."

"Fine. No problem," Chloe said, sitting in one of the chairs at the table. "What a mess."

AJ pulled up a chair next to her. "Nothing a little work can't fix," he said.

"Thank you. I've not had much experience with geese. I didn't have any idea they were that mean."

"Not quite the image of Dickens, is it?" AJ asked, pointing to the goose in the crate. Its squawking had set off sympathetic cries from the other birds, large and small, that he and Chloe had managed to herd into crates and cages. He looked at the door to the garage. Most, if not all, the flying gifts they'd shooed out there had joined the new cacophony.

"Think we got them all?"

"Yes," she said. "I'm going to kill that man. Look at this," she picked up the card that had come with the delivery. "Lovebirds for my love," she read. "What kind of insanity inspires this?" She indicated the wrecked rooms, littered with boxes, cages, and crates. Decorated with feathers of all sizes and colors. Dotted with birdie calling cards.

"The kind that comes from being in love, I guess."

"If love does this to a perfectly reasonable, brilliant man, then I don't want anything to do with it. I'm going to give e-Cupid back to its inventors. All it's done is cause trouble."

Was that sadness he heard in her voice? "Come on, Chloe. The Eternal Optimist. You don't want to give up on love before you've found it, do you?" He was just beginning to think this true love thing wasn't all that far-fetched, and his primary cheerleader was thinking of quitting.

"You're sweet to try to cheer me up, but it won't work. Time to face the truth—e-Cupid is a failure.

It just proves how strong the power of suggestion is—true love doesn't really exist, people just create fantasies to satisfy some inner longing not to be all alone." She said the words so quietly he almost didn't hear them.

"Nonsense. It matched Barb and McKinnett, didn't it? I'm confident it'll find Ralph's one-and-only as soon as he has a chance to look at it again. Everybody's got somebody." Now he was spouting nonsense. He was the free and unattached bachelor who had to focus on getting his struggling company back on its feet. He had no business trying to reassure a naive woman—who kissed like she had years of experience—that there was someone for her. Someone. Somewhere out there.

Him, for instance. He could certainly act as a stand-in.

She stood, dusted off her jeans and said, "Well, be that as it may, I've got to get this mess cleared up. Thank you for bringing me home. And for helping."

"My pleasure." He should be leaving, she was right.

"Oh, and thanks for helping with Andrew and Barb. They seemed pretty happy, didn't they?"

"As clams. Although, I don't really know how happy clams can be." Personally, if he'd been a clam, he'd have been lonely. One to a shell was a rotten way to live. Of course, a double-wide shell could accommodate a lady clam and then, well, he *would* be happy. As a clam.

"Good." She looked forlornly around the kitchen. He could almost see her calculating the time it would take to rectify Ralph's misadventure in courting. "I guess I could call Leann. She'd let me stay in the guest room. I certainly can't sleep here tonight." She spoke to herself.

"Allergic?"

"What? Oh, to the feathers? No, but the noise and the smell are a little off-putting. Not to mention the mess the goose made of my bed."

He hadn't taken note of much else during the Great Goose Rescue, but he had noticed that Chloe's bed had been used as a makeshift nest and was soiled and wet. "No, I guess not."

She picked up the phone and dialed. He watched her wait through two minutes of ringing before she hung up. "Guess they're not home."

"Look, I've got extra space at my place and nice freshly painted walls. Why not stay with me tonight?" he offered.

Chloe could think of two dozen reasons why that wouldn't be a good idea at all. And one that was wonderful. That kiss. She knew that she hadn't dated a lot. That she had limited experience with romance. That she was a fool to even be considering what she was considering. *But, sweetcheeks,* a voice told her, *you're practically thirty and AJ is the first man who's kissed you like that.*

Suddenly, she wanted more.

"Okay. Let me go get my toothbrush and some stuff." She spun on her heel before she could change her mind. Her heart was racing. Sweetcheeks, indeed. She didn't need help deciding to take some risks in her personal life.

It was time. Time she started acting like a woman. Time she experienced the full range of woman-ness. She'd tried the steel-heeled businesswoman bit. She needed to explore her other self. The one that steadfastly believed in everyone else's dreams. It was time to act on some of her own wishes. She could be a businesswoman for the rest of her life.

As she shoved clothes into a small bag, she decided it was time to give herself an early Halloween treat.

AJ.

* * *

"This is where you live?" Chloe asked as she walked into the classic Virginia town house. As far as she could tell, it was basically divided into three levels. They now stood in the living room/dining room/ kitchen sort of area, off of which two sets of stairs were visible. She assumed one led up to the bedrooms and the other down to a den. It was clean and homey, with watercolors on the walls and an antique windup phonograph in place of the standard yuppie electronic excesses. Of course, the wide-screen TV, DVD player, eighteen speakers, and assorted gadgets were probably lurking downstairs. AJ was too much a modern man to have completely abandoned technology.

It smelled of fresh paint.

"For the time being," AJ said, tossing his car keys into a large, frog-shaped ashtray filled with loose change.

"I need to freshen up," Chloe said.

"It's a one-bath town house," he said. "It's next to the bedroom." He pointed up. "Let me help you with your bag."

Bedroom, singular. "Where are you sleeping?" It was the question uppermost in her mind.

"I'll take the couch," he said. He shed his leather jacket, dropping it over the back of the incredibly uncomfortable looking Victorian-era sofa, and picked up her bag. "This way."

As she rounded the last turn in the stairs behind AJ, she understood why there was only one bedroom.

The entire top floor had been converted into a huge master bedroom suite. In one end of the room was a complete set of exercise equipment, enough to put her paltry treadmill to shame. Free weights and a punching bag she could identify. Everything else looked like medieval torture machines.

The bed was large and rumpled, as though AJ had simply pulled the bedspread up in a hurry. Built into a low, sleep frame with a minimalist headboard and attached bedside tables, it looked very comfortable. He set down her bag and grinned. "Bathroom's in there. I'll get you clean towels. It isn't as fancy as your place, but it's home."

She took off her ankle boots. Much more comfortable. "Thanks, AJ."

"No problem. Clean towels are in the basement. I'll be right back." He sauntered back down the stairs and she watched him go with growing heat in her belly. Tonight. It would be tonight or never.

She looked around. The table beside the bed held a lamp, a clock radio, and a book. If she was expecting the latest Grisham novel, or a treatise on football, she was pleasantly surprised. AJ, it appeared, read classics. *The Complete Plays of William Shakespeare* was open to *A Midsummer Night's Dream*.

A mixture of scents teased her nose—the fresh smell of clean laundry, the lingering scent of a very masculine cologne, and something undefinable but uniquely AJ.

She set her small bag on the end of the bed and went into the bath. The scent of cologne increased, mingled with the odor of soap. She scanned the large, decadent room, taking in details. Navy blue towels, huge soaking tub, larger shower, two sinks. With a twinge of guilt, she wondered again if AJ had a woman in his life. He'd never mentioned one, but a guy this good-looking rarely wandered around solo. She opened the medicine cabinet, just to check on indications of a feminine presence. Nothing. She sighed with relief. She'd only really thought about AJ in terms of how he could affect the future of CI.

It had never occurred to her that he had a life outside his work. And Charlene, of course.

She wasn't sure she liked how that made her feel. Normally, she delved into people's lives, trying to pin down exactly what drove them to create their products or business ideas.

She'd been so focused on saving CI, she'd totally neglected to find out much about AJ.

No time like the present.

AJ had moved to the town house's lowest level and was sitting in an ugly green recliner, folding laundry. Chloe stopped short and scanned the room. Yep, every electronic excess she could name, and several she couldn't, were displayed in a wall-sized unit. "What haven't you got here?" she asked.

"I don't have one of those cool flat screen TVs that hang on the wall. The ones shaped like movie screens so everything looks better? Can't afford one yet."

"I thought consultants were rich," she said, trying to keep her tone light.

He shrugged. "The economy hasn't been kind to smaller companies like mine. We'll be okay, though, so don't worry about us."

"I'd like to meet the rest of your firm," she said.

"Probably not a good idea," he said, setting down a beer. "You'd fall for Tommy and that would simply distract him from his job. And you'd want to adopt Joanie and she wouldn't stand for that. She's an independent, modern woman."

"I've met Tommy and I'm pretty sure I could resist him." AJ was the one she was having trouble resisting. "The other consultants, then. I could meet them at least."

"Sorry. There aren't others."

"Maybe I'd be less trouble in a hotel. I'll just call up the Willard and see if they have a room." She headed toward the phone when AJ stopped her by reaching out and grabbing a handful of her shirt.

"What are you doing?" she asked.

"You really want to leave?"

She tried to pry his fingers away from her shirt. The warmth and electricity that zinged through her as she touched him made her stop. There was that funky tingly feeling in the pit of her being again. Low, just beneath her belly button, a blaze of epic proportions was brewing. Threatening to engulf her. "Isn't it a little hot in here?" she said.

Still holding on to her shirt, AJ slid out of the recliner. He cocked an eyebrow and then spun her around so she was facing him. Close. Very close. Too close. Her gaze started mid-chest and traveled up until she was staring into his eyes. Clear. Blue. Dangerous.

Okay, this was too much too fast. And not at all the kind of personal information she'd thought she wanted. She tried to pull back from AJ.

Instead of letting her, his arms circled her in a gentle embrace, pulling her even closer. "Don't be frightened, Chloe. I'm not going to hurt you." One of his large, capable hands slid up her back until it held her head. His touch was soft, enticing. She relaxed a millimeter or two, the memory of the kiss among the birds fresh in her mind.

"I'm not afraid of you."

"Good, because I'm a really nice guy."

"You're working for my brother. How nice can that be?" It was her first and stupidest reaction. He'd said repeatedly he wasn't out to close CI. Why couldn't she let it go? And enjoy the moment. Because she was feeling light-headed and out of control, two sensations she didn't like.

"So what? You think too much. Quit worrying about Oz. I'll take care of him." He tipped her head back and stared into her eyes.

Hot. It was so hot she was melting. Her bones were turning to mush. And, her brain wasn't far behind. She closed her eyes, wanting him to kiss her. Wanting that delirious sensation she'd experienced in her kitchen, amid the feathers and bird poop, to happen once more.

Now, he could kiss her now, and she'd be able to float once more on those imaginary clouds that had lifted her and caressed her. Just one small kiss. That's all she wanted. She was confident that if he'd simply kiss her, she could either banish him from her brain, or convince him to continue to kiss her. Maybe even more.

But she needed the kiss. She opened one eye. He was smiling at her, an amused look similar to one a teacher might give a student who wanted to do higher math before she'd mastered simple addition.

"What?" she asked.

"I love watching you. When you make up your mind, it's an amazing thing. I can certainly see why people come to you with ideas." He released her head and shoved his hands in his pockets.

He was just like many of her projects. They needed a little prodding. So, she'd prod.

He was standing in front of that ugly green recliner. She narrowed her eyes, calculating. If she shoved just there . . . She put her hands on his chest and pushed. AJ, hands wedged tightly in his jeans pockets, wasn't expecting her assault. He toppled over, landing in the recliner.

"What the . . . ?" he began.

"Don't talk," she said, climbing on top of him. "I'm in charge here." And she kissed him. Was she that unattractive that he couldn't take a very basic and very obvious hint.

* * *

For a moment, he resisted her. Then he shrugged and gave in to the inevitable. He rearranged himself so the recliner would recline instead of bucking the two of them out onto the floor, and struggled to get his hands out of his pockets.

Trouble was, with Chloe on top of him, her hands caressing the back of his head and her tongue doing a marvelous repeat performance of the Kiss Among the Birds, he had no room to maneuver. His hands were stuck. Her knees had him pinned in the chair, helpless.

Hmmm, he thought. Isn't this an interesting development? His physical reaction was immediate. The fact that Chloe rubbed against him as she maintained control of the kiss made his position in the chair all that more uncomfortable. Uncomfortable and amazing. What Chloe was doing to him with a simple kiss should be banned in Boston.

His heart pounded and he began to feel sweat trickle down the back of his neck. Where had this woman learned to use her mouth like that?

Chloe nibbled on his lips and then kissed his forehead before she ran a moist tongue across his eyebrow, down the side of his face and into his left ear. Ohmygod, he thought, as shudders of pure lust racked his body.

As she attacked his ear, he heard a hoarse, sluggish voice say, "If you'd slow down just a little and let me get my hands free, this would be a lot more fun." He barely recognized the choked sound as coming from his own vocal cords.

"But I'm having fun already," she whispered, soft and wet, in his right ear, where she renewed her assault. She worked her way down his neck, to the edge of his T-shirt. Suddenly, she sat back and jerked his shirt out of the waistband of his pants and began tugging it up over his torso. He finally managed to free his hands, only to find himself captured once more by Chloe's simple move of sliding his T-shirt up his arms and twisting it into cloth handcuffs. Not that he minded.

"Oh, my," she said. "Muscles." And she touched him with her hands, delicately at first, tracing the edges of the pectorals he'd worked so hard to define.

All those hours in the gym were paying off and *he couldn't do anything about it.* When she started kissing his chest, making the black jeans all that much more tight, he remembered his personal trainer insisting all that conditioning would come in handy some day.

That day had arrived. With effort, he arched his back, pushed down with his legs and forced the recliner to un-recline. The movement was rapid and unexpected. Chloe tumbled backwards, landing on the floor between his feet.

He pulled his hands out of their T-shirt shackles and tossed it aside. He grabbed her shoulders, lifting her to her feet as he stood. "Now we can do this properly," he said, and picked her up, one arm under her knees and the other around her shoulders.

"Wait," she said, struggling, "where are you taking me?"

"Where we should have been all along," he said, climbing the steps two at a time. "I wanted to wait, to take things slowly, to try to be a sensitive, new-age kind of guy. But if you're going to take the initiative, then I have no choice but to respond." He made it up the two flights of stairs in record time, tossed her onto the bed, and kicked off his boots. When he unbuckled his belt, he saw her eyes go wide.

Rhett Butler couldn't have done better, Chloe thought, her heart pounding with excitement, at least with the stair climb. Maybe she should revise her conclusions about e-Cupid. *This* was definitely a true-love kind of feeling.

"Be careful what you wish for, Chloe Phillips," he said. "You just might get it." He undid the buckle slowly, as though trying to gauge her reaction. With careful precision he unbuttoned the top stud on his 501s.

As the stud was released from its buttonhole with a soft pop, Chloe scrambled to the top of the bed, wearing what she was sure resembled a cat-ate-the-canary grin. He took up a lot more space half naked than he did fully clothed. This, this was more like how she'd imagined she would feel when she met someone. Flushed, excited, somewhat nervous. But marvelous. "E. Rose and Milo just might have been right," she said.

AJ quirked an eyebrow, flexed his biceps, and undid the next stud on the black jeans. A curl of his black hair had fallen across his forehead. Her heart picked up its beating as he reached for the third stud. "Wait," she squeaked. Where was his undying declaration of devotion? His promise to love her forever? She blinked and tried to calm the buzzing inside her head. "Really, you don't need to demonstrate how masculine you are. I can see that quite well from here, what with the muscles and the hair and . . . the . . . oh, my." She stumbled to a stop, her mouth open wide as AJ undid the last stud on the jeans and shoved them down.

She'd heard about men who didn't wear underwear, but she'd dismissed it as idle chatter, or as something that happened in *those* kinds of magazines. She swallowed, a difficult task since her mouth and throat were drier than Kansas in a dust storm.

Standing in front of her was the most magnificent

specimen of well-put-together manhood she'd ever seen. Not that she'd seen that many, you understand.

Certainly not one fully aroused.

She forgot about e-Cupid, forgot about the uncertain future of CI, forgot everything except the moment. Her pink pheromones had finally met their match. And they narrowed her world to AJ and the rapidly growing heat she could no longer ignore. She gulped when he stepped forward and then closed her eyes.

She felt his weight on the bed and her heart pounded into her throat. What was she going to do? A disturbing tickley hot sensation between her legs made her want to fling herself at him in wanton and tawdry ways she had only imagined. Made her want to rip her own clothes off and join AJ in sweaty, united passion.

She heard him open a drawer beside the bed, and then the sound of ripping foil.

"You can open your eyes now, Chloe."

She opened one eye a slit. He was sitting on the end of the bed, broad shoulders just as broad as they had been the last time she looked.

"I have to ask you to do something before we go any further," he said, his voice husky.

"Whatever you want," she said.

"Fire me."

"What?"

"Tell me I'm fired."

"You're fired," she replied, puzzled.

"Thank you." He grabbed her ankles and pulled her down in the bed. "You are wearing entirely too many clothes," he whispered, his voice husky.

Blinking, she shuddered as he slid a hot hand under her sweater, moving slowly over her ribs until he reached the front catch on her bra. The lacy purple one Leann had insisted she buy. With one swift movement, the clasp came open and there was nothing between her breasts and AJ's hands but heat.

Ohmygodohmygodohmygod. He'd pushed the sweater up and she helped him take it off, while his mouth followed his hand, targeting first one taut nipple and then the other. She was having trouble breathing.

Besides, she needed AJ. Now.

She struggled out of her slacks and matching purple panties, kicking one leg free so she could guide him to her, to that urgent demanding need she had no will to resist.

"Now," she whimpered. "Now would be good."

"You sure?" he asked. "We don't need to rush this, you know."

"Yes. We. Do." She arched into him and he responded to her body's demands. Their joining was swift, hard, and infinitely satisfying.

As her world exploded in a shower of multicolor stars, she abandoned herself to the sensation. When she came back to earth she felt AJ move beside her. "I'm sorry, Chloe. I didn't mean for things to go so quickly."

"No apologies necessary," she murmured. "You're exactly what I needed." She felt drowsy and safe. She snuggled next to him, happy, satisfied, and composing thank-you notes to E. Rose and Milo.

"Chlo?"

"Hmmm?"

How to put this, AJ wondered. After the glow of their lovemaking cooled, she'd take a deep breath and realize that mixed with the fragrance of good sex was a little too much of AJ's own sweaty body odor. He needed a shower before he could properly attend to the next, and significantly slower, course of love, Chloe-style.

"I'm sorry, AJ, I didn't mean to . . ."

"Of course you did. You meant every moist, tongue-led kiss of it."

He leaned over and planted a wet one on her cheek. "I'm going to take a shower." He grinned insolently. "You're welcome to join me, you know. Conserve water, shower with a friend."

# Chapter Fifteen
# "Wild Women Do"

Chloe curled up on the bed, listening to the water in the shower. Imagining the water sluicing over AJ. Oh, my. That itch was back. That growing need that AJ had begun to satisfy was back.

She rolled over and opened the drawer where she found a supply of foil packets. She grabbed one and slid off the bed. She padded across the carpet and went to the bathroom door, turning the foil packet over and over in her hand. The shower was still running. She pressed her ear against the door. Was he singing?

Damn. All that and a voice, too.

"Wild women do, and they don't regret it," he sang.

A woman who could see potential in Satelhat and Fish-in-a-Dish could handle anything. She was that woman. And it was AJ she wanted to handle.

She opened the bathroom door and went in, closing the door behind her.

Breathing in the fresh fragrance of soap, she opened the shower door and slipped inside. The mini concert didn't falter one beat when she entered. "Wild women do and they don't regret it," he belted out, again.

One wild woman, coming up.

"Hey, what's going on?" AJ asked as she circled his slim waist with her arms, rested her cheek against his strong back.

"I decided you were right about water conservation," she said.

She took the bar of soap out of his hand and, still standing behind him, began to lather his chest and stomach. AJ tipped his head back, letting water run over his face. His hair dripped onto her and she shuddered with anticipation. "All done," she announced, holding the blue bar out.

He took it. Carefully, he turned so she was positioned in front of him, the shower pummeling his back. Holding the soap in one hand, he lifted her chin with his other. "You sure this is what you want?"

She nodded. "Absolutely." Goose bumps flocked all over her body when she saw his eyes go suddenly dark and smoky. He hugged her to him and began soaping her back, his hands confident and capable. They moved across her shoulders, tracing lazy circles lower and lower until they held her bottom, one cheek for each hand.

Of course, the effect of that particular move was to press her body tightly against his. Up close and personal, there was no denying AJ's readiness for passion. He ducked his head and whispered in her ear, "You are so beautiful. I've wanted you since the day you kissed me in your office."

Sure, bring up her past sins. She stood there watching the water run in rivulets across his chest and down, following the path his dark hair offered, to his erection, eager to participate in a compatibility test. She dragged her eyes away from the enormity—pun definitely intended—of what she was doing, back to AJ's face.

He turned her once more, so the shower crashed over her head, wetting her hair.

Despite the hot water all around her and AJ's hands in her hair, she felt a chill. Accompanied by a white-hot twist of desire deep in her belly. Elation and trepidation coursed through her being, singeing the edges of her soul with want.

He ripped open the foil packet with his teeth and rolled the condom on. "Come to me, Chloe. Make my soul sing." His voice was husky, his hands insistent. He lathered her hair and gently rinsed it in the steaming shower.

Every now and then, his hands would dip lower and graze her breasts. Each time he did, she wanted him to ignore her hair. The intense tightness in her breasts and between her legs was almost too much to bear. She'd been ready for him the minute he'd left the bed.

And now she had him. Better go for it, Chloe, her more wild, more passionate side urged. This might be all there is. Make the best of it.

She turned around and reached behind him, to trace the indentation of his backbone all the way down to his butt and grab him the way he'd held her. She pulled him to her, rubbing against him, feeling the evidence of his arousal, amazed and rather impressed that she could cause such a reaction.

AJ sucked in his breath. "You keep doing that, Miss Venture Capitalist, and we won't make it back to the bed."

"Hey, you're the one who insisted on washing my hair," she said, working her hands around and over the tops of his hips, his slim, strong hips. Carefully, gently, she circled AJ's erection with her hands, stroking the length of him.

"Ahhhh," AJ said. "I've dreamed about this."

She stroked him once more, long and slow.

He grabbed her shoulders and kissed her, ignoring the suds slipping over her shoulders. The kiss wasn't the gentle one he'd delivered amidst bird feathers, or the one she'd coaxed from him on the recliner. Or even the hasty one they'd shared moments ago in his bed. This was a kiss of possession, of taking. Fierce and strong, hot and hungry, this kiss blazed straight to her heart and stamped it "Property of AJ Lockhart. No Trespassing."

"Put your arms around my neck," he said hoarsely. "Now."

She did as required, barely aware that he was picking her up and pressing her against the wall of the shower. Instinctively, she looped her legs around him, putting those insistent, yearning parts of her anatomy in direct contact with insistent, yearning parts of his anatomy.

He was kissing her again, his hands on either side of her head. "I told you we wouldn't make it to the bed," he said, his lips trailing heat down her neck.

Suddenly, one of his hands moved between them, between her legs, stroking, probing, finding the entrance to her being. She clung to him, drowning in the sensations that washed over her the way the shower did: hot water pounding on her, hot throbbing between her legs, hot kisses from a man she'd only dreamed about.

He entered her slowly at first, carefully, pressing her up against the wall, letting her absorb as much of him as she could. She felt herself adjust to him, and he began to thrust more insistently, seeming to lose himself in her. She hugged him with her legs, increasing the contact as he began rocking, driving himself toward release. She felt herself begin to shudder and explode, and he increased his pace.

She arched her back as much as possible, pressing against him, wanting to make the joining complete, wanting more of him. The pulsing shower matched the pulsing rhythm of a dance older than time. She closed her eyes and cried out as AJ took her to the edge of the universe and stars exploded around them.

When they'd both spent their collective passion, they stood in the shower, clinging to each other. As the water began to turn cold, AJ whispered, "We should probably take this discussion someplace else." He nipped her ear and then kissed her swollen lips gently. Still slick with soap, he eased himself out and away, quickly rinsing off. He grabbed the washcloth and softly wiped away the soap between her breasts. "Besides, I haven't really gotten started." He turned off the faucet, opened the glass door and took a towel from the stack. "In case you want to cover up for the trip to the bed."

She blinked water out of her eyes and looked up at him. There was more? "How?" How could he possibly think he could top the sensations that were even now clinging to the edges of her very being, taunting her with an experience so fresh, so new, so totally overwhelming she wasn't sure she could walk, much less do this again. At least not right now.

"Watch and learn," he said, patting her bottom as she got out of the shower, suddenly chilly. Not bothering with anything as mundane as a towel, AJ put his arm around her shoulders and guided her to the bedroom. He flung back the chenille bedspread, a blue blanket, and the top sheet. He sat on the edge of the mattress and pulled her down with him, rolling over so they lay side by side.

"I couldn't properly pleasure you the first time. Too fast. And pleasuring you standing up, although very enjoyable, wasn't exactly the way I had imagined us," he said, stroking her breast.

Whatever part of her that had thought twice was enough was swiftly silenced and ordered to keep quiet. The chill from her wet skin quickly fled in favor of heat. She moaned, reaching for him. That darned itch was back. Maybe it was the shower, the water, that had gotten in the way of completely satisfying it.

"Oh, no. This time we go slow," AJ said, catching her hand before it found its target. Deftly, he caught her other wrist and held her hands over her head, rolling on top of her just enough so she couldn't move. Not that she wanted to.

"Slow? I can't go slow," she gasped.

He smiled at her. "I can," he said, and proceeded to capture her nipple between his teeth and tug gently. He spent forever teasing one breast and then, not to show favoritism, concentrated on the other.

Chloe squirmed, trying to rub against his leg or any other part of his anatomy that presented itself for rubbing. He chuckled. "Not yet, my sweet. Not yet."

*When!* she shouted inside her head. *When?* The delightful tension and torturous pressure she felt threatened to push her past sanity. She'd about decided, with what little part of her brain that was still functioning normally, to demand he give her release, when he shifted.

Down.

Down her body, kissing a path from her breasts to her belly button to the triangle of fire that marked her essence. At least he'd let go of her arms. Without thinking, she tangled her fingers in his hair, wishing without words that he would do what she thought he was about to do.

He kissed the curly mass of red fire between her legs, pausing long enough to remark, "I see you're a natural redhead." Then, instead of tending to the need that was within inches of his tongue, he kissed the inside of her thigh, getting so close she could feel his hot breath.

He was trying to drive her mad.

And he was succeeding.

Then she felt him and her release was immediate. She arched into his most intimate of kisses, crying out, shuddering in the total absorption of the act. Again and again, waves of the most incredible sensation rushed over her from one source, AJ. AJ. Absolute Joy.

She began to come down from heights she hadn't thought possible when he moved up her body once more, replacing his hot mouth with his manhood. This time, he didn't dawdle, entering her swiftly and powerfully. "God, you're beautiful," he said, thrusting more and more quickly, seeking his own oblivion. She joined him on the climb up to the heavens and, miraculously, they exploded together, their souls and their voices joining in an unambiguous declaration of shared passion.

Later, as they lay covered by the sheet alone, AJ thought to himself that he'd had good sex before, but nothing came close to what he'd experienced with Chloe. Nothing. Her breathing, slow and regular, told him she'd been satisfied. He studied the ceiling. Just thinking about her made him hard.

"I hope that was satisfactory," he said. He traced the tops of her breasts and slipped the sheet off them so he could look at her, really look at her. As he edged the sheet off her totally, she curled into him, seeking his warmth.

"Definitely." She moved her hand across the expanse of his chest, then traced the crooked line of his nose. "How'd you break it?"

"A couple of guys in high school made rude comments about my mother. I defended her honor, but they got in a few good punches."

"I'm sorry."

"It was a long time ago."

He twisted her hair in his fingers. "What was your father like?" he asked.

"My father? Aloof, powerful, always right. Why?"

"He was successful. He raised two children by himself."

"With the help of a string of nannies and au pairs."

"But he stuck." AJ rolled over and opened the drawer of the bedside table. He brought back an old photograph. "This is my father," he said, showing her the picture.

"You look just like him."

"Unfortunately."

"Why unfortunate? He's a handsome devil. I'll bet your mother loved him."

"You got the devil part right. She loved him unquestioningly and he left her just the same." The pain in his voice was barely under control.

"AJ, I'm so sorry."

"Like I said, it was a long time ago." He rolled over and kissed her, tenderly and then fiercely, as if the kiss could block out the past and make the ache go away.

"Tell me about your mother," she asked.

"Amazing woman," AJ said, between kisses. "Bright. Never really had a chance to do what she wanted until I managed a scholarship that paid for my four years of college."

"No siblings?"

"Just me, and, believe me, when you meet her, my mom will tell you one was enough."

So, he wanted her to meet his mother. "She lives around here?"

AJ nodded. "Leesburg. She teaches piano to kids too poor to afford lessons any other way," AJ smiled. "It doesn't pay much, but she loves it."

Chloe shifted so she faced him. "I envy you," she said. "You had a mother."

"You had a father."

"Not really. The only times he was around, other than major holidays, he was too busy for his kids, especially his overimaginative daughter." She wound a strand of AJ's hair around her finger. "Although maybe he did pay more attention to all my wild scheming than I thought at the time," she said. "I think that's why he left CI to me and not to Oz."

AJ smoothed her curls back from her face. "He's an odd one, your brother," he said. "It'd be interesting to take a look at his companies, you know, compare them to CI. Just to see the differences."

Chloe snuggled closer, resting her cheek against AJ's chest. "That spreadsheet you were worried about? I found some other files attached to it, smaller spreadsheets," she said, tracing the line of hair from AJ's chest down to his belly button. "I think they've got some of Oz's numbers on them."

She stuck her finger in his belly button.

"Hey!" He reached for her hand. "That tickles."

"Really?" She attacked his ribs. "How about this?"

"You're asking for trouble, Miss I-have-great-ideas," he said, laughing.

"I'll stop if you tell me what AJ stands for," she giggled.

"Amazing Journey," he said and grabbed her,

pushing her down on the bed and straddling her.

Her skin was the classic ivory that went with red hair. Her arms and legs were dusted with a soft scattering of freckles. Her lips, swollen from his kisses, were ripe red. She was the most beautiful woman he'd ever seen.

And her computer program, e-Cupid, had paired them together. Maybe he should take Cupid.com more seriously. Chloe definitely had a way of making him in believe in her projects, he mused. Although her greatest feat—and scariest—to date was that she had him half-convinced that true love did in fact exist. Was it possible the woman who funded other people's dreams had set his own heart dreaming?

And thinking like a damned Hallmark card! AJ felt his mouth curve in a self-deprecating grin.

He leaned over and brushed Chloe's forehead with a kiss, then moved down and captured her lips. He was ready for her again, hard and hot. She settled more closely to him, turning onto her back as his hand moved from her waist to her hip.

She was warm and moist and opened herself to him with a welcoming sigh.

Chloe rolled over and looked at the clock beside AJ's bed. Eight-thirty, it announced, in a blinding green digital shriek. AJ, warm and sleeping, curled closer to her.

So much for I'll-try-this-once-and-get-it-out-of-my-system sex, she thought. There was nothing about their night together that had the remotest relationship to tentative, lukewarm sex. No, it had been soul shattering. Regardless of what happened next in their lives, Chloe knew with absolute certainty that, whether AJ was her true love or not, she'd never have that kind of experience with anyone else. Ever.

But a new day dawned. She ran a hand through her hair, trying to control the cinnamon and red mess she knew had come from too little sleep and lots of love. "Time to get up," she said.

AJ opened one sleepy eye, smiled at her, and said, "Up?"

"Not that kind of up. You, even you, need a break. Besides, we've got bird cleanup duty today. Edgar needs food." She kissed the end of his nose. "You stay in bed. I'm going to shower," she held out a hand in warning, "just me. I'll make sure there's enough hot water for you."

"You're the boss," he said, his voice heavy with spent passion and sleep. "You could easily take the day off."

"Tempting, very tempting," she said. She grabbed AJ's T-shirt, discarded so long ago, and pulled it on. She didn't need to provide any more stimulation or they'd really never get out of bed.

Not that that idea didn't have a strong appeal.

She padded into the bathroom, coloring a little as she remembered what had happened in the shower last night. She looked in the mirror. Yikes. Her hair was worse than she'd thought. It stuck out in all directions, like a demented dandelion. A shower would fix that, she told herself and turned on the water.

She kept her promise to leave AJ some hot water and was looking through his medicine cabinet when he came into the bathroom, wrapped in a towel. "Can I help you with something?" he asked.

"Looking for a spare toothbrush. I can't seem to find mine."

He reached around her and fished one out of a drawer under the sink. "Always keep a spare, just in case," he said, winking. He stepped into the shower, tossed his towel over the top, and turned on the water.

"You said something last night," he said. "Something about Oz's numbers in a spreadsheet."

"Yep. You'd be proud of me. I figured out how to make the program divulge information. You can look at it if you want," she offered.

Chloe dressed in the clothes she'd hastily packed the night before, trying to smooth out the wrinkles. It didn't matter, she told herself. They were going straight to her house anyway. Which reminded her. She needed to call someone to come get the birds. She skipped down the stairs to the kitchen.

When AJ joined her, wearing a fresh T-shirt and jeans, she winced, more aware than ever of her disheveled appearance and the overwhelming urge to get him right back out of those clean clothes.

Instead, she said, "Bernie, down at the pet store, said he'd be at my house before ten. With a van and a helper. He apologized for the mistake in the delivery yesterday."

"I knew that had to be wrong. Even Ralph isn't that stupid."

"He was merely offering the pet store alternatives if they couldn't find the pair of lovebirds he'd originally ordered. Apparently, someone at the store read the order wrong and sent everything. Bernie even said he'd pay to have the house cleaned."

"Only proper, although I think Ralph ought to donate something. It was his idea to send birds in the first place." AJ opened the refrigerator and took out a pitcher of orange juice. "OJ from AJ?" he asked.

Chloe looked at him. "Was that a joke?"

"My mother always thought it was funny," he said pouring himself a glass. He gestured with the pitcher, offering once more.

"Sure," she said. "You still haven't told me what your name is, other than initials."

"AJ is my name, and breakfast is my game," he said. "How do you like your eggs?"

They arrived at Chloe's house about the same time Bernie did. He was unloading bird-catching gear as they drove up.

AJ parked in front of the house and helped carry the various nets and snares while Chloe unlocked the door. Slowly, she opened it, hoping that no winged creature was waiting to attack her. "Coast is clear," she said, and the team of intrepid bird hunters entered the devastation area.

After filling Edgar's water dish and serving her a can of cat food, Chloe took Bernie to the garage where several gaggles of winged animals were waiting for them. "Wow, Miss Phillips," Bernie said. "I had no idea this would happen." He signaled his helper to begin hauling crates with birds out to the van. "I don't know how they could have gotten out. Usually, these clasps are solid." He pointed to the closure on the closest cage. "You sure there wasn't someone here who opened them?"

"The only person with a key to my place is Mrs. Hutchins, my next-door neighbor. I assume she let the delivery people in and locked up after, but she wouldn't set birds loose in my house. She's a veteran neatnik who probably lectured your driver on the insanity of birds in a house in the first place." Chloe figured it didn't much matter how the winged creatures had gotten out. It was just one more crazy incident in her out of control life. Maybe the driver had decided to play a practical joke. Whatever the explanation, she didn't really care at this point.

As the last of the cages were removed and Bernie set about rounding up any wildlife she and AJ hadn't managed to corral the night before, Chloe's doorbell rang. "Maybe that's Ralph, come to apologize," she said, heading toward the entryway. "Yes?" she said, to the young woman she found standing on her porch.

"Good morning," the woman said. "Are you Chloe Phillips?"

Chloe nodded.

The woman reached into her briefcase and withdrew an envelope, which she handed to Chloe. "Have a nice day, Miss Phillips. You've been served." She turned and went back down the steps to her car.

"Served?" Chloe opened the envelope and pulled out a handful of official papers.

AJ came up behind her, nuzzling her neck. "What's that?"

"Another attempt by Ralph Higgenbotham to get my attention, I guess. He's suing me for breach of contract."

# Chapter Sixteen
# "Can't Buy Me Love"

"Let me see that," said AJ, taking the papers. He flipped through them quickly, scanning their contents. "He's not kidding, Chloe."

She took the documents back and read the first few paragraphs. They were littered with "parties of the first part" and "wherases" and references to an implied contract. "What is he talking about?" Chloe asked. "The only contract I have with Ralph is for the funding of SatelHat, and it's been vetted by half a dozen of my brother's best lawyers. There isn't any way he could be suing about that. In fact, I could sue him," she said. "He hasn't made one development or report on time."

AJ raised an eyebrow. "I expect your board might feel a bit of sympathy for the man in that regard."

Chloe narrowed her eyes and smiled at AJ. "No need to bring that up." She shrugged. "I guess I'll just have to call Oz and see what to do."

"Nonsense," AJ said, snatching the papers once more. "Let me handle it."

She took a step back. "Look, I don't want to involve you in this mess."

"I'm already involved," he said, kissing her cheek. "Besides, Tommy's a lawyer. He can help you out here. You don't want to include your brother, do you? Really? He's already wavering in his support for you. This would be the last red flag required, don't you think?"

She thought about that for a minute. "You're right, of course. I'm supposed to be able to handle anything the world tosses at me. This is just one more hot potato to be cooled off and disposed of."

"I doubt Ralph would appreciate being called a potato, but you're right." He draped his arm around her and steered her back into the ruined house. "Here, this chair isn't too bad. Sit down and I'll get the phone."

As he reached for the telephone, it rang. He handed it to Chloe. "Hello? . . . Uh-huh . . . No . . . Tuesday, I see . . . No sooner? . . . Fumigate? Are you sure? . . . Okay, see you next week then." She hung up and her shoulders slumped.

"Not the news you were hoping for, I presume?"

"The cleaning crew came by earlier this morning. Mrs. Hutchins let them in." She was really going to rethink giving her neighbor her key. "They say they'll have to set off some kind of germ eradication bomb in here and let it sit for three days before they can clean."

"So, you're going to have to stay with me," AJ said, a satisfied, lust-filled look on his face. "What a pity."

"I'm going to have to think about that, AJ. Last night was . . ."

"Amazing. Dazzling. Beyond real. Exceptional sex, with a capital X?" AJ pulled her to her feet and folded her in an easy embrace.

"Yes."

"I hear a 'but' coming."

"But I've got responsibilities at the office, reports to prepare, projects to review."

"And you've asked me to help. That doesn't mean we can't be together after all the work's done, does it?"

"I remember firing you last night," she said.

"This help's on the house. Pro bono."

She thought about that for a full minute. Was it a good idea for them to continue to work together? Was there any way to avoid it? She needed him to help her prove to the board what a great manager she was. She would just have to trust him—to assist her with CI and not to trample all over her heart. "I can stay with you. I'll have to get a few things, however." She accepted a quick kiss and ran up the stairs.

"I'll call Tommy while you're packing," AJ called out, grabbing the phone again. "Tommy? I've got a problem," AJ said when his friend answered.

"So, tell the Tomster all."

AJ related, in much abbreviated format, the bird episode, his night with Chloe, and her lawsuit. "Can you take this on?"

"Is there money in it?" Tommy asked. "The check from Phillips still hasn't cleared the bank and the copy machine people are threatening to take ours away unless we pay our bills."

"Don't worry about money, pal. It's covered," AJ said. "This sounds like a classic nuisance suit to me. Think you can talk a judge into dismissing it?"

"When did you turn into a protector of the innocent and overworked? If I didn't know better, I'd say you were in love, my friend." AJ let Tommy's comment sink into his head. Was it possible? Sure, Chloe and he made the universe tip when they were together, but love? "On the subject of getting the suit dismissed," Tommy went on, "I'll try. Drop off the papers on your way to wherever you and the Bird Woman of Virginia are going."

"Very funny. We're going to her office. See you in a few." AJ hung up the phone, thinking about what Tommy had said. In love. Well, Chloe *was* different from other women. Setting aside her amazing abilities in bed, she had an optimism he missed when he wasn't around her. Kooky ideas aside, she always saw the good in what life served up. He liked that. And, she knew what growing up with an absent father was like. He knew she'd listen to him if he wanted to talk about his own dad and what a jerk he'd been.

Exactly what he intended to do with this revelation he didn't know. He chewed the inside of his cheek. He'd planned to make enough money on this job to pay all the company's bills. He'd planned to get settled in and make a boatload of money. He hadn't planned on a sweet little redhead waltzing into his life and turning things upside down.

He hadn't planned on falling in love.

"All ready," Chloe said.

AJ's heart started a staccato beat that insisted he haul her right back up those stairs and do what any manly man would when faced with the vision in front of him.

Chloe was dressed in a pair of black leather pants, a pale yellow sweater, black ankle boots, and a smile. She was stunning. Her hair still stuck out in all directions, but he was getting used to that. It was her signature, a reminder that she was one of a kind.

Instead of sweeping her back up the stairs, he shrugged into his leather jacket and said, "Great. Tommy wants us to stop by and give him the papers. He says he'll take your case."

"Thank you. I wasn't looking forward to Ozzie's reaction when I told him I'd been sued, and by a client!" Chloe waved to Bernie. "Have Mrs. Hutchins lock up after you're done, will you?"

"Sure thing, Miss Phillips," Bernie said, wrestling a recalcitrant swan into a crate. "We'll be out of here in no time." With a loud hiss and a lunge, the swan twisted out of Bernie's hold and flapped around the living room, protesting loudly. "Really. Trust me." Bernie grimaced.

Chloe closed the door on the chaos that inhabited her house. Poltergeists would have been easier to deal with than Ralph's birds d'amour. And now he was suing her. Because she didn't want to date him.

Half an hour later, Chloe chewed her fingernail and watched as Tommy reviewed the papers she'd been served with. AJ sat next to her, almost as nervous. Finally, Tommy put down the papers and took off his reading glasses. He cleared his throat. "First off, let me tell you that no judge will hesitate to throw this out, on its face. Your matchmaking software is an interesting idea, Chloe, but no one can possibly believe that it could actually find you your true love. Right?"

Chloe and AJ nodded. "Right." They said in unison. Chloe knew they both viewed e-Cupid as simply a cool idea with a ton of marketing potential. Software might balance your checkbook, but it would never find your true love. "What are we up against?" she asked.

"Basically, Mr. Higgenbotham's position is that you and he have an implied contract to be each other's true love, based on a prototype software you showed him. He further alleges that you've stained his sterling reputation in the scientific community by refusing to go out with him, thus making him look like a fool." Tommy raised his eyebrows.

"Well, he's mistaken," Chloe said. "The software can't promise anything from a legal stand point. You said it yourself. How could a software program actually *know* who your soul mate was anyway? Besides, there's something wrong with the software that makes my picture come up each time a man uses it." Chloe sat forward, anxious for Tommy to believe her insane tale.

"As crazy as this all sounds, it's true," AJ said. "I was in her office when both Ralph and Andrew viewed e-Cupid, and subsequently lost their marbles. Although Officer McKinnett seems to have regained his senses, unlike our lonely inventor friend."

"I'd like to question this policeman and I'd like to view the software program myself," Tommy said. "Then I'll file a motion to dismiss and we'll see if we can't get this wrapped up."

Chloe shifted in her chair, staring at her feet. "Couldn't we proceed without you looking at e-Cupid? I really don't need any more men chasing me around the city. I'm kind of, um, seeing someone."

Tommy cocked an eyebrow and looked first at Chloe and then at AJ. "You sound like you believe it really works."

"No," she said, "but Andrew and Ralph certainly acted goofy and I don't want to take any chances that you'll react similarly. As far-fetched as this whole situation sounds, I really can't deal with another love-struck Romeo hot on my trail."

"I understand your concern, but I still think it would be a good idea for me to see it. I need to know what I'm defending you against." He grinned. "Besides, I suspect a certain friend of mine would promise bodily damage if I entertained any romantic thoughts of you. And that's a huge deterrent to my losing my marbles, as AJ so eloquently described Ralph and Andrew's behavior."

Chloe blushed. "If you're sure." She stood up. "My laptop's in the car, um, Charlene," she said holding out her hand to AJ.

"Yes?"

"Give me the keys and I'll go get the program."

"I'll get it," he said. "Charlene is the jealous type."

"Oh, please. She and I get along just fine." Chloe grabbed the keys and left the office.

On the way out, Joanie said, "AJ giving you grief about his car?"

Chloe nodded.

"He must care about you an awful lot to let you take the keys," Joanie said and smiled. "It's about time he found someone to share Charlene with."

"Right," said Chloe and went into the parking lot to retrieve the laptop with the wounded software. "You've known him longer than I have," she told the Corvette as she unlocked the door and reached behind the seat. "What is it with him anyway?"

Charlene was silent.

"Yeah, he takes my breath away, too." She closed the door, careful not to slam it, then patted the roof. "You're lucky to have him, you know."

Back in the office, Tommy opened the laptop and turned it on. "Now what?"

"Follow the flashing heart," said Chloe.

Minutes later, with a stupid half smile, Tommy sat back in his chair. "This is amazing, Chloe. May I call you Chloe?"

"Oh, no," Chloe said, standing up quickly and leaning on the desk. "I told you it would just cause trouble. Save yourself the time, Tom, I won't go out with you, I don't love you, I can't love you."

"Oh, come on. I'm not that ugly. Not like AJ, and you seem to be fine around him." He closed the computer. "For the record, then, I did not, repeat, did not, see your picture in this program. If it was broken before, it's somehow fixed itself."

Chloe sat down, stunned. "This is good, right?"

"Well, it depends. If a judge concludes that the software is genuine and does give you your true love," Tommy said with a silly smile "then Higgenbotham may have a case."

"If you didn't see Chloe, pal, who did you see?" AJ asked. "Inquiring minds want to know."

Tommy grinned at his friend. "On the other hand, if it was broken and is now fixed, perhaps the solution is to have Higgenbotham try it again and find his real true love." He picked up a pencil. "Assuming that you aren't his true love."

"Trust me," said AJ. "She's not."

Chloe looked at AJ. What had he just said? Heat flooded through her body. Was he saying *he* was her true love? She shook her head. No way. Sure, he liked her and the sex had been otherworldly, but love?

"I see." Tommy scratched the side of his head with the eraser end of his pencil. "Still, he *thinks* he is. Do you have a proposal or a signed contract with the software's inventors?" he asked Chloe. "Anything that would indicate what the program promised?"

"I've got their initial business proposal, of course. And," Chloe dug into her purse, "I've got this." She handed Tommy the purple beeper Milo had given her the first day.

"Looks like a Barbie computer," he said, opening the gadget and touching the tiny keyboard with the end of his pencil. "What is this supposed to do?"

"Two things. There should be a picture of your true love on the screen, and it vibrates when you're around her, or him," Chloe explained. "Just turn it on."

Tommy pushed the switch on the side of the pager and grinned as he watched the miniscule screen. "Cool." The pager vibrated wildly in his hands. He set the purple pulsing plastic on his desk and the three of them watched it shake its way across the desk and plop into AJ's lap.

AJ caught the little computer and turned it off. "Still not going to tell us who you've seen?" Tommy shook his head. "Fine." AJ tossed the purple gizmo back to Tommy. "You keep it. For evidence."

Tommy turned the beeper in his hands, his broad smile widening. "Chloe? Do you have the e-Cupid information in your briefcase as well?" She nodded. "Go get it please."

When she'd left, Tommy put the pager on his palm. It vibrated and his smile lit up the office. "See," said AJ. "Proof positive the product doesn't work. Chloe's not even in the room." Good God, what was he saying? After last night, well, he wouldn't call it love, exactly, but he'd certainly been considering the idea that Chloe might *have* a true love wandering around out there. And it might be him. He. Whatever. If he thought about it, he might get used to the idea of Chloe in his life.

At that moment said woman reappeared with a handful of papers and Tommy turned off the pager. "Thanks," he said, hefting the tiny instrument in his hand. "I'll make a few calls and see what I can do to get this lawsuit dismissed. We should be able to make Ralph see how wrong he is." Tommy stood and shook hands with Chloe. "It's been a true delight, Miss Phillips. I'll let you know what I manage."

Outside Tommy's office, Chloe said, "What did you guys do with the pager?"

"Tommy just left it on to see if it'd vibrate while you weren't there."

"And?"

"It vibrated. No big deal, right?"

"Maybe, maybe not," she said. "I really thought it only worked when you and I were together."

"Now you're a believer in e-Cupid?"

"No," she said. "Absolutely not. But he looked pretty happy after he'd tried it." She opened the car door and gave him an impish smile, obviously teasing. "But if it works when I'm not there, then maybe Tommy's true love was close by."

"I doubt that," he said. Tommy was hot for an assistant U.S. attorney who worked on the hill. But AJ didn't like the idea that his fate was in the hands of a software program, assuming software actually had hands. No, there was no way a little purple gizmo was going to put him in a position to act like his father had. Not now. Not ever. Even if its target for his devotion was the woman next to him who made him crazy with lust. That was just chemistry. Love had nothing to do with it—regardless of his earlier, clearly hormone-driven thoughts to the contrary.

"I suppose you're right," she said. She straightened in her seat. "I'll just have to find E. Rose and Milo, that's all there is to it. When we get to the office, you work on reports for Oz and I'll track down two errant inventors."

"I'm done preparing my presentation for the board," AJ announced, coming into Chloe's office.

"Good," she said, pushing an empty box of Cracker Jack around on her desk.

"What's wrong?"

"I just talked with Webster. The board has called an emergency meeting to hear your report and probably to yell at me because of Ralph's suit." She turned the empty box upside down and shook it.

"And there was no prize in my Cracker Jack."

AJ walked behind her and rubbed her shoulders. "I'm sure Tommy will make this whole thing disappear. In the interim, I have good news."

"I could certainly use some," she said.

"I'm recommending that the board give you their full support and declare the requirements of your father's will fulfilled." He spun her chair around and bent to kiss her. She smiled.

"Hey, lady, I just gave you your company on a platter," he said. "Aren't you going to be just a little bit excited?"

She jumped up and threw her arms around him. "Of course I am," she said. "It's the best news, AJ. The best." She undid his tie. "Now, my day would be complete if you would just tell me one little thing."

"What's that?"

"What does AJ stand for?"

"Absentminded Juggler," he said, picking her up and swinging her around. When he set her down, he looked at her computer screen. "Is that the infamous spreadsheet?"

"The very one."

"Can you show me what you found?"

"Sure," she said. "Just click here and, voilà, a whole new page of numbers."

"Nice work, Chlo. Nice work," AJ said. It looked like she'd discovered revenue figures and expenses for Oz's companies. If he could take a little time, AJ was certain he'd figure out why the bank hadn't released his check yet. But first things first.

AJ had leaned over the desk to claim a kiss from Chloe when Gloria breezed in unannounced. "Ahem, excuse me for interrupting, Ms. Phillips, but there's a call for you. Your brother. Sounds quite urgent."

Chloe jerked back from AJ. "Thank you. Transfer it in here, please."

Gloria raised a knowing eyebrow, smiled, and left the office. Seconds later, the phone on Chloe's desk rang. "Oz, what can I do for you?" She held up the express mail envelope that Gloria had handed her. AJ took it.

"Chloe," Oz said. "I just found out about the lawsuit. What's going on over there? Are you okay?"

"I'm fine, Oz. I've got a good lawyer and he tells me it'll be dismissed. No problem."

"Oh, good. I know the board of directors has called a meeting for later today and I wanted to be sure you were going to be there."

"What's wrong, Oz? You sound funny."

"Nothing. I'll see you later," Oz said and hung up.

"That was weird," Chloe said. "Oz is up to something."

"Don't worry about him," AJ said. "Maybe this is good news." He handed her back the envelope.

She opened it and read the contents. "I'm really beginning to hate the government," she said. "It's Spuddy Buddy. Something's wrong and the FDA isn't going to approve our design."

"Ah, but they haven't seen the new, improved version yet. Don't worry, we'll get it through," AJ said. "And forget about Oz." AJ looked once more at the spreadsheet open on Chloe's computer. "You can review my presentation right now. Then you can quit worrying and maybe we can spend a bit of time doing something more interesting."

Chloe came around the end of the desk and put her finger in the center of AJ's chest. "Listen, without a flawless presentation, I will lose my business. It's the only thing I've ever really wanted, other than a pony for my sixth birthday, but that's irrelevant. As for something interesting . . ." She traced his ear and hugged him. "Well, let's just see how long it takes to go over your presentation."

"You're the boss."

# Chapter Seventeen
# "Prisoner of Love"

"Here." AJ dropped a three-inch stack of papers on Oz Phillips' sleek black desk. "Here are your damned reports."

Phillips looked at him from heavy-lidded, blank eyes. "And?"

"And what? I've done the job. Gotten your sister's reports completed. Just like you asked. Everything's ready for the board presentation." AJ had concluded already that Chloe and Oz couldn't be related. She always looked for the positives, and he was after only the grimy underbelly.

"Did you find irregularities?"

"Every company has a few mistakes in their financials, you know that. I'd bet the obscene fee you're supposed to be paying me and all the wonderful publicity you've planned that I'd find an equal number of errors in any one of your companies." AJ had spent enough time with the spreadsheet Chloe'd uncovered to know exactly how many irregularities Oz had in each of his companies.

"What does that mean?" Oz arched an eyebrow.

"You know damn well your check is on hold at the bank." Anger threaded through AJ's tone. Anger laced with fear.

"Right." Oz stood and walked across his expansive office. "I planned it that way, actually, once I realized Chloe was interested in you." His smile was thin, oily.

AJ's apprehension upped a notch. "Really?" Oz had better not hurt Chloe. "Did you plan this?" AJ pulled another file out of his briefcase and tossed it on the desk. "Or this?" A second and third file followed. With grim satisfaction AJ knew he'd hit Oz where it hurt most.

"What are these?" Oz said, his calm demeanor starting to crack.

"A little bonus work I've done for you—no extra charge." AJ flipped open the first file folder. "According to this, you're not the hot manager you keep telling Chloe you are." And not half the person Chloe was.

"Where did you get this?" Oz's eyes were granite gray and just as hard. He was most assuredly not amused with AJ's revelations.

Good. "You helped Chloe set up a spreadsheet program that would track her business, right? Well, you linked it to your own balance sheet and income statement so that positive balances from CI automatically transferred to your companies. A masterful deception, Oz. Chloe found it but didn't know what it was." AJ was on his feet now leaning close to Oz, his anger beginning to spill out. "I do." And Chloe would as well, when AJ explained what her loving brother was really up to.

"Sit down, Lockhart and let me explain to you how real companies work," Oz said. He leaned against his desk, waiting for AJ to sit.

"Fine, I'm sitting."

"Setting the spreadsheet aside for the moment, you have figured out that I'm plagued by some financial challenges, shall we say. That my construction group is deep in the red because of delays and that it's affecting everything I do."

An understatement.

"You're concerned that your fee won't be paid, am I right?" Oz walked across his deep scarlet carpet and opened his briefcase. He extracted an envelope. "In here you'll find a check that will clear." He approached AJ and handed it to him. "It's twice your fee," he said. "Call it a bonus."

AJ turned the envelope in his hand, then tossed it on the table. "What do I have to do to earn this unexpected largess?"

"Simply complete your assignment, Lockhart. You've uncovered some spectacular products in all the goofy things Chloe funds. FrogVision alone is going to make millions." He pulled a letter from his desk drawer and handed it to AJ. "A little early warning from my friend Senator Salton. The Pentagon has asked for funding to the tune of a hundred million for FrogVision. The senator will see to it that the request is approved." He walked around his desk and poured himself a tumbler of whiskey. He offered to pour one for AJ.

"No thanks. Too early for me."

Oz sat at his desk and sipped. "I need her company, Lockhart. The only way for that to happen is for you to find such serious trouble that the board puts me in charge. Then I can use her venture fund to fix my short-term troubles and her successes to make me whole."

"You bastard," AJ said.

"I doubt it," Oz replied, swirling the aged Scotch in the crystal tumbler. "My mother wasn't the type."

"There's no way I'm going to betray Chloe, *Oswald,* so you're out of luck."

"Perhaps. I know you're on the brink of financial failure yourself, my friend. You have no phone service, your landlord is evicting you, and you're about to lose your computers. Are you certain you're willing to let that lovely, pregnant assistant try to find work, much less insurance, in her condition?"

AJ stood up, his heart pounding with anger. "You're a pig."

"No, just a man who will do what's necessary. A man like your father, for example." Oz steepled his fingers. "I think you're your father's son, Lockhart. You'll walk away from Chloe just as your father left you and your mother when the going got rough. You're going to help me or there will be no money from Phillips International."

AJ's ears rang with rage. For an instant he was ten years old once more, watching his dad walk away. Hearing again his smug laugh. "I suppose you'll arrange it so Chloe can't pay me either, but if I do as you ask, there'll be more work for my company." All his life he'd fought not to be like his father. He knew exactly what his father would have done in this situation. Abandon the woman who trusted him with her future.

"You catch on quickly, Lockhart. I like that about you. Now, do we have an understanding?"

God, he hated that supercilious pose. AJ picked up the envelope once more. Inside was the answer to his troubles. Money for Joanie and her baby. Funding for a year, at least, at Lockhart Associates. Cash to fix Charlene. He tossed the envelope down again. "Not on a bet."

Oz raised one eyebrow, his only indication of surprise. "I can certainly see how your friend Mr. Morales will land on his feet, and your assistant can probably get by on welfare, but if you defy me, I'll make sure you never work in this town again." His tone assured AJ that he could carry out his threat.

"You are one son of a bitch, Phillips, you know that? If I give in, the board will take away the one thing your sister wants. And then you'll have everything." AJ hadn't been in a fight since high school, but he wanted more than anything to punch Oz in his aristocratic nose. Just once.

"Precisely."

Instead, he took a deep breath and stood. "I'm due in court," he said. "I feel sorry for you, Phillips. You've missed the point." He spun on his heel and strode out the door.

"I need your answer," Oz shouted after him.

"There's more to life than money, you miserable excuse for a man," AJ shouted back.

Once he was outside the building, he stopped and took another deep breath. What a mess. Either he betrayed Chloe and got the money he needed to keep the business going and by extension save his friends, or he stood up to her brother and let his business and his friends go under. His father would simply have run away.

Question was, would AJ do the same?

"Your Honor, we'd like to enter into evidence this laptop computer containing the disputed software program e-Cupid," Tommy said, brandishing the technological troublemaker.

"Very well," said Judge Julio Ramirez. "Continue with your witness."

For reasons known only to the judicial system, the judge had denied Tommy's request to dismiss the suit that Ralph Higgenbotham had filed against Chloe. Consequently, here she was, the day before

Halloween, mere hours before the board meeting, testifying instead of working.

"Miss Phillips, do you recognize this laptop?" Tommy held up the machine.

"Yes. It's the one that E. Rose and Milo brought for our first meeting to discuss their software project, e-Cupid." A meeting she more and more frequently wished she'd never taken.

"What claims, if any, did these two men make regarding the software?"

"They indicated that it was designed to link a person with his or her true love." She looked out over the courtroom and caught AJ watching her, a wary expression on his face.

"And what process did you follow in order to know the identity of your true love?"

"I initiated the software and the program did the rest."

"Go on."

"It showed me a picture of a man purported to be my one true love. He was quite handsome and dashing, not at all what I was expecting." Which was nothing, but the court didn't need to know that. "Furthermore, it did not give me any information about him, his name, occupation, how to contact him."

"And have you subsequently met this man of your dreams?"

Chloe coughed slightly, feeling her ears and cheeks heat up. "Yes," she said quietly.

"Would you repeat your answer, please," said the Judge.

"Yes, I have met him," Chloe said, "although I don't believe the software program has anything to do with our attraction."

"Why is that?" Tommy asked.

"Software can't make people fall in love. It can

suggest someone you might be compatible with—that's all. Whether or not two people are attracted to one another has to do with chemistry—their physical reaction to one another. And no computer program can control biological responses.

"Objection," said Ralph's lawyer, Edgar Blatch, a sleazy, rumpled, chubby man with a red face. "Miss Phillips is not an expert on chemistry or interpersonal relationships."

"Overruled, the witness may answer."

"Hormones, pheromones, that's what attracts people to one another initially. Nothing more." Chloe tried not to look at AJ, who was sitting just behind the defendant's table. He was living proof that mones, whether hor- or phero-, just complicated things.

"Thank you. Now, turning to the afternoon in question. Mr. Higgenbotham came to your office?"

She dragged her attention back to the process at hand—saving her company. "Yes. Ralph and I had an appointment to discuss the latest developments on his project, the Satelhat. He was falling behind in his—"

"Objection," Ralph's lawyer said.

"Overruled. Miss Phillips is the manager of her own business and is qualified to determine whether or not her clients are meeting their deadlines." Judge Julio smiled at Chloe. "Please continue."

"Thank you, Judge," said Tommy. "So, Higgenbotham was behind?"

"Yes, but it wasn't anything serious. He had some design concerns that we discussed."

"And, after that discussion, did you ask him to look at the e-Cupid program?"

"Yes."

"With what result?"

Chloe felt her face redden. "He saw a picture of me on the screen."

"Then what happened?"

"He got down on his knees and declared his love for me. He begged me to go out with him. I was so surprised, I refused. But I would have refused anyway. I never date clients. It's a matter of ethics."

"Ethics!" shouted Ralph's lawyer. "This woman has no ground to be talking about ethics, Your Honor. She wantonly took advantage of my client by promising him favors and then flaunted her denial in his face, damaging his reputation and humiliating him in one swell foop."

"I believe you mean fell swoop," said Tommy.

"Sit down, Mr. Blatch. Save it for your cross," said the judge.

"You never promised Mr. Higgenbotham anything, did you?" Tommy asked.

"No."

"No further questions, Your Honor." Tommy sat down, smiling at Chloe and nodding that he thought the case was going their way.

"Redirect, your honor. Miss Phillips," said Mr. Blatch. "Why did you decide to fund this e-Cupid project?"

Chloe shifted in the chair. "It appeared to me to be a solid idea with significant potential."

"Uh-huh. Tell me about some of your other projects, Miss Phillips."

"Objection, relevance."

"Goes to motive, Your Honor. It is our contention that Miss Phillips is careless about choosing projects to fund and that her disregard for standard business practices has led directly to the heartbroken state of my client."

"Overruled. You may answer, Miss Phillips."

"I have any number of projects, Mr. Blatch. All of

them show promise or I wouldn't have taken them on."

"For instance?"

"Well," she cleared her throat, "there's a very promising technology for washing windows, an inventive approach to fish farming, and of course, Mr. Higgenbotham's SatelHat, which is by far the most promising of them all." She smiled at Ralph. It was the truth. His ideas were breakthrough and worth the funding she'd given him.

"Did you offer any of those clients the opportunity to try out the e-Cupid software?"

"No."

Blatch got an "ah-ha" look on his face, as if he'd just found the treasure. "So, you singled out my client, is that correct?"

"Ralph happened to be in the office that day. If any of my other clients had had appointments, I probably would have let them try the software as well."

"Probably! But not with certainty."

"I guess."

"Moving on. Did anyone else try the software?"

"Yes, Officer Andrew McKinnett previewed the program. He also saw my picture, which was when I knew there was something wrong with the software."

"Objection, Your Honor," said Blatch. "It is our contention that this woman, lonely and alone, approaching spinster status as she turned thirty, plotted to have multiple men wooing her in order to shore up her own sad life."

"You cannot object to your own questions, Mr. Blatch." Judge Ramirez chuckled. "And save your conclusions for your summation."

"Yes, Your Honor." Blatch consulted his pad of paper. "Did you, in fact, go out with either of these men? My client or Officer McKinnett?"

This felt like a trap. Chloe looked at Tommy for help. He shrugged and nodded. She'd have to answer. "Yes. Officer McKinnett took me out for pizza and later, we arranged to meet for dinner."

"At a bar with the reputation as a place for people of the opposite sex to meet? Am I right?"

"Objection." Tommy rose partway out of his seat. "The presumed reputation of various bars and restaurants that my client may or may not have visited is completely irrelevant."

"I'll allow it."

Chloe cleared her throat. "I've heard people refer to it as a singles bar, yes."

"Why did you choose that particular place for McKinnett and you to go? Did you have plans to pick up some other unsuspecting man?"

"No. I had plans to get Officer McKinnett back together with *his* true love, my friend Barbara. She lives nearby, so it was a logical meeting place."

Blatch sputtered, "His true love?"

"That's what the program said when Barbara tried it out." Chloe turned to the judge. "You see, whenever a woman tries the computer program, it shows her the picture of a man who the software predicts will be her true love. Whenever a man tries it, he sees me. It's a glitch. A bug. Possibly a virus."

"Objection! This witness is neither a computer expert nor an epidemiologist. Move to strike."

"Give it up, Blatch. This is a strange case, borderline at best. One more outburst from you and I'll dismiss it. Understand?" The judge nailed Blatch with a look that rivaled Chloe's best.

"Do you have any proof that this glitch, as you call it, actually exists?"

"Nothing but the program itself."

Blatch paced back and forth in front of the witness

chair. "No more questions for this witness." Blatch walked back to his table and conferred with Higgenbotham. "I call AJ Lockhart."

"What are you trying to do?" AJ asked.

"Make a case for my client. I believe you've been called to the witness stand."

AJ appealed to Tommy, a somewhat desperate expression on his face. "Hey, man," he whispered, "can't you stop this?"

"You should know better, AJ."

AJ made his way to the stand and took the oath. Chloe watched, wondering why AJ was so reluctant to talk. Was it because of their relationship?

"What's wrong with him?" she asked Tommy, who shrugged.

"Ahem, Mr. Lockhart," Blatch began. "Do you know the defendant?"

"Yes," AJ said.

"How do you know her?"

AJ hesitated. "I work for her firm, in a consultative role. I've been helping her compile reports for her board."

"What is your current profession, Mr. Lockhart?"

"I'm a consultant."

"I see. My research indicates that Miss Phillips' brother hired you to help her struggling business. What did he promise you in return for assisting his sister?"

"He promised to give me more business and to allow me to use him as a reference."

"Would you explain to the court what kind of work exactly you have been doing for Miss Phillips, please."

"Your honor," Tommy said. "I fail to see what this line of questioning has to do with the alleged injury to Mr. Higgenbotham."

"I agree. Move along, Mr. Blatch."

"Fine. Let's take up the issue of your relationship to the defendant. Did she show you the e-Cupid program?"

"No."

"So, what you're telling me is that, while she saw your picture in the software, she chose to have e-Cupid tell her that my client was her true love and scorned you." Blatch turned and picked up the black laptop from the evidence table. "Your honor, I ask the court to allow me to test this defective software here and now."

"Proceed."

"Mr. Lockhart, will you please run the program and tell us who you see?" Blatch set the laptop in front of AJ.

AJ opened the computer and turned it on. He worked his way through the program. Since Blatch had hooked the laptop up to a projection screen, the entire courtroom could see what was on the screen. AJ stopped short of having the Cupid figure turn the silver frame around.

"You've got it all wrong. I don't need a software program to tell me whom I love," he said. "When you're in love, you see it reflected in her eyes. You see your future there, your hopes, your joys."

"Are you saying you love Miss Phillips?"

"Yes, I guess I am."

"Do you think she shares your feelings?"

"You'd have to ask her."

All eyes in the courtroom turned to Chloe. She didn't know what to do. AJ was proclaiming his love from the witness box. In all her dreams, all her fantasies, never once had her hero been made to declare his love under oath, in front of a packed courtroom. It had always been a much more private moment.

On the other hand, he had said he loved her. And he was under oath to tell the truth, and nothing but.

She started to speak when Tommy stopped her. "You've already questioned my client, Blatch. Call her back if you want, but please follow a little decorum here."

"Your Honor, they've admitted it, they plotted to humiliate me," Ralph said, jumping to his feet. "*She* lured me into her office, thrust the software under my nose, and forced me to participate in this cruel joke. All the while, *he,*" Ralph jabbed his finger at AJ, "was working behind my back to steal her away from me. Confess, Lockhart, confess the hateful plan you cooked up."

"Order! Order," Judge Ramirez pounded on the bench with his gavel. "I will have order! Mr. Blatch, restrain your client or I'll have him arrested for contempt."

"Yes, Your Honor." Blatch pushed Higgenbotham into his chair and said, "Sit there and shut up. I've got this case won unless you screw it up." He turned his attention back to AJ, a slimy smile on his puffy lips. "Yes, Mr. Lockhart, do tell us about the plan you and Mr. Higgenbotham and Officer McKinnett participated in."

All eyes now shifted back to AJ. "It was no conspiracy. Early on in this, this problem Miss Phillips had with e-Cupid, she didn't know how to handle all the attention McKinnett and Higgenbotham were giving her." He looked directly at her.

"Go on."

"I stepped in, with the idea that I might be able to organize the courting, might be able to make the frenzy these two men were causing go away."

"Did you want to court her yourself?"

"Not at first. My initial motivation was simply to eliminate the distractions so we could continue our work, but things changed after I got to know Chloe."

"Tell the court your plan."

"I set up a contest for Chloe's affections, between the officer and Ralph, here. Each agreed to drop out of the competition if she indicated she really wasn't interested in him, and not to tell her about what we were doing."

Chloe's mouth fell open. She'd been the prize in a boy's game?

"No further questions."

"Your witness," said the judge.

Tommy stood slowly, clearly stumped as to where to take his line of questioning. "AJ, I have only one question for you. After all this planning and plotting and gamesmanship, what has changed?"

AJ looked at Chloe. She detected moisture in his eyes. "I fell in love. With Chloe."

"Nothing further."

Chloe burst through the door to AJ's offices. He'd left the courtroom after his astounding admission of love and she hadn't been able to find him after the judge adjourned the proceedings. She needed to talk to him before they went to the board meeting. He loved her! "What's going on?" she asked Joanie, who was busy packing files into boxes.

"We're being evicted," she said. "Can I help you?"

"Is AJ here?" She watched as the pregnant woman's expression changed from helpful to hurt.

"No," she said. "I don't suppose there's any way you could get the check released from the bank, is there?"

"I don't know what you're talking about."

"The check from Phillips International, paying AJ for all the work he's done. That *is* your company, isn't it?"

"Yes. But I don't understand. Didn't my brother pay you?" She frowned when Joanie shook her head and went back to packing. "Is that why you're leaving?" She turned Joanie's phone around and picked up the receiver.

"Sorry, Miss Phillips. Our phone service was cut off three days ago." Joanie sat down, rubbing her pregnant tummy.

"This can't be happening." Why wouldn't Oz have paid AJ? And why had he lied to her about it? There had to be some logical explanation. She'd have to talk to her brother, but first she'd call the board and get another check issued.

"It is," Joanie said. "But it'll be okay. AJ won't let us down."

"Where is he? Why didn't he tell me about this?"

"He doesn't normally share his problems with clients, Miss Phillips."

"We're a little more than client and consultant," she said. "He's just sworn in open court that he loves me." Even in the face of disaster, that knowledge made her light-headed.

"He loves his car, too, and he's selling it, so don't get your hopes up too high." Joanie jammed files into a box and taped it closed. "He didn't tell you because the only thing he has left is his pride, and begging would have destroyed even that."

Chloe sighed. Damn him anyway. He loved her enough to swear it under oath, but not enough to share his problems with her. "You can quit packing, Joanie. I'll fix this if I have to wring my brother's neck to do it." She raced toward the door. "Where would he go to sell Charlene?"

# Chapter Eighteen
# "Love Changes Everything"

"I want to thank you for taking time out of your evening to attend this emergency meeting of the Board of Directors of Phillips International," said Paul Webster, the chairman. "I know you all have very busy schedules that had to be rearranged to make your presence possible, but this is important. As you know, we've been watching Creative Investments very closely since the general weakening of the market because we felt improvements could be made in the management and because the two years stipulated in Oswald Phillips' will is almost at an end. I'd like to introduce AJ Lockhart, the consultant we hired to help us evaluate what actions to take with regard to CI." He sat down and motioned to AJ.

AJ smiled at Chloe and stood. "Thank you, Mr. Webster." AJ gathered some papers and walked to the front of the room. He handed his computer disk to the secretary. "I must tell you that, when I took on this assignment, I was skeptical about being able to make a positive recommendation. But, after working closely with Miss Phillips, I've come to understand the value of keeping this company in place and encouraging her to continue funding promising ideas. In my opinion Miss Phillips is the best person to run Creative Investments."

Chloe tried not to smile, but AJ's words made her want to stand up and shout. He not only loved her, he respected her abilities in the office. She glanced at Oz. He was sitting at the opposite end of the table, turning a very unhealthy shade of purple.

AJ worked his way through his presentation until he got to a list of projects and the amount of funding Chloe had approved.

"Mr. Chairman?" Chloe's brother stood up. "May I say something?"

"Certainly, Mr. Phillips."

"Thank you." Oz walked to the front of the room and stood next to AJ. "Lockhart's work is excellent, but he's too modest. And too kind. I believe he's leaving out some very important information to spare my sister embarrassment."

"Oz? What are you talking about?" Chloe leaned forward in her chair.

AJ turned his full attention on Oz. "You're right, Oz. But it wasn't Chloe's embarrassment I was worried about." AJ flipped open his folder. "I had planned to talk to the board separately about the analysis I did on your companies." He handed the file to Webster. "Oswald Phillips has been having a lot of financial troubles with his companies. He asked me to write a report that would give the board reason to replace his sister at the head of Creative Investments and put him in charge. He wanted to use the profits from her work to save his own failing businesses."

Chloe gasped. "Oz, no."

Oz ignored her. "It's true. I asked for that report, but not for those reasons. In business, our loyalties are with our shareholders. Let me draw your attention to the first and the last projects on this list." He pointed to AJ's presentation slides, specifically to Task-tender and e-Cupid. "I happen to know for a fact that my sister hasn't been able to contact the e-Cupid inventors since the first day she met them and," he held up his hands to ward off Chloe's protests. "And their software has caused one of her clients to sue her."

"That's true," AJ said, obviously trying to take back control of the meeting. "But it's also true that she hasn't given the e-Cupid inventors a dime."

"What about Ruthie Wheat?" asked Oz, a smile of satisfaction on his face

"I don't know what you mean," AJ said. He fiddled with the pointer in his hands, his jaw tight.

Oz began to pace back and forth. "Let me explain. Wheat is a single mother of two who has absolutely no background in business and an idea that will never succeed." He stopped pacing and put his hands on the back of a chair. "Now, I believe in helping individuals, but value must be delivered for monies paid." He shot a sharp look at AJ. "My sister gave this woman more money than she's given any other project *simply because she felt sorry for her.*" He glared at Chloe. "Furthermore, she hasn't asked for an accounting since she issued the check almost two years ago. I've had financial challenges, it's true, but I haven't indulged in personal whims. Or fraud." He paused. "What has Ruthie done with our money?"

Webster turned to Chloe. "A very good question, Miss Phillips. Do you have an explanation?"

All the color drained from Chloe's face. She stood up, shaking. "Not at this time, no." Her heart pounded and she felt faint, but not because AJ loved her. Because he'd betrayed her. Only he could have told Oz about Ruthie Wheat. He was the only person who knew, the only person she'd trusted with the story.

"You see," Oz went on, "how in good conscience, and keeping in mind your duty to the stockholders of Phillips International, how can the board even consider leaving my sister in charge of Creative Investments?" He gathered the board's attention with his eyes, looking each member in the face before he continued. "I suggest that you cannot and, based on my sister's poor decisions, you must fulfill the wishes of my dead father and dismiss her." He sat down, a smug look on his face.

Chloe did not sit. She faced her brother. "How dare you question my integrity, Oswald Phillips. I thought you were on my side. We're family."

Oz merely shrugged.

"Fine, take the company," Chloe said and began to collect her things. She couldn't leave the room fast enough. At the door she turned and pinned Oz with a cold green gaze. "You finally have it all. I hope you're happy." She ran out the door, AJ on her heels.

"Wait," he said.

She spun to face him. "And you! I trusted you. I thought you actually *were* trying to help me, but all you wanted was inside information you could pass on to my brother so *he* could talk the board into booting me out and giving my lovely projects to him." She jerked her Gucci bag back up on her shoulder and ran down the hall.

She didn't stop until she reached the elevators. When she saw AJ coming after her, she shouted, "Don't. I don't want to hear any excuses from you.

Go back with the boys and finish the job." Fortunately, the elevator arrived and saved her from crying in front of him. Instead, she watched the doors close on AJ's stricken expression.

He'd lied to her. She reviewed all the events of the past week and a half and realized just how big a fool she'd been. All that talk about wanting to help her, about keeping his own company afloat, about helping Joanie and her baby. Lies.

His kisses, their shared passion, his declaration of love? Oh, God! What a fool she'd been.

She drove home quickly, but carefully. When she opened her door, Edgar Allan was waiting for her. The cat meowed at her and followed her into the living room. When Chloe threw herself on the sofa, Edgar jumped up beside her, purring and rubbing her, as if she knew something was seriously amiss and Chloe needed comforting.

"You silly animal," she said. "Why did you pick now to be friends?" Chloe held the cat and cried.

AJ stepped out of his shower Saturday morning, Halloween, angry with himself. He should have realized what a snake Oz was. He should have told Chloe he loved her earlier. He should have done a lot of things differently.

He was in love for the first time in his life. And he'd fallen hard.

Right on his arrogant face.

She'd walked out on him and it was his fault. He looked at his reflection in the bathroom mirror. "You pig," he said, addressing the fool staring back at him through the steam. "She was right, you know. You are a pig, and a jerk, and two dozen less pleasant terms that a woman like Chloe wouldn't know or wouldn't use if she did. Although you'd deserve every one." He squirted shaving cream into his left hand and smeared it on his face. At least the business would survive. He'd gotten just enough for Charlene. Lockhart Associates would go on, even if Phillips tried to follow through with his threat of blackballing AJ's reputation.

Waving his razor in admonition, he said, "The very least you can do before you slink away like the worthless slug you are is fix things with Ralph." He scraped away foam and beard. "Then, and only then, can you go back to your office and try another way to build your business." He finished shaving and splashed his face with water.

He didn't much care without Chloe. He'd realized along the way that his success didn't rest with Oz Phillips. It was Chloe who really mattered.

He'd been a colossal fool.

Hurriedly, he dressed in his signature black. He ran his fingers through his wet hair, grabbed his rental car keys, surpressed a pang of longing for Charlene, and fled his town house with an idea building in his head.

He'd never been a quitter and he wasn't about to start now. Not when the rest of his life was on the line.

Three hours later, he was standing in Ralph Higgenbotham's workshop. "If I can fix this whole thing with Chloe, will you agree to drop the lawsuit?"

Ralph looked inordinately pleased with himself. "Why are you doing this? I thought you were the big charmer who could have any woman he wanted."

The only one he wanted was Chloe and she'd dumped him. "Because I owe it to Chloe to make things right between you two. Because, because I just do, Ralph. Don't make me beg."

Ralph watched him from behind safety goggles. AJ had interrupted his latest flange idea. He had a jagged piece of metal in one hand and a blowtorch in the other. All AJ had to fend off any sort of temper tantrum Ralph might throw was a slim black laptop computer.

He set the laptop on the counter in front of Ralph. "All I'm asking you to do is try e-Cupid one more time. If Chloe's picture comes up for you, then I'll bow out and accept defeat as gracefully as I can. If someone else pops into Cupid's picture frame, then you'll agree to drop your lawsuit and get back to work on your project." He turned the computer on and shoved it towards Ralph. "Agreed?"

Ralph set down the piece of metal he'd been working on, turned off the blowtorch, and set it on the counter. "You'll walk away? No tricks? No further trouble? No regrets?"

Hell, if this didn't work, he'd regret it for the rest of his life. But, after Tommy told him who *he'd* seen in the e-Cupid demo, AJ was pretty sure he'd come out okay. It looked like e-Cupid actually worked, as peculiar as that sounded. Chloe had seen him, hadn't she? He loved her. And she loved him, she just hadn't admitted it yet. "Right," he said, nodding. "I'll be a memory. Try it."

Ralph took off his heavy gloves. He looked at the computer screen and began the process of being Cupidized once more.

As before, the clouds roiled onto the screen and then the Roman villa appeared. When Cupid turned to Ralph holding the silver picture frame, AJ closed his eyes and held his breath. *Please, let this work. Please.*

When Ralph didn't jump up cheering, AJ opened his eyes. There, on the screen, in Cupid's picture frame, was the image of an attractive dark-haired woman with glasses. She was dressed in clashing greens and fuchsia. AJ looked at Ralph, whose mouth was moving but making no sounds. AJ knew the feeling. As crazy as the last few days had been, this latest development took the cake. It was just too screwy to be believed. E-cupid worked. It actually worked. Or maybe love was just clouding his brain.

He smacked the inventor on the back. "What do you think, Ralph old buddy? Is she a hottie, or what?"

"Ah, ah, ah," Ralph sputtered.

"My sentiments, exactly," he said. "And I have more good news. I know where she'll be tonight at," he checked his watch, "about eight o'clock."

Ralph tore his gaze away from the screen. "Where?" he squeaked.

*Good,* thought AJ. *Now, all I have to do is convince the Board of Phillips International that Chloe deserves to stay on at Creative Investments.* It was going to be a busy afternoon.

"Cheer up, Chloe," said Leann, inside the chicken costume she'd borrowed for the Halloween Ball. "You're missing all the fun."

"Fun," Chloe said. "I'm having fun." She was miserable. She'd found out just before she arrived at the ball that the board wanted to have an emergency conference call that evening and it certainly didn't help her mood.

"Liar," Leann said. "Although, may I say, you look fabulous tonight. With the possible exception of the cell phone stuck in your belt. What will the Merry Men think?"

Chloe'd abandoned her poultry costume for Robin Hood. She hadn't felt helpless enough to be trussed up in a long Cinderella dress for the evening, which was Leann's suggestion. Hopeless, perhaps, since she'd sent her true love packing without a backward glance, but definitely not helpless. She'd survive this. She always did.

The Corcoran Gallery was in fine form that evening, displaying the winners of a local school's pumpkin carving contest all around the perimeter of the main floor. Pumpkins carved with her own Punkin' Pal carving kit, thank you. Costumes included the standard witches and goblins, but there were also characters from *Matrix*, a gladiator or two, one Spider-Man, and, by her count, four Cleopatras of various sizes and shapes.

"Looks like we outdid ourselves, in terms of donations this year," Leann said. "Have you checked out the things we have at the silent auction? You might even want to bid on some," she said.

"I'll have to take a look." She adjusted her hat, making sure the feather hadn't drooped. There was nothing so disheartening as a drooping Robin Hood hat. Unless you counted a mysterious board conference call. Her experience with the board had never been all that positive, and something about the secretary's tone when he'd called to tell Chloe about the special conference call convinced her that disaster was imminent. Oz and AJ had won. The board would probably hire AJ to take over for her.

"You do look great, Chlo," Leann said. "I'm sorry things didn't work out with AJ. But, as my mother always said: Lots of fish in the river."

"Your mother never went fishing in her life."

"What does that have to do with the price of persimmons in Paris?" Leann waved to her husband, or what Chloe assumed was her husband. A tall rooster strode proudly over and put a wing around the chicken that was Leann.

"Cock-a-doodle-doo?" he said.

"Doodle cock to you, too," Leann answered. "Oh, Chloe, look there." Leann pointed up the broad stairs. "It's Cupid. Isn't he cute?"

Chloe watched a slender blond youth with shining

white wings descend the steps slowly. On his arm was an exquisitely beautiful woman with long blond hair. A short, balding gnome followed them, carrying a quiver of arrows. She knew these two! They'd started the whole ugly mess. E. Rose and Milo. E. Rose. Eros. *Cupid?* She shook her head. Couldn't be. It was just her imagination in overdrive. They were probably here to give her another pitch for e-Cupid. She had a few carefully chosen words for them. "Excuse me a moment, will you?" she said. And headed up the steps toward the duo who were partially responsible for the three-ring circus her life had been as of late.

"Hey, sweetcheeks," said E. Rose. "Where's your true love? Have you met my lovely wife, Psyche?"

"Don't start with me, you fraud! If you hadn't pitched me that stupid software idea I wouldn't be in this mess."

"Mess?" E. Rose said, batting his eyes with extreme innocence. "What mess would that be?"

"The one starring me as the ex-executive of my own company. The same one where the true love you promised me turned out to be more interested in plotting with my brother than being in love, that's the mess I'm talking about."

"Oh, *that* mess," said Cupid. "I didn't promise you success in business, dearie. Merely success in love."

"You did meet your true love, right?" asked Psyche, her voice like a musical breeze.

"Theoretically."

"Cupid, my dear, we must talk. That wasn't the way it was supposed to play out. There was one more step, as I recall."

"The evening is still young, my love," E. Rose smiled serenely at his lovely companion.

"Uh, Boss?" said Milo. "There might possibly maybe almost be a problem."

"Couldn't be. Psyche, you said use technology. I used technology, she fell in love, end of story."

"Didn't happen," said Milo.

"Beg your pardon?" said E. Rose.

"The technology didn't have anything to do with her falling in love," whispered Milo. "It wasn't working when she looked at it and he never did see it."

"Of course it worked," said E. Rose. "If we hadn't put the idea into her head, would she have kissed him that first time? No. Would she have needed his help getting rid of her two unwanted suitors? No." He crossed his arms and nodded once. "It was our technology that brought them together at last."

"What are you talking about?" Chloe asked.

E. Rose shrugged. "It was never about e-Cupid, Chloe. You and AJ were destined to be together. Milo and I simply helped push the process along a little." She thought she saw a little twinkle in his eye. "Helping all your friends to find true love was just an added bonus."

Before she had time to digest what she'd heard, there was a commotion at the far end of the gallery. She looked up. Someone was climbing onto the railing of the upstairs balcony. Good grief, what was this?

The figure, a tall man dressed as Zorro, was standing on the railing, holding on to what looked like a rope. Attached to what, Chloe wondered, as she, along with the other guests, watched the man launch himself into the air and swing down, down into the crowd. He landed, without toppling either himself or anyone else, in front of Chloe.

The rope he'd come in on retracted back to the second floor. "Very dangerous stunt," Chloe said, readying herself to give this interloper a large piece of her mind. "You could have injured someone."

"Ah, my lady Robin Hood, but it is I who am injured, and mortally, too, I fear."

"How is that, you fool? Jumping off the balcony into a crowd. Think what could have happened!" She didn't like being the center of all this attention. Didn't like feeling foolish. Besides, Zorro was tall and all too familiar. Her heart didn't care about being foolish. It skipped beats. Several of them. Destined, E. Rose had said.

"But it didn't," Zorro protested.

"No excuse."

"What better way to demonstrate my new idea to the most creative venture capitalist in town, may I ask?"

"You did this to get my attention?" He'd held her attention since their first meeting.

"Just so. And it appears to have worked, because you are paying attention." His voice took on that honeyed quality and she started to melt.

"Couldn't we talk about this next week in my office."

"No. This is something so outrageous, so inventive, that it won't wait."

"Fine. What is it, El Zorro?"

The man in black cleared his throat and reached into his shirt. He pulled out an envelope. "For you, oh Princess of Thieves." He handed the missive to Chloe. "My first boon to you, this evening."

Chloe pulled out a sheet of paper and read it. "Is this some kind of joke? This says that Ralph has dropped his lawsuit." She studied Zorro's masked face, seeing AJ's sparkling eyes behind it. "What's this about?"

"I'm victim of a cruel fate, my lady. You have stolen my heart and I want it back."

"AJ? You're not making any sense."

"Unfortunately, that AJ fellow couldn't make it tonight. He asked me to extend his regrets and his sincerest apologies." He smiled and stroked his slim mustache. "He also begs your forgiveness. He admits he is a colossal fool and hopes his creative resolution of the Higgenbotham situation meets with your approval."

"If you mean am I glad the lawsuit is gone, yes. I don't know anything else about Ralph."

"Ralph is up there," Zorro pointed up the stairs to where a man dressed as Einstein was happily chatting with one of the Cleopatras she'd seen earlier. The one with glasses.

"It's Gloria! How? What?"

"According to the new and improved e-Cupid, your secretary is Ralph's true love."

"Come on, AJ, what's this about? I am not amused." She was confused. She'd been the prize in a game, then she'd been sued, and then her true love betrayed her.

"As unbelievable as it sounds, the second time ol' Ralph tried e-Cupid it actually *did* show him his true love—Gloria."

Cupid, Psyche and Milo stood on the steps, nodding and smiling. This was too much. She had to have her wits about her for the board conference call.

As if on cue, her cell phone rang. She closed her eyes and pulled it from her sword belt. "Excuse me, please," she said and answered the call.

The knot of people surrounding her didn't let her out of their human corral as she'd expected. Instead, they watched as she listened and responded to Webster's deep voice. "I see. . . . Really? That's wonderful, but . . . Okay. . . . I could do that. . . . Monday? . . . Great. . . . Thank you so much." She closed her phone.

"Well?" asked Zorro.

"That was the board! They're initiating a formal investigation of Oz's companies." She took a deep breath. "They reviewed all the reports, your presentation, and they're so happy with them that they've offered me a seat on the board as executive director." She looked around the circle. "They don't want to fire me, they want me to help them expand Creative Investments!"

The collective applause was almost deafening. Something had happened to make the board change their minds about her. To make them overlook Oz's accusations. She looked at AJ standing there, all heroic and masked. Was he her knight in shining armor or the evil villain?

"Congratulations, Chloe. The board made the correct decision," said Zorro. "If you're not too overwhelmed," he began and pulled a small box from his pocket. "I'm here to admit, in front of all these fine people, the astronauts, the kings, the clowns, the chickens, that I am a complete fool, the worst kind of fool. I don't want to lose you." He went down on one knee. "I love you and I want to marry you. If you'll have me, that is." He opened the box and held it up.

Chloe took out the ring inside and blew on it. The tiny yellow whistle was barely audible above the sound of the crowd that had gathered to witness the madness AJ was promoting. "I thought you were a big-time consultant with a fat fee from my brother. Surely you can afford more than a Cracker Jack ring."

"I don't know about the big-time part, but there is no fat fee and no recommendations. You're still in business and that means I failed. The cash I got from selling Charlene went to the company. So I'm broke and Cracker Jack rings are about all my meager budget can handle at the moment." AJ stood and bowed over Chloe's hand, slipping the ring on her finger. "What's your answer, my lady? Are you going to give me back my heart or keep it and take the man as well?"

She'd spent hours after the board meeting thinking about what she would say if AJ tried to win her back. She was used to projecting into the future. She did it with every person who came into her office, asking for her money and her promise to believe in them.

She'd played out so many imaginary scenarios with AJ that she was having trouble keeping them straight. But she knew one thing. This man had lied to her, had told her brother things only she and AJ had known. "One of the sexiest things any man can do for the woman he professes to love, AJ, is to tell the truth. You haven't done that."

"This time I am. Chloe, I didn't mean to hurt you. I didn't know what Oz would do with the story about Ruthie. I didn't plan on falling in love with you."

"I certainly didn't plan on falling in love with you either, and I wish I never had," she said, turning away.

"Chloe. Stop, please," said AJ. "All we need to do to clear this up is talk to one another. You know, talk, like you do with the people whose goofy ideas you love so much? Talk to me about my goofy idea."

"You may be startled to learn, Mr. Lockhart, that I have been paying attention to your business lessons. You've exhorted me on several occasions to be more circumspect when I take on new ideas. I'm doing that right now."

"Look, Robin Hood. You can't just steal my heart, abuse it, make it feel feelings it didn't know it was capable of feeling, and then stomp on it."

She raised an eyebrow and adjusted her hat. "I trusted you, AJ. It's something I don't do lightly. I don't think I could stand to have my trust betrayed again. I'm a businesswoman. I can handle the disappointments of day-to-day work. I can even manage to deal with my brother. If you think you've had your heart stomped on, then consider mine. It's shattered. Humpty Dumpty had a better chance of being put back together again." She hitched up her loden green tights and walked swiftly away, losing herself in the crowd.

"I'll tell you what AJ stands for," Zorro mumbled to himself as he watched the woman of his dreams walk away.

"Bad luck," said Leann. "She loves you, really she does. But you're her first experience with this emotion, so you should expect her to be crushed."

"Well, she's the first woman I've loved and I'm not crushed."

"Really?" said her husband, Karl. "Looks like classic crushed to me, Leann. What do you think?"

"Classic." Leann walked around his deflated Zorro, critically sizing him up. "Crushed."

"Don't talk about me like I'm a can of soda. I'm fine. I'll be fine." Chloe'd accused him of lying and, damn, here he was, doing it again. Maybe she was right.

"I'm not fine," he said, registering the pain saying those words brought to his chest. "I've just let the best thing to happen to me since I learned how to ride a bike walk away. Tell me it wasn't the stupidest thing I've ever done."

By then, he'd gathered a larger crowd of sympathizers, assembled in a semicircle. Tommy, recognizable behind his molded plastic Batman muscles, his arm around a very pregnant pumpkin—Joanie. "Tommy, I see you went in search of the woman in the silver picture frame."

"I did indeed. Chloe's software, man. It showed me what I'd really known all along but didn't have sense enough to do anything about. Joanie has agreed, just this night, to become Mrs. Tomas Jesus Diego Morales." Tommy hugged his fiancée.

Officer McKinnett, dressed as a convict in a really unattractive striped pajama-like outfit, was securely shackled to Barb, dressed, not unexpectedly, as a police officer. "Chloe gave up an awful lot to get Barb and me together where we belonged. This isn't the way to repay that risk, you know."

So he was a jerk and stupid to boot. "She rejected me."

Einstein, aka Ralph Higgenbotham, elbowed his way into the circle. "AJ, if you don't go after her, you'll hate yourself. Even though she isn't *my* true love, she is *yours.* She said so. Her program said so. You know it. By the way, have you met Gloria?" He put his arm around Cleopatra. "You were absolutely right about her being a great lady."

"Thank you, AJ," said Gloria. "I've been trying to get Ralph's attention since he first came in to see Chloe, but I didn't realize what a charming and wonderful man he really was until I met him tonight. I understand you're responsible for his coming to the ball."

Oh, yes, he was responsible. For the mess his life was in. For blowing it with the woman he loved. "You're welcome. I'm glad you're so happy." It was right in front of him—proof positive that e-Cupid worked. Which meant Chloe *did* love him. He just had to get her to admit it.

"And," said Ralph. "It looks like SatelHat is taking off big time. We just got an order from the NFL for five hundred thousand units. Five hundred thousand!"

That should make Chloe happy.

"She isn't here, AJ," a voice said, behind him.

AJ turned around. His sword caught the kneecap of a man dressed as Cupid. "Should I know you?"

"E. Rose, at your service," said Cupid, bowing low. "Listen, pal, if you don't get your butt out that door and find Chloe, I can't go back home." He turned AJ around and gave him a shove. "Go. Now, or I'll have to resort to violence." He pulled a golden arrow from his quiver. "You two belong together. If you don't go after her, I'll make life miserable for you."

The collection of Chloe's friends and his friends nodded in unison, then parted, like the Red Sea. "She went outside," Barb said helpfully.

"All right. I can take a hint." AJ spun around, heedless of the people scattering before his sword, and ran down the steps and out the doors of the Corcoran Gallery.

"Well, I'm glad that's fixed," Cupid announced.

"What are we going to do about Henry the Eighth?" asked Milo, pointing to Oz Phillips milling around on the other side of the room. "He's done nothing but cause trouble here."

"No problemo, my friend," said Cupid, as he shot Oz with an arrow. "I always said the old ways work best."

Oz Phillips stopped midstride, shook his head, and grinned stupidly. He walked slowly toward a woman dressed as a construction worker. "Excuse me," he said. "Aren't you Mathilda O'Reilly?"

The startled woman adjusted her tool belt and nodded. "Yes. Do I know you?"

"Not yet, but my sister tells me you have a wonderful idea for a way to keep track of remote controls for all kinds of technology," Oz said. "Let me get you a glass of punch and we can talk."

"I love it when that happens," said Milo.

* * *

Skidding to a damp stop at the bottom of the steps outside the gallery, AJ ignored the falling rain and scanned the sidewalk for an errant Robin Hood. All he saw was traffic.

Wait. There, across the street and headed for the White House, he saw a bobbing feathered hat. Holding out a gloved hand, he dashed between cars and sprinted after the retreating figure. His cape flew behind him, his knee-high black boots squishing rhythmically in the mud as he hurried to catch up with Chloe.

He was confident that the Park Police, the White House Security Team, and the Secret Service, all of whom could come after him, had never seen Zorro streaking across the grass before. "Hey, Robin," he shouted, pulling even with Chloe, "your feather's getting all droopy in this rain. Come back to the Corcoran."

He wondered if she was using the rain as cover for her tears. She was soaked through and shivering. AJ took off his cape and draped it over her shoulders. "Come on, the head of a very successful venture capital firm should know better than to stand out in this kind of weather."

"I'm not standing, I'm walking."

"You're running. Running away. From the truth."

"You're not one to throw truth in my face."

"Look. I know you think I conspired with Oz, but in fact I made him call Webster this evening, before the ball, and admit everything. I've done everything I can to make things right between us." He spun her around. "Face it, Chloe, you're in love with me. Your friends say so, I say so, even your software program says so."

"The software is bogus!"

"You love me. Say it."

"I love you. I love you. I love you," she said. "Satisfied?"

"No," he said, taking off his Zorro hat and kneeling in the mud in front of the White House. "I understand why you don't trust me. I'm a jerk. I misled you. I lied and if you tell me to go away, I will. But I'm telling you the truth now, the way I did under oath in that court room. I love you. You. Chloe Phillips. And I want to spend my life with you." He held up the whistle ring one more time. "I'll get a better one tomorrow."

"Stand up, you're getting your pants all dirty."

He stood, dripping hair hanging across his forehead in the most adorable way. "You are the most irritating, frustrating, sexy woman I've ever met. I know how much you value promises, so let me give you one. I will love you all the days of my life. And that's the truth."

Chloe blinked away raindrops and made a decision. She reached up, standing on tiptoe, and put her hands on AJ's sopping wet black shirt, feeling his muscular chest and his pounding heart beneath. "I love you," she whispered.

Then she kissed him.

When they finally pulled apart again, she grinned at him and asked, "So, what does AJ stand for? I should know if I'm going to be Mrs. AJ, shouldn't I?"

AJ grimaced. "Promise you won't laugh?"

"Promise."

"Abner Jedidiah," he said and stopped her laugh with a kiss.

# *Epilogue*
# *"Lovers and Friends"*

AJ bounced Elena on his knee. Joanie's daughter was four months old and her mother was dancing with her new husband of six months. "Let me hold her," said Gloria. "You go dance with your wife."

"Thanks," AJ said and went in search of Chloe. They'd been married for almost three hours and he was floating. He couldn't believe she'd said yes that cold, rainy night, but she had and here he was, a married man. He had to give Cupid—otherwise known as E. Rose—credit. He'd done his homework on Chloe and her friends. Heck, on AJ's as well. Joanie and Tommy. Andrew and Barb. Ralph and Gloria.

And Chloe. His wife. He grinned.

He and Chloe had never really been able to figure out just who E. Rose was. He'd swept out of their lives as quickly as he'd descended, taking e-Cupid with him. But having found true love in each other's arms neither AJ nor Chloe was willing to discount the possibility that Cupid really did exist. If nothing else, it added a delightfully romantic quirk to the tale of their courtship.

AJ spotted his bride at a table with a few familiar faces. Leann and her husband, Karl, waved to him as he approached. "I can't believe your name is Abner," Leann said, laughing.

"It's a family thing."

"Well," said Andrew, his arm around Barb. "I hope you aren't going to carry on the tradition. This world only needs one Abner Jedidiah Lockhart."

"Hey, you guys. Can't a fellow dance with his bride on his wedding day?"

He leaned down and gave Chloe a kiss. "I happen to think Abner is kind of cute," she said.

"AJ," said Ralph, saluting with his champagne glass. "Great news. SatelHat is going international."

"I'm happy for you, but I've got other things on my mind right now." He took Chloe's hand and pulled her up. "Dance with me, wife."

"Bossing me around already," Chloe said, laughing. "I was trying to save your girlfriend's dignity, is all."

"Charlene?" AJ was suddenly worried. "What were they planning to do with my wedding present?"

"Oh, cans and streamers, I guess." She shrugged. "Maybe we ought to skip the dance and just leave."

He kissed her thoroughly. "Excellent idea and one I don't believe needs a business case." He took her hand and escorted her across the dance floor, to the band. He signaled for the group to stop and took the microphone. "Ladies and gentlemen. Thank you for joining us on this perfect day. I want you to know that, before you can destroy my award-winning classic Corvette, my bride and I are leaving."

Chloe laughed beside him. "Hard to argue with the new president of Phillips International, folks. See you next month." Then she followed him out of the reception hall through the grape arbor. "Where are we going, Abner?"

AJ winced. "A long time ago you suggested that I should take my fat bonus and go to Tahiti, so I thought I'd take my wife there instead."

"Tahiti, huh? Works for me," Chloe said. "I've got this interesting idea for a sunblock applicator."

"Nope," said AJ. "No work on this honeymoon. All we're going to explore is each other."

Dear Reader,

I hope you enjoyed Chloe and AJ's wild and wacky courtship. I had a lot of fun dreaming up a different way for Cupid to bring people together, even if it didn't work out quite the way he first planned. I love casting classic mythical figures into the "real" world. However, all the zany projects Chloe and AJ work on together came strictly from my overactive imagination. Any resemblance they bear to actual products is pure coincidence. I, myself, am still waiting for a version of the remote remote to come on the market. Until then, I'm off to search for the stereo remote control. . . . Happy reading!

Best,
Karen Lee

# SHOCKING BEHAVIOR
# JENNIFER ARCHER

J.T. Drake has always felt he pales in comparison to his father's outrageous inventions. But with the push of a button, one of the professor's madcap gadgets actually renders him *invisible*.

Roselyn Peabody's electrifying caress arouses him from his stupor. The beautiful scientist claims his tingling nerve endings are a result of his unique state, but J. T. knows sparks of attraction when he feels them. And while Rosy promises to help him regain his image, J.T. plots to dazzle her with his sex appeal. Only one question remains: When J.T. finally materializes, will their sizzling chemistry disappear or reveal itself as true love?